MILTON PLACE

Persephone Book Nº 131
First published by Persephone Books Ltd 2019

© The Estate of Elisabeth de Waal 2019

Preface © Victor de Waal
Afterword © Peter Stansky

Royalties from the sale of this book
will go to the Refugee Council

Endpapers taken from a mid 1950s textile design SB469
by Sheila Bownas © Sheila Bownas Archive Ltd

Typeset in ITC Baskerville by
Keystroke, Wolverhampton

Printed and bound in Germany by
GGP Media GmbH, Poessneck

978 191 0263 211

Persephone Books Ltd
59 Lamb's Conduit Street
London WC1N 3NB
020 7242 9292

www.persephonebooks.co.uk

MILTON PLACE

by

ELISABETH DE WAAL

with a new preface by

VICTOR DE WAAL

and a new afterword by

PETER STANSKY

PERSEPHONE BOOKS
LONDON

CONTENTS

PREFACE

Elisabeth, my mother, was born with many talents, or rather she had the ability to enter into herself to acquire them as she needed them.

The eldest of four children, she grew up in the Jewish haute-bourgeois family home in Vienna at the turn of the twentieth century, a golden age of music and the arts to which her young diaries testify, and which so sadly 1914 brought to an end.

Branching off, she enrolled as a student of law and economics in the University of Vienna, from which she graduated *summa cum laude* after the war that had ended the Hapsburg Empire and left Austria in ruins. Her experience of the economic depression and the havoc of rampant inflation never left her and influenced her political outlook after the second world war.

But in the 1920s America beckoned, and she won a Rockefeller scholarship to Columbia University where she began a lifelong friendship with the distinguished international historian Eric Voegelin, who had likewise studied in Vienna. She went on to explore the United States and Canada for another year. Later she told of her adventures to us when we were children, but sadly her descriptive letters to her parents did not survive the destruction of the family home by the Nazis in 1938.

In 1927 she moved to Paris and it was there she began to write and correspond with, among others, the poet Rainer Maria Rilke, She also contributed as a journalist to the *Figaro*. In Paris she met my father and they fell in love. They married in Vienna and settled in Holland where I was born in 1929, after which we lived in Paris, the South Tyrol and Switzerland. These were happy times, but overshadowed by the rise of Hitler. It was from Switzerland that my mother, in 1938, bravely travelled to Vienna to rescue her parents evicted from their home by the Nazis. And it was from Switzerland that a year later the family came to England, fearing a possible Nazi invasion.

As was usual in those days, on her marriage Elisabeth relinquished her career to follow her husband and care for her family; and as was also usual then in a middle-class household she was supported by nannies and a cook. When these vanished with the outbreak of war in 1939, our mother had to acquire yet more skills. Having never cooked in her life, she embarked on a correspondence course with her own mother's old cook now living in London. Some of these instructions and recipes survive, each beginning deferentially (in German) – 'Madam takes . . . Madam then does . . . Madam . . .' Needless to say she soon excelled, and when rationing allowed became expert even in Viennese dishes.

Our mother nevertheless made Tunbridge Wells, with the Battle of Britain overhead and then on the Luftwaffe's fly-path to the Blitz on London, a most comfortable home; while our father commuted to his office in the City (until it was bombed, after which he worked for the Dutch Government in exile, and later for the United Nations) while the boys went daily to school.

After the war, with our father retired, and her sons first at university and then married and with their own careers, Elisabeth continued to develop her gifts of friendship, and in particular formed a group of women friends who explored with her and learned from her the riches of spirituality – a group that continued until she was in her late eighties. She had, since Paris days, developed from her Jewish heritage and entered deeply into the Christian mystical tradition, particularly of Teresa of Avila and John of the Cross. This profound side of her was known to very few.

Alongside this, and most significantly, Elisabeth returned to her long-neglected talent of writing.

My parents' house did not have a 'drawing room'. The room where we sat comfortably by the fire and as children played family games was 'the library'. It had bookshelves from floor to ceiling on every wall, deep enough for two layers of literature in the languages of Europe, as well as history and politics. But my parents were not academics. It was just that they had been educated in the rich tradition of European culture: my father in Holland in a merchant family, my mother in Vienna in a household where English was as familiar as German and French.

They wrote poetry to one another, and letters to family and friends, not only about daily happenings, but discussing reading and ideas. I still have boxes of letters from my mother from my teenage years. When I was a university undergraduate studying European literature she shared her own great knowledge in letters full of love that were also additional tutorials. And there is a cache of correspondence with her friend from student days in America, Eric Voegelin, among whose papers this novel has surfaced.

So it was natural for Elisabeth to find time to write for herself. A little extra bedroom in the house became her study and there she retreated most days. In her twenties she had composed a dramatic poem about Michelangelo which Rilke admired. Then in the second half of life she wrote the novels in which she explored the issues thrown up by her own experience, illumined now by her familiarity with and absorption in European literature.

One theme of that experience surfaces in her first novel to be published, though not in her lifetime: *The Exiles Return*, Persephone Book No. 102. In this novel Elisabeth's autobiographical voice can be heard as she draws on her own feelings of hope and disappointment and memories of the home from which in 1938 her parents had been so cruelly evicted. We hear her in the struggles for recognition of the Jewish academic Kuno Adler, and in Resi the young woman trying to find her feet in the troubling relationships of a new world.

These passions of hope, love and betrayal surface again in a new form in *Milton Place*, set now after the war in a country town very like the immediate post-war Tunbridge Wells in which she was now living in the deceptive middle-class calm of the English home counties – a town of shops and cafés and local businesses and politics, whose surface concealed alongside a strong sense of neighbourhood, many unacknowledged rivalries, jealousies and disappointments.

Milton Place is a story in which the tragedy of *King Lear* finds a contemporary setting. Mr Barlow, widowed and in old age cared for by two faithful old servants, in his country house, now mostly shut up, has kept alive as he sits in his beautiful walled garden, the memory of a long lost Austrian girl of his youth. That memory takes on unexpected flesh in the coming of Anita, the daughter of that old love.

Here too Elisabeth's autobiographical voice can surely be heard again in Anita's love for Mr Barlow's favourite grandson Tony, a student on the cusp of adulthood, reminiscent of one of my own undergraduate friends to whom my mother became very close. Both bring renewed happiness to the old man and yet there is inevitably a dark side to the story, for like Lear Mr Barlow has two daughters, Emily and Cecilia, who between them in their professed love for their father ensure that there can be no happy ending.

Although *Milton Place* is a quintessential English country house, yet it implicitly pays homage to a house in Slovakia called Kovecses, 'a very large and very plain eighteenth century house ["a large square box such as children draw" in Elisabeth's words] set in a flat landscape of fields, with belts *of* willows, birch forests and streams' wrote my son Edmund de Waal in *The Hare with Amber Eyes*). It was only about two hours from Vienna and was where my mother used to spend every September and October when she was a girl. It had been her own mother's family home and was now lived in by her younger brother, Elisabeth's uncle Baron Philippe von Schey known as 'Pips'. He had spent several years in England before the First World War and never forgot the cultured Edwardian world of which he had for a while been a part.

Like Milton Place, Kovecses grew increasingly run down. By 1918 'there are only two old man to tend the gardens, and the roses on the long veranda are unkempt' (*Hare*). Yet Pips continued to live there during the inter-war years and in the early spring of 1934 the English writer Patrick Leigh-Fermor came to stay with him. He described the house as having the 'charm of a large and rambling rectory occupied by a long line of bookish and well-to-do incumbents torn between rival passions for field sports and their library. . . . The library was so crammed that most of the panelling was hidden and the books, in German and French and English, had overflowed in neat piles on the floor. . . . There were shaded lamps and leather armchairs beside a huge open stove, a basket of logs and a spaniel asleep in front of it. . . . From his demeanour and the excellence of his English I think a stranger in a railway carriage would have taken [Pips] for an Englishman but of a half-patrician, half-scholarly kind which even then seemed threatened with extinction.'

It was thus not Kovecses alone that influenced my mother's evocation of Milton Place, it was also Pips' gift for friendship. When Leigh-Fermor writes 'these long walks are wonderful and we talk about every possible thing and there are frequently the same silences of perfect company' there is a strong echo of Mr Barlow's walks with Anita Seiler.

Sadly, with the ascendancy of fascism and anti-semitism, by the mid-1930s life became increasing difficult for my grandparents. They finally left Vienna after the Anschluss (so well described by Edmund in *The Hare with Amber Eyes*) and headed for the relative safety of Kovecses. This 'looks much the same as it has done, a jumble of grand and informal . . . [but] the roses are more unkempt. . . . The house is much emptier' (*Hare*). My grandmother died there on 12th October and was buried in the nearby churchyard. Elisabeth managed to secure permission for her family to come to England and in early March 1939 her father left for Britain, where he lived in Tunbridge Wells until his death in 1945. Elisabeth remained there for the rest of her life.

Elisabeth berated herself a little for having been 'so withdrawn, never having "pushed" myself'. Yet she had a deeply fulfilled life. She ended her page of introspection: 'I wanted a woman's life, a husband to love and children, all the more difficult to achieve because I was not attractive to men, the kind of man I wanted. I had plenty of men friends, but none I would have wanted to marry. And then I did marry the man I wanted, oh great, oh unspeakable good fortune! About this I have never been in doubt and it explained all the sacrifices I made (if they were sacrifices) to my marriage. And I have had, I have, two remarkable sons. That is real fulfilment. I have no regrets.'

Victor de Waal, London 2018

MILTON PLACE

CHAPTER ONE

The envelope bore a foreign stamp. The writing of the address, too, looked foreign – large, flowing, slightly angular, obviously shaped on a different type of script from the one taught in English schools. But it was elegant and well-bred.

Mr Barlow held it in his hand, contemplating it critically, dubiously. It was something out of the ordinary and, these days, he didn't much care for unusual things. His daily papers, his weekly *Economist*, a letter, from time to time, from his daughter Cecilia who had married a doctor and lived in Torquay, an occasional communication from his banker or stockbroker; these made up the accustomed and staple postal nourishment served to him on a silver salver by his old butler Sims.

Still postponing for a moment or two this adventure into the unknown, the opening of the letter, Mr Barlow scrutinised more closely the postmark and the stamp. And so doing, he felt the slight unease, caused by the unfamiliarity of the envelope, quicken to something like excitement, a little fluttering at the base of his throat, which at first he resented and which then made him shake his head and smile at himself for an old fool. He glanced slowly round the room: at the old, heavy, familiar furniture, and out of the window at the majestic cedar spreading its dark branches against the pale, wintry sky over the damp lawn. Having thus assured himself of the permanence and stability of his surroundings, he took an ivory paperknife and slit the envelope.

He knew, of course, before he unfolded the letter, that it came from Vienna, but the name at the bottom of the last page meant nothing to him.

'Anita Seiler – never heard of the woman,' he told himself, 'wonder what she wants, how she got hold of me?'

His composure had returned, together with a slight sense of disappointment. This could be nothing personal, nothing to disturb or remind him. Yet, in another moment the fluttering in his throat had returned, it was almost a throb. He read quickly, without pause, as if swallowing a large glass of water in a hurry, at one continuous gulp.

'Dear Mr Barlow,' he read, 'you do not know me, but I believe you knew my mother before she was married. It is a very long time ago, but as she remembered you so well and so kindly, and often spoke about you to me in the last years of her life, I thought perhaps you would remember her, too. Perhaps you also remember my aunt. She was older than my mother and married a Mr Osborne, a friend of yours, I think. She died before the war and I don't know whether her husband is still alive. So you are the only person I know of in England. My mother had your address, but, of course, you may not live there any more and this may never reach you. It is all so long ago. But if you get this letter, please forgive it, please forgive me for troubling you.

I am very anxious to get away from here for a while, to come over to England, if I can. I thought perhaps I might find a post, as a governess, or housekeeper, or simply a cook. I am told such persons are difficult to find now and I might have a chance. I am a widow, my daughter has just got married, so I have no ties. I don't mind what I do, if only I can get away. Perhaps, knowing my background, even if you don't know me, you would be kind enough to recommend me. I should be so very grateful.

Again, please forgive the trouble. And thank you very much in advance.

Yours sincerely,
Anita Seiler.'

When he had finished reading, he put the letter down slowly on his desk at which he had been sitting, and again looked round the room and out of the window. The fact that nothing had changed came as a kind of shock to him. The high looming bookcases full of his books in their dark bindings, the worn leather armchairs, his big oak desk and the old-fashioned brass lamp with its green glass shade, which had once burned oil and had later been wired for electricity, they had been with him all his life, whenever he had been at home. They were infused with his own being and were part of it. Nothing could possibly happen now to make any change in them. He remembered his father sitting here where he now sat, and, especially, he remembered his hands as they lay on the desk, veined and mottled, like his own. He glanced at them. His own hands, or his father's? And for the space of a second, time seemed to waver and identities to be confused. He recalled himself.

A glint of sunshine had come through the grey wintry sky and the inky darkness of the cedar had somehow been enriched and become a living green. The tree was now throwing a shadow on the lawn. Mr Barlow opened the door into the big stone hall, his footsteps sounded on the black and white marble floor. He found his hat, coat and muffler on their usual peg in the closet and went out into the garden.

The morning was indulging in one of the brief sunny periods promised by the weather forecasters. A gravelled terrace ran along the front of the house and a low stone balustrade, stained and patchy with the growth of lichen, separated it from the lawn and the big cypress. Not far beyond, the lawn merged into the rough grass of a meadow which sloped away gently down to another and broader field beyond which ran the road. Thus the terrace commanded a wide view of grassland, dotted about with several large oak trees, their trunks and bare branches a pen-and-ink drawing enriched with a delicate colour wash for the grass, the clouds and the sky.

For a long time Mr Barlow stood on the terrace and looked. He looked at each tree in turn that he knew so well, at a flock of starlings wheeling in the distance, at the blue haze beyond the road and the river, where the land rose again in a gentle swell towards the horizon. From time to time the sound of a car drifted up when a breath of wind carried it towards the house, but the traffic remained out of sight, as the road was sunk below the hedge bounding the estate.

All this, too, was part and parcel of Mr Barlow's life. But, whereas the furniture of his study was, in a manner of speaking, bone of his bone, rigid and fixed in an unalterable pattern, the landscape was breath of his breath. It was alive and full of the endless possibilities of life, just as Mr Barlow, in spite of his seventy-five years, was alive. And life means that nothing is set, nothing is finished, because beyond every end there is always another beginning.

To the west of the house, and divided from it by the drive which swept up to the big front door under a glass canopy, was an old brick wall. The paint was blistered on the door and some of the glass panes in the overhanging roof were cracked, but the old brick wall, much older than the mansion it faced, seemed to glory and mellow in its age. The little green-painted door that led through it had not been neglected; having paced up and down the terrace several times, Mr Barlow crossed the drive, opened it and went through. Here he found himself in one of his favourite spots: a square enclosure, surrounded on all sides by walls of the same rose-coloured brick. They had at one time been part of a much older building, farm or manor house fallen into ruin, next to which Milton Place had been built. Two sides of what might have been a courtyard had been standing. Mr Barlow himself had completed the quadrangle with the same old bricks, carefully collected from the remains of older structures. Not a single new brick of harsh colour was amongst them. The walled garden enclosed a small lawn with rose beds in the middle and broad borders along two adjoining sides. Two benches were placed against the other walls which gave shelter from the east and north. On one of these Mr Barlow decided to sit for as long as the sun should bestow on it as much warmth as it could muster on this February morning, and in this seclusion he would now allow himself to indulge in the imaginings he had hitherto always excluded from his conscious mind.

* * *

It was summer now, in his mind's eye. The walled garden was ablaze with flowers, and he himself was a young man. The green door opened, and a young girl came towards him, a slender girl with fair hair piled high upon her head. She wore a white embroidered blouse with a high collar, emphasising her long neck, and her little, round chin rested on its edge in a manner both pert and appealing. Her white skirt fitted closely round her incredibly small waist and then fell down in a bell-shaped sweep to her white-shod feet. At her appearance, all the bright colours in the flower beds seemed to glow with an even greater brightness, and the very air quivered and sang in his ears.

He rose to meet her and, taking her by the hand, he walked with her slowly along the borders, telling her the name of each flower as they came to it, the English and the Latin, which she repeated like a good little girl learning a lesson. She knew them all, of course; they had done this so often, but he liked to repeat this scene in its most minute detail. It made it seem real.

He closed his eyes, straining to recall her voice saying the names of the flowers. That was always his last effort. Then the picture faded. Never, in his most vivid imaginings, had he embraced her or kissed her lips. If he had not allowed his daydream to go any further, it was because, at one time, the pain of awakening from it would have been unbearable; because, if he had indulged in it beyond a certain point, it would have wrecked his life. So, with iron determination, he had kept it within bounds. And later, in the middle years, when his work and his responsibilities had crowded his days, the dream had practically vanished. If ever it flitted across his mind, he dismissed it with a nod and a smile as a foible no longer dangerous, no longer disturbing. Only in recent years, since the death of his wife and his retirement, since he had come back to Milton Place and lived here alone, he had, from time to time, intentionally recalled it, dwelt on it and suc-cumbed to its fascination. Now it was all purely visual, a figment in his mind's eye, since it no longer evoked the scorching thirst of desire, no longer tortured the senses with unfulfilment, since the girl and the young man he had been lay buried in the past, beautiful and inaccessible, as in a glass coffin.

It was such a brief encounter from which this dream had sprung, a quite ephemeral incident, yet he was sure that it had been one of the most important events of his life. In one sense, *the* most important. True, it had not deflected him from his career, nor from leading what the world called a normal family life. But in another dimension of his being, a dimension in which he was neither an administrator, nor

7

a husband, nor a father, the one in which he was alone with himself, it had never been forgotten.

He had seen the girl only twice, forty-five years ago, when he had gone to Vienna with a former school friend to act as best man at his wedding. Mariella was the bride's younger sister. He had seen her entering the big drawing room in her father's house, at the ball on the eve of the wedding, in a white dress of some shimmering, diaphanous material in which she had seemed to float into the room. All the evening he had not been able to take his eyes off her. He had danced with her twice and they had spoken a few conventional words, but at the touch of her hand in its white glove, the cradling of her tiny waist in his arm, there had been an immediate, unspoken understanding between them. He had danced with no one else, and when she had another partner, he had stood against the wall and watched her. Then, at the wedding, he had seen her for the second time, as a bridesmaid to her sister, this time in blue. White and blue, those were her colours. In his mind's eye, she never wore anything else.

On that day she looked at him as he was looking at her, with a smile and a question in her eyes, and an agony went through his heart, because he knew this was love, his only and eternal love – and it was without hope. For he himself was engaged. His forthcoming marriage had been publicly announced, a suitable and profitable match for which settlements had already been discussed between the young lady's father and his own.

In those days, one did not jilt a girl when things had gone as far as this. It was almost as unthinkable as a divorce. Even had he attempted it, after such a scandal, what kind of a reception would a girl from abroad, who had occasioned it, have found amongst his family and friends? In the very instant that his love was born he knew that he had lost it; in the same heartbeat he felt the intensity of delight and the shock of despair. He ought to have left immediately, found some excuse and departed. It was the honourable thing to do, and yet he had stayed. He had seen her look and her smile, and he wanted to explain.

After the wedding breakfast at which his eyes never left her, looking on her, as he knew, for the last time, he saw her disappear through a side door of the big drawing room. He followed her, down a narrow passage, into a little room lined with cupboards, overlooking, as he remembered, a courtyard. Every detail of it was stamped on his mind because he was ashamed. The scene that followed ought never to have happened.

He shut the door behind him, and she turned and looked up at him from under her bridesmaid's wreath of forget-me-nots. He spread out his arms, she came to him and he enfolded her.

'Darling,' he said, 'this is goodbye.'

And standing there, with her cheek against his shoulder, he told her everything. Talking over her head at the bleak window, interspersing his story with words of love which he should not have uttered, he felt her quiver and bent his head to kiss her cheek, which was wet with tears. Then she broke from his embrace and ran out of the room.

Somehow he found his way out of the house, wrote a letter of apology to his host, mentioning an urgent telegram

recalling him to London, and left Vienna. He never saw Mariella again.

Three months later he had been married.

* * *

All through that winter's day, during his solitary luncheon which Sims brought to him in his study, and after he had cleared it away, he indulged his reminiscences. There was no harm, no pain in them now. It was all so long ago. For him, Mariella had never grown old. For him, she had never changed. She was dead.

He took up her daughter's letter: 'My mother often spoke of you, she remembered you so well.' It was written in the past tense. For him, she had died on that day, when he had broken his heart. A silly phrase, or, rather, a debased one, but it had been true.

Nevertheless, he had lived his life and she, it seemed, had lived hers. She had married, had had a daughter, and had spoken of him to her. He had never spoken of her to anyone. He had shut her away in another world, in a realm of dreams.

But here was this letter, an actual, tangible fact, come to him by the post, written by an actual, living person, a total stranger, and yet . . . Something, he realised, would have to be done about it. And so, before going upstairs to bed that night, he wrote to Mariella's daughter and invited her to come and stay at Milton Place.

CHAPTER TWO

He would have to tell Emily. That, Mr Barlow said to himself next morning while going over his face with a safety razor, was an inescapable fact. His hand, he realised, while contemplating this necessity with distaste, was not quite as steady as it used to be. Although these contraptions were supposed to be foolproof, he had made a nasty scratch in front of his ear, and it was bleeding. Of course, it would have dried by the time Emily arrived, but she was bound to notice it. In the old days he had used cut-throat razors, a beautiful set of seven, one for each day of the week, in a leather case. He had never cut himself with those. He didn't care for this newfangled gadget, though it seemed everybody used them now. It had scratched him. He rubbed the place with a haemostatic pencil, but Emily would see it and say she was afraid his hands were getting shaky. She was always looking for signs of old age in him. She probably meant to be kind, but it was the sort of kindness that annoyed.

He would have to tell her about the letter and his reply to it, and he wondered what she would say. Not that it mattered, he told himself, it was none of her business. He did not have to

ask her permission to ask whomever he liked to stay in his own house.

Emily Mannering was Mr Barlow's younger daughter, a trim, tailored woman in her early forties who carried herself upright, walked briskly and was never tired. Her marriage to John Mannering, a company director in the City, was childless, and she made up for the dearth of home duties by a wide variety of outside activities. She sat on the board of several charitable societies, was a great organiser of bazaars, jumblesales and bridge tournaments at which she excelled as a swift and competent player, and she was also, with her husband, a member of two golf clubs. In fact, there was hardly a moment on any day of the week which, as she put it, she could call her own, though one might be tempted to ask whose they were, since they were all filled with self-chosen occupations. It was a pity, if one came to think of it, that Emily Barlow had not taken up a profession instead of marrying. She would have made an excellent political organiser, or a production engineer, if she had had the technical training, for she loved manipulating people, cutting out waste, getting things done. These traits she had most definitely inherited from her father. But in him they had been coupled with a creative imagination and backed by professional competence. He had been a civil engineer and administrator, and in that capacity had spent many years as adviser to governments in Africa and in Burma. But in Emily they seemed somehow out of scale, or misapplied, for with all her brains and willpower she lacked that complementary grace, so essential in a woman, the intelligence of the heart. For all her good works, she seemed a barren kind of person, not only physically, but spiritually as well.

It was Wednesday, the day marked in her schedule for coming to Milton Place. Everybody was a little tense on Wednesday mornings, a little apprehensive and somehow on their best behaviour, as before an inspection by a commanding officer. Everybody, however, is a big word to apply to such a very small number of people. It comprised, apart from Mr Barlow himself, the old butler Sims and his wife Alice, who were assisted, at irregular intervals, by Mrs Brown or Mrs Smith who came up from the village to give a hand with the rough and partake of a cup of tea. These ladies always kept well out of the way on Wednesday mornings. The outdoor staff consisted of Nichols, head gardener and chauffeur, a second man and a boy, who worked under him. They, too, were occupied in the more distant parts of the grounds this morning, but Nichols felt it to be his duty to be there.

At eleven o'clock, Mr Barlow heard the crunch of the car wheels on the gravel, and then Emily's voice calling out to Sims. He remained in his study, as this was what was expected of him. Emily would first want to talk to Sims and enquire about any occurrences during the week. Then she would go through the kitchen to Alice's little private den beyond.

The kitchen was a vast place, paved with flagstones, and had an enormous range. It must have been a warm and cheerful place in the old days, when the fire was alight and there was a bustle of maids about. But now the electric cooker, so small in comparison, tucked away in a corner next to the big stone sink, gave it a deserted look, made even more desolate

by the white wintry light filtering in through the high-placed windows, which were at ground level out of doors and afforded no outlook from within.

Ridiculous place, thought Emily, to cook in for a single old gentleman. For here in the domestic quarters, as everywhere else, the great house hung like a vast garment many times too big for the shrunken stature of its diminished inhabitants.

Diminished in the flesh they might be, but not diminished in spirit, as long as Alice Sims was one of them. Although she had no one now to order about, except her husband and the occasional Mrs Brown or Mrs Smith, she who had once been at the head of a large staff, as long as she had the use of her limbs she did not intend to abdicate. In vain did Emily try to persuade her that it was all too much for her and that she must say so to Mr Barlow. She was not, Alice said, going to live in one of them homes! It was not a question of comfort or convenience, but one of dignity and position. She had been at Milton Place for forty years and there she would stay as long as Mr Barlow stayed there. What would become of him without her? But what, Emily sometimes argued, if Mr Barlow gave up the house? That, said Alice, was for Mr Barlow to decide. She would certainly not wish him to do so. Sims himself would have been more amenable. He, for one, did not enjoy carrying trays, laying fires and sweeping the great expanse of hall and staircase. He would be quite prepared to retire, but he could not go against his wife. It was she who laid down the law.

Therefore, having provisionally renewed the armed truce which marked her relationship with Alice, Emily then had a few confidential words with Sims. She felt that he needed her protection and encouragement.

'This cannot go on, Sims, it positively can't, not for another winter. It's too much both for you and Alice, and Mr Barlow will catch his death of cold. I really shall have to do something about it.' To which Sims, who had heard this many times before, dutifully, resignedly and, perhaps, incredulously shook his head.

Emily bustled into the study with her usual 'Good morning Father!'

'Good morning, my dear.'

'How are you, Father?' She stooped to give him a peck on the forehead.

'I am perfectly well, thank you. I have no complaints. Has Sims got any? I heard you having a confabulation outside my door.' Mr Barlow's hearing was remarkably good.

Emily gave a little shrug.

'Well, you had better tell me. Was he disapproving of something, or were you?'

'Oh no, Father, nothing in particular,' Emily said without quite keeping the irritation out of her voice. 'It's only that you really ought not to be living here. Each time I come, I'm appalled again at how cold and uncomfortable it is. Somehow each week seems worse than the last. And it seems such a waste of effort, and money, and everything. When I think how well looked-after you could be, if only you would listen to reason. It tries my patience, it really does!'

'I'm sorry, Emily,' said Mr Barlow gently, 'but we've discussed all this before, haven't we? So we won't go over it

15

again. I like living here, in my own house. It may be inconvenient – you say it is, I don't find it so, and, anyway, I like it. I'm sorry if I try your patience, I may not do so very much longer. Who can tell?'

'Oh, Father, you know I don't mean to imply any such thing!' Emily took refuge in being annoyed. 'You know I am only worried for your sake, afraid of your catching cold.'

'I don't incline that way, my dear, sorry to disappoint you. I'm afraid you'll have to bear with me a little longer. So let's change the conversation. How's John?'

John, Emily said, was well and sent his love. He was very busy. She had been very busy too.

Changing the conversation was all very well, but there was always something laboured and contrived about anything she and her father tried to talk about on these weekly occasions. Mr Barlow had given up asking her in detail about what she had been doing, for she would then reel off a whole string of committee meetings and social engagements, as if she were reciting a catalogue. Her tone of voice, in answering any questions he might put, was compounded of: 'What's the use of explaining when you don't know anyone I am talking about', and 'I wish you'd mind your own business'. These words were, of course, never spoken, but Mr Barlow could hear them, nevertheless, just as clearly as if she had articulated them with the utmost precision. They didn't encourage him to take an interest in her activities. Emily, for her part, was incapable of being interested in any activities but her own. Thus, conversation was apt to hang fire, while Mr Barlow looked dreamily over his daughter's head, not being over-anxious to stare her in the face, and Emily desperately searched her mind for something to say.

A fretful silence ensued, in which Mr Barlow played with a paper-knife and Emily instituted a search of her handbag. Mr Barlow knew he would now have to broach the matter of the visitor before she got up to go. Best get it over, as casually as possible.

He opened a drawer and handed her Mrs Seiler's letter. 'You may be interested to read this,' he said.

'A letter? From whom?' Emily was immediately alert.

'Well, read it.' And Mr Barlow watched her face, under half-closed eyelids, while she did so.

'Fancy writing to you on such a very thin excuse!' she exclaimed at last when she had finished. 'What presumption! Asking for a recommendation on the strength of your having met her mother! It must have been ages ago. I don't suppose you even remember her?'

'I do remember her,' he said.

'You do? Did you know her well, then? This woman seems to imply that you did?'

'I only saw her twice in my life.'

'Then it is an imposition, writing to you like this out of the blue!'

'I should like to help,' said Mr Barlow slowly.

'Would you really? Well, in that case, I suppose I could do something about it,' said Emily, folding the letter and preparing to put it in her bag. 'I might easily hear of a situation for her, if you say she comes of respectable people. It is quite true that women prepared to take domestic jobs are in great demand. So, don't worry, Father, I'll deal with it.' She got up.

'No, Emily. Please give me back the letter,' Mr Barlow said gently. 'There is nothing you need do at this stage. I have already dealt with it. Perhaps, later on, when Mrs Seiler is here, I may ask for your assistance.'

'When Mrs Seiler is here, did you say?'

Mr Barlow took the letter from Emily's hand and put it carefully back into the drawer.

'Yes. I have written and asked Mrs Seiler to come and stay here, at Milton Place, for a little while.'

Emily was too dumbfounded, for a moment, to speak.

'You have asked her to come and stay here?'

'Yes. Is there any objection? I'm old enough to be her father, my dear.'

'Oh, of course,' Emily replied impatiently. 'I was thinking of Alice, and Sims. They won't be able to cope, they're too old, you don't realise, Father. And the state the rooms are in! They've all been shut up for so long. I don't suppose there's one fit to sleep in.'

'I admit I hadn't thought much about it.' Mr Barlow was slightly disconcerted. 'But there's Cecilia's room, that must be in a fairly reasonable condition. She was here in the summer. I think Alice does keep it in order for her. It's next to Tony's.'

'Yes, well, I suppose she can have Cecilia's. Since you've already written and asked the woman without consulting me, we must see how we can manage. I'll go and speak to Alice.'

'I'll speak to Alice myself, dear, you needn't bother.'

But Emily did speak to Alice, as Mr Barlow noticed when, in the evening, he broke the news to her of his expected guest.

'Lady coming to stay with you, Sir, so Mrs Mannering tells me. From abroad, I think she said. I'm very glad, Sir, you're to have a little company. Not so lonesome for you, Sir. I always thinks that it's dreadful how lonesome you are, Sir. The lady speaks English, I hope?'

'Indeed she does, Alice. She's written me a very nice letter.'

'Mrs Mannering says as you've known her a very long time, Sir. There's no friends like old friends, that's what I thinks, especially at our time of life.'

'But, Alice,' Mr Barlow corrected her, smiling, 'it's the lady's *mother* I knew a long time ago. Mrs Seiler must be – rather young.'

'Well, I hope she's no worse for that, Sir, though I don't hold much with the young ones, nowadays, I must say.'

'She's not exactly a girl, Alice.'

'So much the better, Sir. I'll get Mrs Crawfurd's room ready for her, Sir, so don't you worry.'

CHAPTER THREE

Anita arrived two weeks later, towards the end of a February afternoon which was clinging to daylight with quite noticeable success for appreciably longer than of late. Mr Barlow had sent Nichols in the old, shabby Bentley to fetch her from the station in Waterington. Mr Barlow rarely used the car these days, having very few neighbours now whom he cared to call on, and practically never driving into Waterington himself. So, apart from an occasional trip to the station, like the present one, only Nichols used it to fetch and carry for Alice or himself. But Mr Barlow stubbornly refused to sell it and buy a more practical one, much to Emily's annoyance.

'Can't afford a new car,' he would say, 'cost the earth nowadays, as well you know. As for these little tin cans they put on the road now, I couldn't get into them, in the first place, and should be rattled to death in them, if I could. No, my dear, the Bentley will last my lifetime.' So it would, being practically indestructible, though it did, as Emily said, drink petrol by the gallon.

Nichols, therefore, was sent in it to fetch Mrs Seiler, following a telegram announcing her arrival. She would wear

a bunch of violets on her coat as a means of recognition, she had written, and Nichols was duly instructed to look out for this sign.

Mr Barlow, who had spent the first week after despatching his invitation wrestling with growing misgivings as to the wisdom of his action, had been, somewhat irrationally, comforted by the mention of the violets. She might have said she would be wearing a green coat, or have a red feather in her hat, and his apprehension would have been increased. He was already dreading the invasion of his privacy, which he had, so unguardedly, brought upon himself, and the mention of any such crude detail as a green coat or a red feather would have made the threat more tangible and more fearsome. But a bunch of violets held something of a promise – violets in February, too. Mr Barlow spent the last half-hour thinking more about them than about their wearer.

As the time approached for the car to return, Mr Barlow put on his coat and went into the big drawing room which was cold and swathed in dust sheets, and stood by one of its windows that overlooked the drive. Now that the trees were bare, he could see quite a distance along its length, as far as the bend where the rhododendrons began. They were a dark wall in the background and the smooth boles of the limes which lined the avenue marched towards it like columns of grey stone. But on the right, where the drive widened in its final sweep up to the front door, stood a willow, and glancing towards it Mr Barlow saw that its slender and drooping branches were yellow with the rising sap. Mr Barlow smiled. The yellowing of the willow's trellis of twigs was the first sign of spring, and the first time he noticed it called for a little silent celebration in his mind. He had noticed it now, for the first time this year, and greeting the sign with the unspoken welcome he always gave it, he added the hope that the omen be favourable. Then the Bentley came into view, swerved and drew up at the door. Mr Barlow went out to greet his guest.

All he knew of her at first was that she was tall, that her voice was throaty and rather deep for a woman, that she wore a long fur coat that had seen better days, and a matching fur cap on her head. There, also, was the bunch of violets which, strange to say, were still fresh and fragrant. She unpinned them and held them out to him.

'Here I am,' she said, 'and here they are, so you know I am the right person. I kept them in a glass of water all the way in the train, and they haven't faded, see? Thank you so very, very much for inviting me.' Then she stopped, a delayed embarrassment overtaking her, as if she felt she had been too impetuous, too familiar.

Mr Barlow had bowed a little too ceremoniously, perhaps, a little defensively too, and that had given her pause. In the hall she pulled off her fur cap and uncovered an abundance of fair hair, not cut short, but coiled and piled up on her head, while wisps of it escaped about her ears and on her forehead, disarranged from travelling and its confinement under the fur cap. The colour was that of burnt straw and appeared faintly powdered, from a sprinkling of whiteness in it, hardly discernible in itself, but casting a sheen over the whole of it. The eyebrows were rather darker than the hair and rather thick, which made the eyes below them look more violet than blue. It was a fine, arresting face, but at the moment it looked drawn and pale, the nostrils were almost transparent and there were tiny lines round her eyes and at the corners of her mouth. She was tired from her long journey, no doubt, but a deeper weariness lay below this superficial fatigue. Yet, in spite of this, there was so much warmth and vitality in her very presence, in her smile and her gestures, that Mr Barlow felt his initial constraint giving way to ease almost at once.

'Will you come in and have tea with me before you go to your room?' he asked. 'Or would you prefer Alice to take you there first?'

'Oh, I should like very much to have tea, if you don't mind my being so untidy,' she said, and slipping off her coat she looked down rather doubtfully at the suit she was wearing – a very good one, but so worn that much of the resilience and resistance to crushing had gone out of it.

So Nichols was left to take care of the luggage: two shabby suitcases and a hold-all, while Mr Barlow led his guest into his study and installed her by the fire. Sims brought the tea. She made no move to pour it, but let him do it for her, taking it with sugar, but no milk, in Continental fashion, and just sat still and relaxed, looking around her with slightly parted lips and a smile that lay more in her eyes than her mouth.

'It is good to be here,' she said again, very softly, and fell silent. She seemed too tired to speak.

Mr Barlow felt it, and made no attempt to talk to her. He sat, sipping his tea, glancing at her now and again when her eyes wandered round the room, and trying to compare this living presence with his memories, with the half-recollected,

half-imagined dream figure he had lived with for so long. But try as he would, from the moment he had set eyes on this real woman, the dream-figure seemed to have faded completely from his mind. He could not say whether there was, or was not, any likeness between the two. He had lost Mariella. Anita was here.

Later she went to her room. Alice having been summoned to show her the way, she followed her up the wide staircase, round the gallery that ran at first-floor level round the hall, and down a wide corridor leading off it, until Alice opened a door. It was a large room, and after the chilliness of the stairs and landing, it struck warm and cheerful with a fire burning brightly in the wide grate. Alice and Sims between them had been nursing it carefully since morning. The curtains of large-flowered chintz, rather faded, were drawn across two large windows. Alice switched on the light.

All the way upstairs Alice had been chattering, giving information about the house: twelve bedrooms, all shut up now, apologising for the cold, telling her about the lack of servants, the maids who had not come back after the war. Her country accent made it difficult for Anita to understand her. So she only repeated 'Thank you, thank you' and 'Do not trouble' over and over again. 'Would Madam like a bath?' The water had been heated specially. Yes, Anita would be grateful for a bath, if Alice would show her the way, and dinner, she understood, would be at eight in the master's study. Did she think she could find it? She was sure she would.

So Anita unpacked her two not-very-large suitcases. And the big, non-committal room with its four-poster, its heavy, carved mahogany wardrobe and chest of drawers, its draped dressing table and rather forbidding chairs, began to unbend and make little friendly, familiar gestures to Anita as she put her photographs on the chest of drawers, her brush and comb and sundry small bottles on the dressing table, hung up her scanty wardrobe in the cupboard and spread her dressing gown and slippers in front of the fire to warm. It was indeed, as she had said, good to be here. This was a generous, dignified room. That dear old soul in her long black skirts who had brought her to it – she seemed like someone out of a book. Did such people really still exist in this country? That charming old gentleman downstairs ... But she must not think, must not reflect too much. Too much relief, suddenly, would destroy her self-possession: she must not embarrass her host by her emotions.

She had her bath and returned to dress in a soft, dark-red woollen dress, she brushed and coiled up her hair again, allowing no wisps to stray now. When she had finished, she looked both older and younger, more tidy and sedate in bearing, and more relaxed from her bath and her short rest.

Meanwhile Mr Barlow had been walking up and down in his study, wondering and pondering, and wishing that dinner and the evening were over, so that he could go to sleep and wonder and ponder no more. He had brought this upon himself: he had asked a strange woman to come and share his home with him, and had not specified for how long. He liked her. Yes, undoubtedly he liked her. She might have been dreadful, and she was not. But inevitably his daily routine would be disrupted, incidents would occur that he could not

foresee. He would, in some manner, have to entertain her. How would she get on with Emily, or, rather, Emily with her? Not, he thought, very well. In that quarter there was probably trouble ahead. And it had all been quite unnecessary. He had acted on an impulse – at his age! Ah, well, perhaps she would not stay very long. It would soon be over.

Sims came in and unfolded the table on which his dinner was served. He pulled out both leaves where usually one was enough, and spread a tablecloth over it instead of a napkin. He laid two places. Mr Barlow watched. Then the door opened again and Anita came in.

CHAPTER FOUR

For the second time that morning Cecilia Crawfurd unfolded her sister's letter and reread it over her mid-morning cup of tea. She smoothed out the wad of thick writing paper on a corner of the kitchen table on which she had placed the teapot and her cup, and sat down with a sigh, only to jump up again for a cloth with which to wipe the table which was wet again, of course, and was smudging the ink. There, the last page was blurred, but not illegible. She hoped she could now settle down in peace for at least quarter of an hour.

Emily did not write very often and Cecilia hungered for her letters, which took her out of herself and her immediate surroundings, and then mostly resented them when they came. Emily's life was so very different from her own; it always had been. Emily's life was interesting, she was in the midst of things, she had a part to play, people listened to what she said and took her seriously. And as if that were not enough satisfaction, she also had a gay life: she played golf, dined out with her husband, went away for weekends. But then, she had married John, dear John who had been such a jolly boy

and who was such an easy-going, pleasure-loving, pleasure-giving man. Whereas she, Cecilia, had married Dr Crawfurd.

'I won't think about it now,' Cecilia said to herself, 'I'll read Emily's letter.' There was a curious piece of news in it, that much she already knew, as she had skimmed through it at breakfast, but she had not yet been able, among all her morning chores, to take it in properly. Now she must concentrate. She glanced anxiously at the loud-ticking clock on the dresser; the minute-hand was moving, she hadn't got much time even now. Soon Mrs Blizzard would be down. She could hear her stamping about upstairs. What a hard-fisted, heavy-footed woman she was, and so ruthless going about her job. She's bound to smash the lamp on the dressing table one of these days. Cecilia wished she had put it in Tony's room, out of harm's way. It was not Mrs Blizzard's day to do Tony's room. Cecilia always removed all the more obviously breakable things from any room exposed to Mrs Blizzard's ministrations. However, I mustn't go up and take it away now, she thought, the hint would be too obvious. Mrs Blizzard might take offence, she took offence so quickly, at the slightest opportunity. But she was honest – and pretty regular. Cecilia sighed. Charwomen were getting more and more difficult to replace. 'I won't think about Mrs Blizzard, either,' she admonished herself again. 'I'll get down to Emily's letter.'

'Dear Cecilia,' she read, 'an unusually busy fortnight [it always was] – two nights in town last week, a very good play at the Lyric, but rather a dull revue to which John had to take some business people whom the firm was entertaining –

dinner at the Savoy. John always insists on my acting hostess on these occasions, rather a bore, but he says I'm an asset, and I must allow him to exploit me. [Exploit her, indeed! What a hypocrite she is, she loves it all the time!] The Maitlands down for the weekend – took them out to lunch on Sunday, to a delightful pub we've discovered near Alderhurst. The food is first-class, and I didn't have the fag of cooking on Sunday morning, thank goodness. [Ah, here it is!] Father has done such an amazing thing. You never know what old people will get up to. They're like children, they really want watching all the time. He's invited an Austrian woman to stay at Milton Place. He only told me about it after he'd written and sent off the invitation, so there was nothing I could do about it. She's the daughter of someone he met ages ago in Vienna when he was a young man. I didn't know he'd ever been there, did you? The woman asked whether he could find her a job as a governess or something. It seems her mother had kept a record of his name and address – can you imagine, after all these years? He showed me the letter, it wasn't even a sob-story as you might have expected, just a request to find her a job in this country, as cool as you please. I was going to advise him to put it in the waste-paper basket, when he told me he had already answered it and invited her to stay with him. What can have possessed him, I can't think! He hardly sees anybody these days and he detests strangers. I'm sure he'll hate her once she's here, and I shall have to take on the chore of removing her. I always have to do all the work. [Cecilia snorted at this.] Well, I suppose I shall be able to find her a post, she won't have to stay there long.'

There was a postscript. 'I have just rung up and heard that she has actually arrived. I wish I could go immediately, but I can't fit it in. But when I go next Wednesday, I shall <u>see</u>.' This last word was heavily underlined.

Cecilia put down the letter and finished her tea. Emily's special piece of news had not impressed her particularly. She wondered why Emily was in such a dither about it. Obviously, she would cope with this situation as she did with everything else. She let her thoughts hover for a moment about the dinner at the Savoy. What had Emily been wearing? She wished she had told her that, it would have been more interesting than finding a place for a foreign governess. She herself hadn't had an evening dress – if it *was* an evening dress – for years.

She hurried to put her cup away and set out a plain white one and the bottle of coffee essence for Mrs Blizzard's elevenses. She could hear her already tramping downstairs. One thing she could not face was having to sit down to a 'cuppa' with Mrs Blizzard. It was not that she thought Mrs Blizzard inferior to herself, she honestly accepted the creed that we are all equal. Goodness knows, her husband had dinned it into her – or, perhaps, 'sneered' it into her would be more correct – all the years of their marriage: 'Think yourself so grand, don't you? You, of course, are out of the top drawer.' But Mrs Blizzard sucked her coffee through her teeth and slobbered. She also smelled of perspiration. Cecilia *knew* it was honest sweat – but she could not endure it.

She put the letter in her overall pocket and left the kitchen as Mrs Blizzard came in. If only she had someone to talk to, someone with whom she could discuss Emily's news. But Emily and her news were out of another world. She could not explain them to anyone she knew without seeming to set herself apart, without appearing 'grand'. Her husband wouldn't listen to her. He would dash in for his dinner in a couple of hours' time, read the paper over his meal, ask for the list of people who had telephoned during the morning and be off to see whether everything was ready for his surgery. It was useless to try to talk to him. 'Noises off' he called any attempt she made at conversation. But even if he happened to be in a more receptive mood, she avoided as much as possible all references to Milton Place, for then he would immediately purse his lips, the corners of his mouth would come down in that intolerably ironic expression which made Cecilia sick at heart when she saw it. 'Ah, news from your ancestral home!' he would say, and Cecilia would stop short and look the other way, in case her eyes should begin to glisten.

From time to time, however, the subject could not be avoided, and that was when Tony was at Milton Place. The boy had a veritable passion for it and spent as much of his holidays there as he was allowed to. As he was away at boarding school during term-time, Cecilia, to her grief, did not see much of him, though she worshipped him with the complete abandon of her otherwise frustrated emotions. In sending Tony to public school she had defeated her husband, but defeated herself as well. Dr Crawfurd, the son of a Birmingham printer, had made his way through Grammar School and Medical School by his own hard work and natural ability, and he had held, very strongly, that Tony should do the same. The idea that a man should think himself privileged because the school he had been to had a famous name, was poison to him. But Cecilia, timid and ineffectual as she was, always anxious to adapt herself to her husband's habits, to accept his opinions and comply with his standards, had stood at bay over the education of her son. Her uncompromising stand on this one occasion sprang from deep-seated instinct rather than from reason. She had no clear views as to the merits of one school or another. But that her son must do what her father and her brother had done – her brother had died in early manhood – that seemed to her a necessity beyond doubt and discussion. She knew her husband could not afford the fees, so she had begged her father, whom she had never asked for anything before, to send Tony to his old school. Mr Barlow had agreed, and Dr Crawfurd, after making some satirical comments and observing a stony silence for several days, had then, quite suddenly, given in.

Cecilia now sat upstairs at her bedroom window, looking down onto the little square of front garden, the empty street, the blackened brick semi-detached houses opposite, each with its green-painted front door and its bay-window, exactly like her own. She sat there waiting for Mrs Blizzard to finish in the kitchen, so that she could go down again and put on the potatoes. Meanwhile she ought to get on with the mending. But she just hadn't got the energy to go and fetch it. She simply sat there, doing nothing, twisting and turning Emily's letter in her nervous, work-roughened fingers, while her thoughts, all the odd bits and pieces of petty worries and deeper sorrows, regrets, reminiscences and self-questionings, went round and round in her head. They were all in such a muddle, she could never sort them out. Why, she kept asking herself, had everything always gone wrong with her? Why had Emily had all the luck? Hardly out of her teens, she had married John, and hers had been such a 'suitable' marriage. John's mother and her own had been girlhood friends. Emily and John had known each other from nursery days and had grown up having the same ideas about life and how to live it. But she, the elder sister, had not been attractive to the young men of her set. They had all got married, one after the other, and she had been left behind. Yet, two or three times she had believed that one of them was going to propose to her, only to see him get engaged to someone else. She never could make out why. Then her mother's health had begun to fail, and finding Milton Place too damp and lonely in the winter while her father was away out East, they had come to live in Torquay. Here the old doctor who attended her mother had himself been taken ill and had sent his partner, recently arrived from the Midlands, to take his place. Dr Crawfurd had done wonders for Mrs Barlow, so she said, and she had liked him exceedingly. Cecilia knew it was her mother who had suggested to him that he should marry her, and when he actually did propose, she who had by then turned thirty accepted him without hesitation.

Her mother had always said that he was a remarkable man, and she had been right in her opinion, but Dr Crawfurd was also a frustrated man. And Cecilia was too limited of understanding to overcome the very real difficulties of living with him in harmony. He was very able, but somewhere, after his achievements at school and as a medical student, something had gone wrong with his career and he had not succeeded in becoming the specialist and consultant which had been the goal of his ambition. He himself attributed this ultimate failure to the harshness and narrowness of his childhood, the strain of too early struggles; but whether for this reason or because it was born in him, there was a lack of breadth, a cramped parsimoniousness and pettiness in his nature for which all his devotion to his profession could not compensate. Cecilia's dullness had not helped to sweeten his temper. Yet, she had been so willing and, she told herself, she had tried so hard. Only once, in this matter of Tony, she had insisted on going against his wishes. She had paid a heavy price for it. She saw very little of Tony. Dr Crawfurd said that since he had been forced to allow the boy's grandfather to pay for his schooling, Mr Barlow must also be allowed to have him in the holidays whenever he wished. 'That's the way you wanted it,' he would say, 'you must take the consequences.' And he always referred to Tony as 'your son'. 'When does your son's term end?', 'How long will your son reside with us before leaving for your father's estate?' – such questions and the tone of voice in which they were asked made Cecilia wince, but they would not have continued to inflict pain if Tony had, in feeling and affection, really been 'her son'. But Tony, even when at home, was unbearably aloof. He told her nothing that concerned him closely. He never kissed her spontaneously, only if she asked him, and she was ashamed of asking. She now thought that her husband had foreseen that it would be so, and that he had given in to her in order to punish her. And she wished in her heart of hearts, now that it was too late, that she had kept Tony at home, had let him go to school in the town and make friends there. Perhaps even her marriage would have come right if she had done that.

Emily's letter was really smudged now, because of those tears that kept welling up and had fallen on it. She tore it up. Then she heard the front door bang and, looking out, she saw Mrs Blizzard's ample figure under her elaborate hat proceeding down the street. Cecilia heaved a sigh of relief at her departure and went downstairs to cook.

CHAPTER FIVE

Mr Barlow and Anita Seiler found it much easier to talk to each other than either of them had expected.

'How do you pronounce your name?' he asked her as they sat down to dinner.

'As if it were written in English with a 'y', 'Syler',' she said, 'but, please, could you call me Anita, because we are going to be old friends. Will you think me – how shall I say – too familiar, if I tell you that already I feel so very much at home?'

'I am delighted to hear you say so, and I hope, indeed, that you will be comfortable.'

'It is not comfortable that I mean,' she replied, lifting her head and looking slowly round the room where the book-cases rose into the shadows and the tall curtains fell from their stiff velvet pelmets. 'I do not mean comfortable,' she repeated, 'but I feel so – comforted.'

He smiled. 'You make fine distinctions,' he said, 'but I understand your point. As for creature comforts, as we call them, I must beg your forbearance. Things are not as they used to be. There are no servants. Mine are very old, like myself. The house is too big. We can only live in a very few rooms, and in the winter it is difficult to keep even those warm. I have come not to mind, for myself. One gets used to things, you know. But now that you have come, I can see what my daughter means when she says the place is no longer fit to receive guests. It was very rash of me to ask you to come, especially in the winter. When my daughter pointed out to me how inhospitable the house is, my letter had already gone.'

'How very lucky for me,' she said laughing, 'that you did not consult your daughter before you wrote. If you had, I might not have been here tonight. And I am so very, very grateful that you have let me come. Please, do not worry about me. All the things you talk about I do not mind at all, not at all.'

She smiled and looked with a tender, more lingering look at the old gentleman sitting opposite her, very upright, his sparse silvery hair above his high forehead, the white, bushy eyebrows and the strong, thin nose. She would have liked to stretch out her hand and touch one of his as it rested beside his plate, a long hand veined with blue and covered all over with little brown specks like freckles on the golden, translucent skin. But she restrained herself. He was too remote.

'I am sorry for your sake, Mr Barlow, that there are all these changes you speak of. To me they will not matter. I only feel tonight what has *not* changed – what has endured.'

Feeling that she had got into deep waters, she lightly turned the conversation to little incidents of her journey, while Mr Barlow fell to reminiscing about his own travelling days at the turn of the century, along that winding line through the Alps, the long smoky tunnels, how the engine had to be refilled with water every so often from funnels erected on poles and overhanging the line like the arm of a crane. It had been delightful, while this was in progress at some tiny station, to open the windows of the carriage, after having been half-suffocated with the fumes, and to breathe the sweet, cold air of the pastures and the pine forests, until the train chugged on again to the next halt.

No mention was made by either of them of the reason for his one-time journey to Vienna, nor did they allude to the long and tenuous thread of circumstance that, starting from there, had brought Mrs Seiler to sit opposite him in his half-lit study that February evening. In this avoidance there was no feeling of intention or constraint. They chatted easily for a while, and very early, asking Mr Barlow's indulgence for her tiredness, Anita went up to bed.

The first evening was over, and Mr Barlow, too, was tired. It had been a day of emotion for him, and he no longer wanted emotion. He had felt disturbed, and he hated disturbances. For him: the unruffled flow of days and nights, the regular recurrence of small daily and weekly events, the repeated mechanical actions of physical life and, unimpeded by these, withdrawn from any involvement in decisions and conflicts, a deep and pure enjoyment of simple and beautiful things – of the things he loved. His trees and his grasslands, his garden paths in their seclusion, and the play of light, the changing skies above them, according to the seasons and the hours – on these his spirit dwelt with delight, as it did in the evening on his books. And sometimes, when the mood overtook him, he played in his mind with the love he had

never had and no longer wanted, but which he was now free to remember without disappointment or regret, because it had never been real. It was because of this daydream that he had responded to Anita's letter, and ever since he had been dreading the consequences of that act. He did not want anything to touch his dream.

Anita had not touched it. She had made no allusions, asked no questions, had not tried to pick up threads of the past. In her person she reminded him of no one. She was just herself, and he liked her. Her voice was low-pitched, her command of English excellent, though some turns of phrase were, perhaps, unexpected, her accent barely perceptible, but just sufficient to give her speech an unaccustomed flavour, like some unusual spice which would be offensive to the taste if too pronounced, but the faint trace of which is interesting, even alluring. Mr Barlow sighed with relief as he lay down between the sheets. He did not think the visit was going to be too difficult.

Anita, too, relaxed with contentment as she lay down to sleep. She was, above all, physically worn out tonight, and the sheer comfort of the big bed, the large, restful room, the silence of the night outside the windows, for which she was unutterably grateful. She, too, had liked her host, his charm and dignity, his slightly ceremonious politeness. And she was grateful that he had asked no questions, neither about her family, nor her past life or her present circumstances, nor why she had wanted to come. All that might happen later, but for tonight at least he had accepted her as she was. She was in a place where, for tonight, perhaps for a little while, if that were granted to her, she could lay down her burden of sorrow, fear and disgust, and, stretching out her limbs under the protecting blankets, she fell asleep like a child.

Next morning she slept late and it was in that blissfully hazy state between dreaming and waking that she faintly perceived Alice's light tap on her door. The old woman had brought her a tray of breakfast, and finding the visitor awake at last, came in to draw the curtains. Anita was full of apologies and thanks. She was, she said, not used to being waited on and would not allow it to happen again. She made Alice sit down and talk while she enjoyed her breakfast. Alice objected that she was not used to sitting down and chatting with ladies in their bedrooms, but Anita laughed and said it was an unusual day and they must behave in an unusual fashion. Anita wanted to know about the house, and there was nothing Alice loved better than speaking about it and about the old days (nostalgically) and the new ways (disapprovingly). To find such an eager and understanding listener was very gratifying to her. When, at last, Anita decided that she would have to get up, and Alice exclaimed that, dear me, she was forgetting herself and her work this morning, the two women were friends.

Sims was relieved to find his wife in such a good temper in spite of her repeated trips upstairs to see whether the foreign lady had woken up, but that was as nothing compared to Emily's amazement, later on, when she found that in Alice's eyes Mrs Seiler could do no wrong. Amongst the many problems to which Anita's coming was going to give rise, this one would seem to Mrs Mannering the most inexplicable one and would puzzle her to the end.

Anita had certainly not set herself, that morning, any far-reaching purpose to captivate old Alice. She just found old Alice delightful. Alice was exactly what she had imagined an old English housekeeper ought to be. True, she was not wearing a black silk dress and a lace cap. Her hands were roughened with tasks such as, in the novels Anita had read, no traditional housekeeper would ever have had to perform. There had been changes. But Anita's perceptions were attuned not to the changes but, as she had said the night before, to everything that had not changed, to all that had endured. Alice as a character, Alice as a philosophy of life had endured. And Milton Place itself, in spite of closed rooms and cold passages and other changes which she would presently discover, had endured also, as had above all, and most emphatically, Mr Barlow himself.

Anita got up and went to the window, which overlooked the terrace. It had been dark when she arrived and she did not know what she should see. Now it was a hazy day with a suggestion of sunshine behind several veils of mist and a soft radiance on the pale green of the lawns, There was a cheerful chirping of birds in the great cedar, and from this majestic tree her eyes wandered to the more distant scattering of oaks and beeches. There was a deep stillness and an exquisite gentleness in it all. She opened the window and looked and listened. How good it was, she thought, just to see and to hear, to let the sight of these things sink into one's consciousness to the exclusion of all else, to immerse one's mind in this silence made audible by the voices of blackbirds and chaffinches.

Later, when she saw Mr Barlow strolling on the terrace below, in his greatcoat and cap, she leaned out of the window and called to him 'good morning!'. He answered, and asked her to come and join him. Together they walked back and forth along the grey stone front of the house, and Mr Barlow told her, with many rambling diversions and loving reminiscences, about its history and the life he had lived in it.

'My grandfather built it,' he said, 'it was not a good period for architecture, and, as you see, it's not beautiful. But I think it has dignity. There was a much older building here before, possibly an abbey, built of brick. Some of the old walls were still standing. I've used them to enclose part of the garden, as you shall see, and when there weren't enough bricks, I used to search the countryside when I was home on leave from the East for more of them to match and complete the enclosure. The walled garden is very old, though I built it. There's not much to be seen in it just now, but of the whole place it is, I think, what I like best.'

The pale winter sunshine was getting warmer towards midday and Mr Barlow unbuttoned his coat. Then, as he talked, and hardly noticing what he did, he put his arm through Anita's for support and as if to engage her attention more closely. For now he was saying aloud the things he so often turned over in his mind, and he was savouring those things which had, perhaps, gone a little stale from their long, solitary confinement in his memory, with renewed relish. He felt Anita's real pleasure in listening, not the politeness veiling impatience which he was wont to encounter when speaking to younger people. Anita, for her part, with the gentle prospect and the muted colours before her eyes, felt confirmed by his talk in her sense of peace and security, in which she relaxed and came to rest.

CHAPTER SIX

Anita had been at Milton Place for two days when Emily put in an appearance. She came in a hurry, and she came annoyed; it was Monday, not her usual Wednesday, and she really couldn't spare the time. But it was obviously her duty to see that Mrs Seiler had been made as comfortable as possible in the circumstances. Of course, she was curious, but Mrs Mannering would never have admitted curiosity as a reason for changing her plans.

It had been raining, but the rain had stopped for a little while. Mr Barlow and Anita were again walking on the terrace before lunch. A new little habit was beginning to form itself; the slightest suggestion as yet of an incipient pattern, but Mr Barlow was already enjoying the recurrence. Then they heard the car come to a stop in the drive and the slamming of the door.

'That must be my daughter Emily,' remarked Mr Barlow, 'though it's not Wednesday, the day she usually honours me with her visit. She never comes on any other day – too many important engagements, you know. She must be terribly curious about you to neglect them.'

Anita caught the trace of irony in his voice and the faint twitch of a smile on his lips. Unconsciously she put up her guard.

Emily came round the corner, introductions were made, the two women shook hands and Emily pecked her father's cheek. She then immediately developed a smoke-screen of words, and from behind this protecting volubility she looked Anita up and down and, as she believed, inside out.

'Ah, Mrs Seiler, I see you are already sharing Father's morning stroll. I'm not staying to lunch, Father, I've already told Alice not to change her preparations. So difficult for her anyhow, poor old dear. It's the committee meeting of Hamley House this afternoon at two and I'm in the chair, so I can't be late. I'll get a snack at the tea-shop on the corner, they give you quite a decent little lunch there, quite enough for me. I don't think it's a good idea to eat a lot in the middle of the day when you have work to do afterwards, do you, Mrs Seiler? Or perhaps you do on the Continent? Now, Mrs Seiler, I've come to see whether you are being made comfortable and what I can do for you. What kind of a job do you want? No, don't tell me now, I'm in such a rush. It takes such a big chunk out of my day when I have to come out here. Darling Father, he is so very obstinate in insisting on living out here, all by himself, aren't you, dear? Well, Mrs Seiler, you must think it over, and so will I, and I'll come and discuss plans with you as soon as ever I can. I shan't come this Wednesday, Father, because I've been here today. You won't need me so much this week because you have Mrs Seiler's company. So I shall be able to go to the golf club luncheon which I would otherwise have had to miss, so it all fits in very well. Now that I have seen you, Mrs Seiler, I think I know exactly what will suit you. In fact, I'm sure I do. So I'll be making the necessary enquiries. It may take a little time to find the right thing, but I can't help it. Father didn't consult me when he asked you over and you arrived before I had time to turn round, or I might have had everything ready for you. Well, now I must rush. Goodbye, Father, goodbye Mrs Seiler, I'll look after you, I promise, so you needn't worry.'

While this was going on, Mr Barlow stood patiently leaning on his stick, as if waiting for the rain to stop. Anita had made a few hesitant attempts to answer what seemed to be questions addressed to her, and had given them up. She had visibly wilted.

'That was my daughter Emily,' Mr Barlow said laconically. 'She is a little tiring. I think I shall now go indoors.' At the door of his study he turned to Anita with a smile. 'She will not come again until next week, on Wednesday,' he said.

Anita went upstairs to her room and moved about there listlessly. The room showed her a cold, indifferent face. The view from her windows was blurred with rain. She began opening drawers that were empty, putting things straight that had not been untidy; futile, aimless gestures that her tense nerves compelled her to perform. How pitifully her two dresses, her suit and her old fur coat hung in that immense wardrobe! How thinly her few pieces of underwear and her three pairs of stockings were spread in one of the wide drawers! But it was not the scantiness of her few possessions that depressed her. They were but a sign that nothing belonged to her and she belonged to no one. It was the sense of her loneliness, of being utterly rootless and cast adrift that overwhelmed her. The last two days in this old house, in Mr Barlow's company, had assuaged it and almost made her forget, as a sedative smooths away pain without curing its cause. Mrs Mannering's brisk intensity had broken the easeful spell. Mrs Mannering was neither rootless nor adrift. She had her purpose and place in life and she would put other people in theirs. She would decide and Anita, who now had no purpose and no place of her own, would accept her decision.

She sat down at the dressing table to look at her photographs. One, in a well-worn leather frame, was of a fine-looking man with a thick moustache, wearing a frock coat and a very high stiff collar. This was the only one her father had ever had taken. She had hardly known him looking like that, but she tried hard to remember him thus, instead of as he had been at the end. There was one of a schoolboy and one of a young girl, in cardboard folders, which she glanced at quickly and looked away, and a faded snapshot of a woman, younger than herself and far more elegant, in a hat with a veil and a fox-fur. At this one she smiled and shaped a kiss with her lips. Catching sight of her own silent greeting in the looking-glass, she suddenly took courage again, as if from an answer received, and went down to lunch.

The afternoon she decided to spend out of doors in spite of a persistent misty drizzle. The air and the earth smelt damp and sweet. Passing through the walled garden and out through the gate in the opposite side, she came to the kitchen garden, a paved path flanked by strips of dark upturned soil.

Behind them, and at right-angles, were the beds where the vegetables would grow; a few cabbages and sprout stalks were still standing. Further on came the raspberry canes and currant bushes. On the right side behind the vegetable plots two long greenhouses stretched all the way down. Beyond the kitchen garden, with the drive on her left, was a kind of garden she had never seen before, a park in miniature, she called it. Clusters of trees and shrubs, most of them leafless and unrecognisable to her untaught eye, grew here in beds of varying shape and size. Between and around them all was lawn; there was no gravel anywhere, but the grass itself formed soft and silent paths, winding in and out and around the trees and bushes, widening to give a view into open country, narrowing as if leading to a secret entrance, to a hidden retreat. There was something mysterious and enchanting in this part of the grounds; even in the bareness of winter it formed a little world of its own, secluded and protected, and disclosing new discoveries at every turn of the paths. Anita wandered around here with the soft rain on her face and the soft turf underfoot, in the stillness of the grey afternoon. Suddenly, at a turn she had not seen before, she came to a break in the ground which fell away steeply into a deep valley or ravine, and all cultivation seemed to cease. It was a wilderness. A row of rocks or huge stones stood along the edge of the valley, piled one on top of the other, polished and pitted as if, long ages ago, they had been rolled and scoured by an immense torrent. Now they were covered with vegetation and even great trees had grown upon them, gripping them on all sides with their powerful roots and drawing their sustenance from cracks and fissures where no soil or moisture was visible to the eye. Down below, the valley was dark with the shiny foliage of evergreens through which bare trunks of leafless trees rose up. The grass at their foot was long and wet. Anita did not venture down. She was already soaked through, so she turned back towards the more domesticated parts of the grounds, where she came out at the entrance to the drive. Going out into the road she followed it and found her way to the bottom of the meadows overlooked by the terrace. Here she opened a wicket gate and climbed up towards the house.

Mr Barlow saw her from his window and waved to her. She waved back. Her fit of depression had passed. Hurrying to the door, she kicked off her sodden shoes before entering the hall and ran upstairs in her stockinged feet to change. She felt younger than she had for years.

Mr Barlow, now sitting by the fire to which Sims had moved the tea table, watched the door through which she would presently come in with a feeling of pleasant anticipation. When she came a few minutes later, she had smoothed her hair and her movements were again quiet and sedate as she poured out the tea. But she had brought with her a smell of fresh air, her face had colour in it and to Mr Barlow, too, she seemed younger than he had thought her to be.

He wanted to know where she had been, and she was able to describe most precisely, as he questioned her, the ins and outs of her wanderings amidst the shrubs and trees, so that he, knowing every inch of the ground, could follow her everywhere in his mind's eye. Time and again he interrupted her to tell her the botanical name of what she had seen growing, and to describe the leaf and the flower that would be appearing in a few weeks, or a couple of months, in one place and another. But the big surprise, he said, would come in the valley, in that forbidding wilderness that lay in the deep fold behind the out-cropping rocks.

'You wait and see,' he said, 'just wait and see, and you will be amazed.'

She looked at him in silence for a moment, slowly sipping her tea. 'I wish I could,' she said with a sigh, 'oh, I do wish I could.'

'And why can't you?' he asked.

'I shall not be here,' she said simply.

He looked up sharply. 'Not be here? What nonsense! Of course you'll be here. You can't leave until you have seen, until I have shown you. But there, I am not going to tell you, you will have to see for yourself. And there is so much else besides. In a few weeks it will all begin.'

Now that he was speaking of his garden, Mr Barlow was launched on the subject nearest his heart and one that, all his life, he alone of his family had cherished. The love of a garden is of all human passions most akin to the love of a beloved person, a child or a woman. It calls for tenderness and care, for years of patience and faith in the future, when for long periods there may be nothing to show. To all this it may respond at times with disappointments, and at others with sudden, renewed promise. It must be guided and planned, yet never constrained; and however lovingly imagined and foreseen, will yet, when come to fulfilment, overwhelm with a spontaneous and divine perfection that surpasses all intention. In maturity it will be a companion for life, renewing its beauty year by year and keeping alive in the heart of its lover, though he himself may age, the resilience of youth. Yet it will suffer no mawkishness or false indulgence, but require from the gardener the discipline and restraint that keeps it from deterioration and excess. Like human love, the love of a garden is not an affair of the heart alone. Knowledge and understanding, study and experience are as needful to it as affection, and if any of these were absent, the others would be of no avail.

These were the things Mr Barlow talked about to Anita while drinking his tea. He spoke chiefly from his knowledge, the emotion remaining implied. Nevertheless, it was present all about him in the room and was as tangible to Anita as the light of the lamp and the taste of her tea. Mr Barlow was showing himself to her in a new dimension and in greater depth. How much better she was beginning to know him now, and how rewarding what she knew! She just sat silent and listened while he felt it quite effortless to talk. Here was someone who was neither critical nor bored, someone eager to learn, someone he could teach almost from the very beginning. Providence could have done him no greater favour.

* * *

Meanwhile, Emily, back from her meeting, was scribbling a note to her sister to give her the news.

'Mrs Seiler,' she wrote, 'is a middle-aged woman of indifferent appearance. She has lots of hair done up in an

unfashionable way and her clothes are rather the worse for wear. She probably is, as Father said she was, a gentlewoman in reduced circumstances, though, being a foreigner with a foreign accent, it is hard to tell. She seems quiet and unassuming, but she doesn't look very efficient and I wonder whether she would be much good in the house. Companion to an old lady will probably be the most suitable thing for her. Anyway, as Father has brought this on himself, he will have to put up with her for a while, and if she upsets Alice and Sims – well then, between you and me – so much the better!'

CHAPTER SEVEN

It was raining again, a cold, penetrating February rain which was half sleet, and the clouds hung low and dark. It went on, day after day, and there seemed no reason why it should ever stop, except for an hour or so to catch its breath, and to come on again. Anita had found herself an absorbing and satisfying occupation. It fulfilled her need for physical activity and, engaging all her attention, kept her mind from useless brooding. She was cleaning the house. A labour of Hercules, she told herself ruefully, far beyond the capacity of one pair of hands and out of all proportion to the time she would have to devote to it. Still, she hoped that by concentrating her efforts she might be able to make some small impact on the dust of neglect that reigned almost everywhere outside Mr Barlow's bedroom and study. Downstairs and upstairs she had opened all the doors, looked into all the rooms. Everywhere shutters were closed and curtains were drawn. Furniture loomed in the darkness. Cupboard doors refused to open or creaked on their hinges, revealing vague shapes of things wrapped and stacked and put away.

Anita decided to start on the dining room and a small drawing room across the hall from Mr Barlow's study, so that he should not be disturbed. She conferred with Alice, for she had to enlist, not her assistance which she did not want, but her benevolent acquiescence which was essential. Alice was at first horrified at the idea, but Anita succeeded in bringing her round. She coaxed the necessary cleaning materials out of her, and Alice finally volunteered to call a man in to move the heavy pieces and to put them back in their place.

'I don't want to think,' Anita explained, 'there is nothing like really hard work to keep you from thinking.' Alice, who had worked hard all her life and had never had to try not to think, was a bit puzzled, but Anita had a most persuasive way with her, so Alice at last put it down to 'foreigners always being a bit queer'. This queerness admitted, the old couple very soon found themselves in a relationship to Anita made easy by the very fact of her foreignness. They were unable to 'place' her. Their instinctive perceptions detected no overtones in her background or speech to embarrass them by an intentional familiarity, or to offend them by a concealed condescension. They thought her strange, but did not find it at all strange to be at ease with her. She made them laugh when she used unusual expressions, and were anxious to explain their own idioms which she had not immediately understood. All this would happen in the middle of the morning when, in her overall, she would join them for a cup of tea, or during the washing-up which she often took over, or even doing a bit of cooking while Alice got on with the ironing and Sims cleaned the silver. She would listen with pleasure to the stories of 'before the war' and 'the old days when Mrs Barlow was alive and Mr Barlow was out East'. Alice enjoyed an audience as much as Mr Barlow did, and like him she found a listener who was both ignorant and interested, the most gratifying of all audiences. And Anita was untiring with her questions. She wanted to know what the ATS were which the maids had joined during the war, and what Sims had done in the Home Guard, and about the Messerschmitt which had been brought down on a neighbouring farm during the Battle of Britain. Why, the very name 'Battle of Britain' was new to her! Long-suppressed springs of garrulity broke forth from the two old people, while Anita steeped herself in the lore of the country, the family and the house.

When Mr Barlow, who during the bad weather confined himself almost entirely to his study and his books, asked her what kept her so busy, she told him she was 'exploring'. He did, indeed, hear her, from time to time, 'rummaging' about, but, absorbed in his reading, gave no further thought to it. Mrs Mannering did not reappear on the following Wednesday, nor on the two next ones, telephoning instead to enquire after Mr Barlow's health and hoping that Mrs Seiler was not getting impatient. She had not yet heard of any suitable employment for her. Mr Barlow sounded contented on the telephone and assured her that there was no hurry. So Emily thought she was justified in giving herself a holiday for once and saving the time and the trouble of going out to Milton Place in this appalling weather, while her father had company of his own choosing.

At last the skies cleared. March had come in and with it a warm spell and a real breath of spring. Yellow and purple crocuses appeared in the grass, and snowdrops in sheltered spots under the trees. Anita got through her morning work in time to walk with Mr Barlow on the terrace in the sun, and on a specially mild day she sat with him on a bench in an angle of the walled garden. Here there were many bright crocuses and the later bulbs were pushing up their green spears through the earth. She was leaning back, half-closing her eyes, and looking through her lashes at the many-shaded rosy bricks of the wall opposite.

'What are you thinking about?' Mr Barlow asked.

'I am looking at the colours of the bricks,' she said, 'I have never seen any quite like them before. They seem to be alive. They answer the sun when it shines on them, each with its own particular shade of pink, some almost orange, some brownish, some mauve – they are all different and all in harmony, like a choir of colours.'

Mr Barlow looked at her curiously. Her description of his cherished wall, which he had so carefully and discriminatingly reconstructed and completed, gave him a thrill of pleasure. But he did not now wish to speak about the wall. Instead, he asked her abruptly: 'Why are you doing so much work in the house?'

She sat up, startled. 'Work in the house?' she echoed lamely.

'Yes. You told me you were "exploring". But now I find that for days on end you have been what Alice calls "spring-cleaning". She tells me it is back-breaking work. She should never have allowed it, only she tells me you insisted.'

'Oh, Mr Barlow, are you angry?' Anita's voice was full of dismay.

'No, I'm not angry. But I don't understand. Surely you do not feel obliged to do servants' work while staying as a guest in my house?'

'Mr Barlow, please do not think of it in that way. It is not at all what I mean. I like the work for its own sake, and just now it is what I need, what is good for me inside. I am like a dog who eats grass because somehow he knows that it is medicine for him. This work is my "eating grass". Besides,' she added with a little laugh, 'nowadays you must not say "servants' work". I do not think of Alice and Sims as servants, I think of them as old friends of yours, part of your household, almost part of your family. I have explained to them what I do, I think they don't mind. Please, you must not mind either.'

Mr Barlow sat silent, drawing lines with his walking stick on the ground before him. He did not know what to make of this declaration.

Anita went on. 'I will now try to explain to you. At first I just wanted to do things for the doing alone, to get tired and not to think. I did not expect to be interested. But now I like the rooms themselves very much indeed. They are so big and dignified, and to work in them is, as I told you before, an adventure of exploring. When I go in it is dark. I don't know what I shall find, but I feel it will be friendly and reassuring. I go and open the shutters and the windows and let in the light and the fresh air. I love the old-fashioned furniture, the carved mahogany, the chairs with the flounces, the glass cupboards, the inlaid tables, the bronze lamps. My great-aunts had furniture like that, so it gives me a family feeling. I like to think I am bringing it back to life. Something of myself comes back to life with it. The big drawing room I have not tackled, I have only looked inside. It is so big and so full of things and of shadows, it is like a forest in which to lose one's way. There will probably not be time for that, which is a pity.' She ended with a sigh.

'Dear me,' said Mr Barlow, 'you make dusting and polishing sound very interesting. But I still don't quite understand why you want to do it. You will only exhaust yourself.'

'Oh no, I promise I will not make myself too tired. Only a little tired, that is very pleasant. Also, at the end of the day I feel I have done something, and in the morning I feel I have something to do. Look, you have told me about keeping order in the garden, and how one has always to fight weeds and get rid of brambles. You said that a large part of cultivation was fighting disorder and decay. Well, what I am doing in the house is just that, only instead of cutting down nettles and brambles, I am getting rid of dust and cobwebs and moths. Something to do,' she added, 'and something worth doing.'

They sat silent for a while and then, very gently, Mr Barlow took her hand and held it for a minute in his own.

'I don't want you to think me curious about your private concerns,' he said, 'and if it distresses you to speak about them, I shall ask no questions. But you have now told me so much, by implication, in wanting to get tired and trying not to think, that perhaps you may want to tell me some more. There is now enough confidence between us, I believe? You would not hesitate to talk to me?'

'Oh, Mr Barlow, why should I burden you, or bore you, with all this. There are so many horror stories – in the main they are simply dull and disgusting. Mine is not at all sensational or very interesting. Much worse things happened to other people, I know. But for me – I think it was chiefly that I couldn't believe that what happened to me could happen at all. It did not seem humanly possible. But it was possible – only, perhaps, not human. Even now, I am still wondering. My mother – you knew her when she was a girl, didn't you? – well, she died before it all happened. She was still far too young to die, and at the time it was a great grief to my father and to me. Afterwards we used to say to each other how thankful we were that she had not lived longer, but it seemed such a distortion of our real feelings to say we were glad she was dead.'

Mr Barlow did not interrupt. Collecting herself, Anita continued: 'I had married very young, and I had a boy and a girl, but after my mother's death I spent a lot of time with my father who was very lonely. Fortunately, we lived very near to each other and I could see him every day. He was much older than my mother and was retired, having been all his life in the service of the State. At the end he was the administrative head of a ministry, you understand, not the political one, because he belonged in his feelings and tradition to the old monarchy. He was a very wonderful man – or at least I thought so – but he certainly was such a gentleman, courteous, scrupulous, single-minded, and so generous. I used to think of him as a gold coin: as he grew older, he wore thinner and lighter, from much use, but he never got tarnished.

'My husband was a geologist and an expert on all kinds of ore. For the first few years of our marriage we lived in Graz, in Styria, where he lectured at the University, until he became a professor in Vienna. He was very good-looking, and I fell in love with him. We were quite happy. In the thirties he began to travel a lot, chiefly in Germany, for study, so he told me. I didn't know he was doing political work. In '38 he was away a great deal, but that was nothing unusual. I had the children to look after and I spent a lot of time with my father, so I didn't have much social life. There was a growing tension and uneasiness amongst people. All sorts of rumours were going about, there were threats and forebodings from some while others laughed them off and made light of them. And some were filled with a kind of secret and uncanny glee which had something sinister about it. So I went out less and less, I just attended to my household and on most days I walked with my father in the park.

'It was warm that spring and we used to sit in the sun, as we are sitting now, and watch the children playing and listen to the birds. We both knew, of course, about the threats and rumours, the secret and not-so-secret Nazi organisations, the struggle of the government to hold its own. But my husband was away, my father was old, his thoughts were remote. I think we neither of us quite realised what was happening – until it actually burst upon us. There it was: German soldiers, German tanks in the streets, march music, shouting crowds, hysteria. And everywhere, from all the buildings, the long, streaming, red banners with the black hooked cross in the centre, like long gashes of blood crawling with spiders.'

Anita paused, remembering. 'It was a horrible sight. It is all gone now, of course, and most people are ready to forget or have already forgotten, as if it had never been. But I cannot forget because of something that happened a little later and was personal to me, and this setting was all a part of it. What made it all so eerie was that on the whole, away from the parades, the flags and the loud-speakers, everything still looked the same: the lilac bushes in the parks were beginning to bloom, and the children still played in the sandpits. Only people's faces were different, and the thoughts they thought. No one looked straight at you, for fear of betraying themselves. One felt fear and despair, and malice watching you to see whether you were afraid. There were types in the streets one used not to see, young fellows, and women, too, who swaggered and lurched against you, talking too loud and using foul language for everyone to hear.

'The schools had been closed for lessons. The children were on organised holidays, they were given flags and badges and marched about the streets. Of course, mine had to go too. I didn't ask them what they thought about it, I didn't want to know. I hoped it was fun for them, that's all, and that it would pass. Father and I went for our usual walks in the park where it was quiet. He was so deeply grieved he could only shake his head in silence, and sometimes I saw him brush away a tear. It would have been better to have stayed at home, but the weather was hot, he needed the fresh air and he hated being shut up. I did my little bit of shopping on the way home.

'One day, about a month later, the schools had been re-opened, my father and I were crossing a wide open square, when we saw a man lying, face downward, in the roadway, sprawled out and jerking with his arms. There was no one near him. Several people passed, and all glanced furtively over their shoulder at him, then pretended they had not seen him and went on. No policeman anywhere, no one to help, no crowd of onlookers, as usually gather round an accident – just this wide square and a wounded man lying there, alone as in a desert. But my father, who had been leaning on my arm, suddenly let go, straightened up and went towards him. Then everything happened terribly quickly. I think I tried to stop him, as a man in the black SS uniform came out of a house near where the man was lying, and shouted two or three times: "Keep away, keep away, you fool, keep away!" But my father either didn't hear or took no notice. He went on and bent over the man on the ground who lifted his head and, I think, spoke to him. At that moment, two men in brown rushed out of the house, there were shots, and my father fell over the prostrate figure.

'I suppose I screamed, but the next thing I knew was that the man in the black uniform, who had shouted "Keep away", was holding me up and putting his hand over my mouth. He half-dragged and half-carried me to a car, still almost smothering me with some black stuff he had thrown over my head. When he uncovered my face, I saw that he was my husband.'

At this point, to Mr Barlow's concern, Anita put her hand to her mouth and laughed, a short, hysterical laugh that ended in a gulp.

'Forgive me,' she said after a while, 'but even now, after so many years, this always happens to me when I think about it, as if it were some horrid stale joke or trick. The story has quite a funny ending, too. My husband took me home, gave me

some brandy and told me to pull myself together. It was bad luck, he said, that we should have happened to pass at that time, and that nothing would have happened if Father had minded his own business – "the old humanitarian fool", he said. But perhaps it was all for the best. People like Father were quite useless, and it was better to be rid of them. I had been wasting far too much time on him, and soon there would be far more important things for me to do. He knew there was going to be a war.'

CHAPTER EIGHT

Mr Barlow sat silent for a long time. He seemed absorbed in his scribbling on the ground, and after a little while Anita began to doubt whether he had been listening at all. She had avoided looking at him while telling her story; she was only putting into words that sequence of events that had gone through her mind a thousand times with obsessional persistence. She had never spoken them out loud before, and that she had now been able to do so came to her almost as a surprise, as if, by becoming articulate, they had detached themselves from her. She could now discard them and put them away; they were no longer the live, quivering, aching part of herself she had been afraid, and yet compelled, to probe and probe again without finding relief.

But, when at last Mr Barlow looked up and when she met his gaze, there was such an expression of pain on his otherwise so clear and serene countenance that a different trouble beset her. She now feared to have done something unforgivable, and a wave of shame overcame her for having exposed herself in such unseemly fashion to the old gentleman's embarrassment and distress.

'Oh, I ought not to have told you!' she exclaimed.

But he answered her quietly: 'You must tell me everything now. What became of your husband?'

'He continued to live in the flat,' Anita went on. 'I moved into another room, and he did not object. He said I would come round in time and get over it. At first I also avoided meals, but after a few days I had to sit down at table because of the children. They were puzzled, and I didn't know what to say to them. But my husband was very often not at home and that made it easier. When the war came he was not at first in the army because he was needed as a technical expert, but later he went to Russia. He did not come back.'

'Then you had the children alone?'

'Yes, I had them alone. They lived with me, of course, but I was alone and so were they. They were growing up, a difficult time at best. We each seemed to be living in a glass case, seeing each other but unable to communicate. Erica admired her father passionately and shared his views. She was, during the war, a fanatical Nazi. I had to be very careful what I said to her, or in front of her, if I wanted to keep the home together. Well, she was very young, she was intoxicated with the big words, the glittering successes of the first years. I was not angry with her, only sorry; and still more sorry for her in her despair at the end. But, do you know, in the shortest possible time, she shook it all off, the enthusiasm and the despair, as if it had never been, like an attack of measles. . . Martin was different. I don't know what he thought, I couldn't encourage him to tell me, it would have been too dangerous, but I think he hated it all as much as I did. We sometimes exchanged a look or a smile, and I kept thinking: some day we will be able to talk. I think he felt that, I try to believe he did. The war lasted just a little too long. They called him up in that last desperate attempt to ward off the final collapse when all was already lost. There was such chaos in those last weeks, nobody really knew what was happening. For a long time I hoped that one day he would ring the bell. . . . I waited three years and then I was told his identity-disc had been found. After that there was no more hope. I still don't know where he was killed. He had just turned sixteen.

'So, you see, with Erica married, and quite uninterested in her old-fashioned mother, and with Martin gone for ever – I have no ties.'

Again, Mr Barlow did not seem to have been listening. He just sat and looked across the rain-dark earth studded with gold and purple crocus-cups, and the silence between them was complete and transparent, as if no heavy words had clouded it with pain.

Then Mr Barlow said: 'Sixteen? A child, only a child. We have much in common, Mrs Seiler. My Christopher was twenty-two when he was killed, and it was not in the first great war when almost all his friends lost their lives. No, he survived that great holocaust, the trenches, the last battles. He was killed two years later, in one of those straggling aftermath actions in the East. It seemed so senseless and harder to bear, so long after the armistice and all that. I don't know why it should have made any difference, but it did. I felt it so, and so did his mother. But she, curiously, was even more unrea- sonable. She took it into her head that it was my fault. She thought I could have got him out of the army before it happened, when the actual war was over. Of course, I could have done nothing about it. He had only got in halfway through – he was still at school when it started – so he had to be late getting out. But my wife would not believe it. Some people find a grief more tolerable if they can turn it into a grievance and settle the blame on someone. That somehow reduces it to manageable proportions. They find it easier to live with anger than with sorrow. It didn't matter much to me – we were never very close to each other and I could not have helped her with my affection. Perhaps in this way I did help her, as a scapegoat. I sincerely hope so. I was so very sorry for her, more perhaps than if I had loved her. So, maybe, I was some use to her, after all, in this rather distorted way. Poor Harriet, she had great qualities, but we were ill-assorted. A woman does not thrive on respect.'

He looked up and saw Anita smile at him. 'How I talk to you!' he said.

'Tell me about your son,' she said gently.

'About Christopher? No, I don't think I can tell you much about him. He would have been, let me see, something like your age now, a grown, mature man. I sometimes try to think what he would have been like, but I never can. How do I know what he would have made of his life, of himself? So, for me, he remains a boy, and as such the picture of him in my mind is always tinged with a quality of hope – a necessary concomitant, I suppose, of his being so young. And since this quality of hope is without sense, it makes him now somewhat unreal. He would probably have become quite different to what I expected. My recollection of him now merges to some extent with my grandson Tony – very much alive, I am glad to say. You will meet him. He comes here for his holidays.'

'How old is Tony?' she asked.

'Eighteen. His last term at school. He is going to Cambridge, with a scholarship. But he will first have to do National Service.' Then, after a pause, he added: 'I am very fond of Tony.'

'I am glad he is coming,' she said. 'When will it be?'

'Next month, in April. As a rule, I don't look forward any more. At my time of life looking forward upsets the balance of the days. But when the time for Tony's holidays approaches, I admit to a little impatience.'

'He must be very nice.'

'He is nice to me. He loves this old place, that I know. So much so that I sometimes think it is unfair to have him here so often, for when I go, it will have to go too. He will not be able to live here. His world will be very different from mine. The things that have seemed good to me will not be his. Would it have been better if he had never known them? I have certainly made life more difficult for him. Love, I suppose, is always selfish.'

'I think life has to be difficult. It is always so for the young. We know it has been so for ourselves. But as parents we then try to make it easier for our children. And we always fail. Our very efforts create new difficulties for them. Or, if we don't make them, they make them themselves – and blame us for them after all. I remember a verse from *Hamlet* which says: "Youth to itself rebels, though none else near".'

'My dear Mrs Seiler! Here I have you quoting Shakespeare to me! How unexpected you are, and how comforting! I do sometimes worry about Tony, helplessly, uselessly, I admit. He has a very unpleasant father, a man with good brains, strong principles and an embittered, cramped and cramping disposition, a man of a different social background who has never got over resenting it, and resenting mine. He has a mother who is both silly and possessive – my daughter Cecilia. The home atmosphere must be distressing. He never speaks about it, but I imagine it is so. Anyway, except for the war years, he has spent most of his holidays here. To cap it all, I have sent him to a school of which his father disapproves. Oh, with his consent, of course, but I gather that, nevertheless, he does not hide his disapproval. What the boy makes of it all, I don't know. He is very quiet and withdrawn and spends much of his time alone.'

'I'm afraid he will not like my being here. I shall disturb his habits. He will want to be alone with you, and with himself. My being here will be awkward, after what you tell me. I had not thought of that before.'

'That, Mrs Seiler, if it *is* a difficulty for Tony, will just be one of those which he will have to deal with. One of those you spoke of yourself. But I don't think so. I think it will be a good thing for Tony to know you, I want him to, and I should like you to know him.'

'Yes, Mr Barlow.'

Mr Barlow thought he heard her catch her breath and looked at her sharply. 'Would it be – very painful to you to have a young boy around the place? After what you told me – I ought to have borne it in mind.'

'No, no! Don't think of that, it would not hurt at all. On the contrary, I should, perhaps, have a special affection for Tony, if I should get to know him . . . And now I will go and finish my polishing.'

She got up. The sun had gone in, a cold wind had sprung up, and all the light had suddenly drained out of the walled garden. The rose, the green, the yellow and mauve of the crocus and early flowering polyanthus looked dull and opaque, with no life in them. The old wall had gone grey.

Anita was anxious to get back to her work and Mr Barlow, mindful of his doctor's warning not to catch a chill, went indoors to his study.

CHAPTER NINE

Mrs Mannering's life was very full. Her first gesture on getting up in the morning – early, in order to drive her husband to the station – was to reach for her diary, and her first feeling on seeing the day's page well-filled, with almost every quarter of an hour accounted for, was one of satisfaction. If there was a gap between two engagements, she would immediately try to think what she could do with it, and some useful employment would almost always come to mind. Her view of society was that it consisted of things that wanted doing, and that the purpose of life was to get things done. Problems were always cropping up – in other people's lives mostly, for she had very few of her own. Her life was so well-ordered and under control that it practically looked after itself.

John was a very busy man, and, when at home, was easy to please. He, too, always knew what he was going to do. It was a pity they had no children, but it had its compensations: far less complications, no measles and suchlike bothers, no school-bills, and more money to spend on what they pleased.

But most people did have problems, and problems, if properly tackled, could be solved. She was the one to deal with them. There were those physically incapable of looking after themselves: the old, the young and the sick; for these she sat on advisory committees and management boards and organised bazaars. But what amazed her as she went about her duties were so-called ordinary people who were forever running into difficulties. They were so muddle-headed or weak-willed they couldn't see the answer to their problems even if it was right there under their noses; or they let things drift and get more and more involved when a little fore-thought and timely action would have kept everything simple and straight. That was why it was a blessing that a woman like herself, with her sound judgment and tireless energy, was left free to devote herself to the welfare of others. It was, after all, a well-ordered world, and she was pleased with it. Had anyone ventured to tell her that in spite of her strong social con-science she was singularly lacking in human sympathy, she would not have believed it. She would not even have under-stood the meaning of the distinction.

This morning, however, lying in her bath, Mrs Mannering was facing a problem of her own. The ten minutes she allowed herself in the steamy-hot and scented water were almost up – longer would have been self-indulgence, and, besides, the water then lost its tang and the edge of pleasure was dulled. That was happening now, and, rallying herself, it came to her as a shock that she had not been out to Milton Place for more than three weeks. She was almost committing what was, in her own eyes, the worst of all offences: letting things drift. There was Mrs Seiler for whom she had promised to find a job, and she had done nothing about it. She would tackle it at once.

But that was only a trivial affair. Her main task was going to be to find the means of persuading her father to give up Milton Place. She had long ago decided that he could not live there another winter. Only a radical solution would serve: the place must be sold and this was the time to do it. It must not be put off much longer. Just now, all kinds of public bodies from the government downwards – county councils, nationalised industries, management boards, and training institutions – were looking for large buildings in which to house their staff or the recipients of their ministrations. During the war, Milton Place had been taken over by the Air Ministry. It was well-suited for one of these newly arising purposes. But there were many Milton Places up and down the country; it would not do to hold back until all the requirements were fulfilled. It would then become wholly unsaleable. Her father would have wasted whatever assets he had, trying to keep it up. He wouldn't do any repairs to the house, but he must be spending a lot on the garden. It was all most wasteful and wrong, and in the end she and Cecilia would be left with nothing but a derelict mansion and grounds that nobody wanted.

If Milton Place were sold and the drain on Mr Barlow's resources were stopped, he would be able to live in a nice, manageable little flat in Waterington or, if he preferred it, in Torquay. Torquay had an excellent climate for old people, any number of them lived there in retirement, and Mr Barlow would be sure to make friends. However, if he wanted to stay in this part of the country, she was only too willing to look after him. She would go and see him every day, and she would find a nice woman to do his housekeeping. Alice and Sims would go to an old people's home, and Nichols could easily be found other employment. It was all beautifully simple, neat and tidy, and the best thing for everyone concerned. But how could it be achieved? It was no use giving advice or dropping hints; she had been doing that for the past year or more and Mr Barlow had met them all with the most obstinate and calculated deafness. She knew that if she put her plan to him clearly, as she saw it herself, he would refuse even to discuss it. It was the wrong approach. Mr Barlow would never change his way of life on his own initiative; old people never did, they were too set in their ways, they would endure discomfort and inflict it on others rather than upset their habits. They clung to things as they were, not for any rational reasons, but because they dreaded the effort, the upheaval of change. But get everything arranged and settled, with nothing to decide, nothing to worry about – so that, in the end, all he need do would be to sign a few papers and drive away in a car – Mr Barlow would acquiesce quite happily, if only because it would be too much effort to resist. Afterwards he would be grateful to her, and, maybe, come to believe that it had all been his own idea from the start.

Having a plan to carry out, an object to achieve, always put Mrs Mannering in high spirits. She telephoned to Milton Place, announced herself for lunch, and then set out to enjoy her drive. From now on, there would be no more of those desultory visits there, laboriously dragged out in rambling conversation, from which she always came away depressed and frustrated. She would take a new interest in the old house, seeing it, in her mind's eye, put to some new and useful purpose. She had still to decide what it should be. And in talking to her father she would carefully and tactfully get him used to the idea of his moving; not suddenly, so as to alarm him, but gradually and gently, as if what was going to happen would take place almost unnoticed, like the change of seasons, but just as inevitably.

After the rain of the last few days, the countryside smelt of wet earth, rising sap, and the faint scent of opening buds. Wisps of mist floated over the treetops and the sky was a pearly grey. Mrs Mannering noticed it perfunctorily as she drove along the winding, hedge-bound roads while, from time to time, drops from the rain-heavy branches overhead pattered onto the roof of her car. Her mind was occupied with her plans and purposes.

Anita had no plans and, as the days went by, hardly a thought of the future. She had stood at her window that morning, lost in the intense concentration of looking, listening and feeling, oblivious of time past and time to come. She saw that the trees in the middle distance had put on an almost transparent pale green drapery through which the articulation of their branches was still accurately visible as through a veil, while the great oaks still lifted the dark tracery of their bare limbs uncompromisingly against the sky. There was no rustle of leaves, but a tiny rush of falling water as a blackbird flew out of the great cedar, causing it to shed a small pool of rain from the edge of a dark-green shelving branch. A soft day, she told herself, a gentle day; the light was soft, filtered through clouds, the air was soft and brushed across one's face like the touch of feathers, and the scent was soft, of grass and leaf

fragrant with rain. When at last she closed the window and turned to her occupations, she was smiling and very quiet in her heart. 'I am being born again,' she thought.

Emily arrived a few minutes before one and went straight to her father's study. Looking round after her usual quick peck on his forehead, and his customary greeting: 'Ah, my dear, nice to see you!', she noticed that no table had been set for lunch. 'Sims is late,' she thought, 'it really is getting too much for him.' But before she had chosen her words for an appropriate remark to that effect, and while she was still drawing off her gloves, Anita came in.

Emily had a split-second of non-recognition. And yet, Anita was wearing the same faded suit that had seen better days, and her hair was still piled in a coil on the top of her head as it had been when she had first seen her – a sufficiently distinctive hairstyle to mark out any woman in the days of close cuts and permanent waves. But Emily had retained in her mind a picture of a tired-looking, middle-aged woman, shabbily dressed. The person who came in and announced that lunch was ready was young; there were hardly any lines in her face. You had to look twice to see the tiny creases round her eyes, and there were none at the corners of her mouth which was full and smiling, revealing a row of remarkably white and even teeth (can they be her own?). Her suit, too, sat smartly on her shoulders, with a crisp, white bow at her throat.

'Lunch is ready,' she said. 'Alice and I thought that the dining room would be warm enough today, with just a little fire to help. It is really quite warm out-of-doors.'

Preceding them across the hall, she held open the door for Mrs Mannering and followed her, while Mr Barlow ceremoniously brought up the rear.

The large, mahogany dining table stood bare, beautifully polished and gleaming, in the middle of the room, but at the far end, between the last window and the fireplace where a log-fire was burning, a small, round table had been set with a damask cloth and the silver and china that had been put away for many years. A silver cup with primroses stood in the middle.

'I picked them yesterday,' Anita said, 'out in the woods. There are only a few buds, so far, but there are going to be masses and masses, judging by the leaves. I am looking forward to them so much.'

The soup plates were filled with a light, clear consommé with little cubes of a custard-like consistency, the same colour as the primroses, floating in it. It was hot and fragrant. Emily was so taken aback by it all that she had hardly spoken since she entered the dining room. Anita cleared the plates and went out to return with a roast chicken, while Sims followed her with the vegetables. Emily had still found nothing to say, except to pass some superficial remarks: 'How nice the table looks! – I haven't been in this room for ages – the soup is very good.' She was incapable of expressing her thoughts because she simply didn't know what to think.

The chicken, too, was excellent, and the potatoes and carrots, sprinkled with minute specks of green, had never tasted so good. Mr Barlow was enjoying himself hugely and was as proud as if he had done it all himself.

There was cheese, and apples from the store-room to finish the meal, and then Anita rose to lead the way back into the study for coffee. When she had poured it, she excused herself, saying she was going to help Alice with the washing-up. 'Especially,' she said, 'because I am responsible for bringing out that lovely old china and Alice is rather nervous of handling it now that her hands are not so steady.'

When she had left the room, Emily at last found her voice. 'What amazes me,' she said, 'is that Alice puts up with all this interference. Mrs Seiler brazens it out with her, I suppose, and the poor old thing is too subdued to protest. Once upon a time she would have been up in arms on far less provocation. Poor dear, she can't give notice now. I'm sure she thinks all this can't last very long, and so she finds it easier to give in.'

Mr Barlow's lips tightened. He did not like his daughter's tone of voice. 'Alice has not complained to me,' he said.

'No, of course not, not to you. I'll be seeing her, though, before I leave. Anyway, one thing I *will* say, Mrs Seiler is a much more capable person than I had supposed when I first saw her. That being so, it should not be too difficult to find her a job. She could cook for a hostel or a home of some sort, it's easy to get labour permits for that kind of employment. I'll set about it at once.'

'There is no hurry, Emily. Mrs Seiler is quite happy here. She is not looking for a position at present.'

'She isn't? Well, isn't that what she came over here for? She has to earn her living, I imagine, or so she said in her letter. She didn't come for a holiday.'

'Mrs Seiler has been doing a great deal of work in this house. You have just seen some evidence of that yourself. You may be sure I didn't ask her to do it, in fact I remonstrated with her repeatedly when I found out – which I didn't at first, she went about it so quietly. However, you couldn't call the way she spends her days "having a holiday".'

'That's not the point, Father. You didn't engage her as a working housekeeper, and if that is the position she is assuming – in spite of your protests, as you say yourself – then she is thrusting herself upon you in that capacity. She will eventually expect you to keep her on indefinitely and to pay her a salary, of course.'

Mr Barlow did not answer. A surge of feeling was rising within him, he recognised it as anger, and until he had control of it, he did not trust himself to speak.

Mistaking his mood, Emily got up and kissed him. 'You hadn't looked at it in that light, had you, dear? For a man of your years and experience you're a darling old innocent where the wiles of women are concerned. You don't know what you are letting yourself in for. Now, don't look upset. I'll have a little word, later on, with the lady, in the nicest possible way, I can assure you. We'll discuss what kind of a post she would prefer and I'll make it my business to find something she will like.'

At last Mr Barlow spoke. He spoke in a tone that Emily had not heard from him for many years past, decisive and cutting, and brooking no reply.

'Emily,' he said, 'you will do me the favour of leaving Mrs Seiler strictly alone. She has been through very harrowing times. She has suffered much sorrow and distress of mind. Here, she is recuperating. She finds the place congenial and restful. I will not have her disturbed. She shall stay here as long as she finds it so – whether it be for a long time or a short one, she herself shall say.'

And as Emily was attempting to interrupt, he continued even more emphatically: 'I hope I have made myself understood. You will not speak to Mrs Seiler about any job or post, you will say nothing to her that might induce her to leave before she is ready to do so. I insist on having your word on that. Promise, Emily!'

'Yes, Father,' – the words came from her almost mechanically, a forced, involuntary reaction.

Mr Barlow's tone softened. 'You have, however, made one good point, for which I am grateful to you. You have brought to my attention the fact that Mrs Seiler needs money to spend and the opportunity of spending it. I admit that I hadn't thought of it. Living here in seclusion, I have rather lost touch with everyday things. Mrs Seiler does seem very poorly equipped, now I come to think of it. I could have asked you to help me with this, it might have come more easily from you. But now, my dear, no, most definitely not. I will deal with it myself.

'And now, Emily, as I have your promise, we will say goodbye. I am a little tired and will have a nap. Thank you for coming.'

And as Emily was opening the door, he called after her, half jestingly, 'And please don't go and upset Alice either. Leave things alone for once, there's a good girl!'

And Emily actually did go straight out to her car, without seeing either Alice or Anita. As she drove back into Waterington, she had a lot to think about regarding what she chose to call the quirks of her father's ageing mind.

CHAPTER TEN

A few days went by. They were lengthening visibly, and round the house everything was green. Spring was no longer coming, it had arrived. But it was colder than it had been in February; the wind that blew from the east across the lawns and meadows had a cutting edge, as of ice, that belied the tender shades of leaf and shoot.

Anita had spent several hours washing windows on the north side of the house. They rattled noisily in their old frames. From time to time she stopped in her work to watch the crowns of the tall beeches that rose from the ravine, swaying in the gale. Then she went down to Mr Barlow's study.

'I think it is too windy for our walk this morning,' she said, 'the windows are simply shaking.'

He smiled at her; her unusual turns of phrase always amused him. She rarely made serious mistakes, but her choice of words was often unexpected.

'Yes, I shall stay indoors this morning,' he said, 'the wind may drop in the afternoon. But don't go away. Sit down, please, I want to talk to you.'

She sat down in a low armchair and folded her arms round her knees. Sitting in that undignified way, she looked absurdly young, almost like a girl. Mr Barlow fumbled with a paper-knife, seeking the way in which to begin. She saw it and suddenly decided that she would take the plunge.

'I, too, want to talk to you,' she said, 'and, if you please, I should like to do my talking first. Because I rather think we want to say the same thing. I know I ought to have said it long ago. We have to talk about my being here.'

'Yes,' said Mr Barlow, 'that is what we must talk about.'

She clasped her hands tighter, so that the knuckles showed white, and went on with a rush. 'I knew it,' she said, 'I ought to have done something about it long ago, and somehow I never had the courage. I am deeply ashamed. Here I am, and here I have stayed, week after week, as if I had meant it to be so when I first came – when I wrote to ask only for your advice where to go. You were so kind and told me to come here. And you have been so kind ever since. But there must be an end of it, I mustn't take advantage any longer. And I must beg you to forgive me.' There was a silence. Her eyes were fixed on the carpet, she was actually studying the pattern – anything rather than look up.

'So now, perhaps, you don't have to talk to me at all,' she said, almost in a whisper, 'and I will go upstairs and write a letter.'

'Don't go, my dear,' he said, 'I still want to talk to you. But tell me first, has my daughter said anything to you that has made you want to leave Milton Place? Is it to her you want to write?'

'Mrs Mannering? No, I have not seen her since she came to lunch. She must have left while I was still in the kitchen. I was not able to say goodbye to her.'

'That is all right, then.'

'I was sorry I missed her, because now I want to write to her, if you will allow me. I think she has many relations, I mean she knows many people, and would be able to find me a place.'

'Listen to me now, Anita,' he said – he had never used her Christian name before – 'it is my turn to have my say. You don't want to find a place. You don't want to go away. *I* don't want you to go. I want you to stay here at Milton Place until – well, until some more suitable time. I don't know when that will be. I am an old man, Anita, and age has some privileges too, not only disabilities. One is that I can say, and will say, straight out what is in my mind. I want you to stay because I like to hear your footstep on the stairs, I like to sit opposite you at meals, I like you to open my door, as you did just now, and say that you will go walking with me – or that it is too windy to walk and that the windows are shaking. And there is another reason. I want you to see the azaleas and rhododendrons in flower. I want to go round the garden with you. It will be like seeing it all for the first time, if I can see it again with your eyes. I think about this every day now. Very soon, and almost every day, there will be something to show you. You can't deprive me of that pleasure – I have been looking forward to it too much.'

She said nothing, still studying the carpet, feeling too intensely happy to speak. He had to ask her: 'Will you stay here with me a little while longer, Anita?'

'Oh, Mr Barlow, I don't *want* to go away!'

'Ah, I am so glad to hear that. Now let me go on. I am asking you, you understand, to give up looking for a place, to put it off for quite a while, until after the summer, perhaps. I am asking you to do that for me. Now, you know that one sometimes has occasion, in professional life, to ask a person to keep himself – or herself – available, not to accept any other employment, because one wants to be able to call on their time. They are giving you something valuable in agreeing to this, and one has to give them something in return. We call it a "retainer". Do you see what I mean?'

'Yes, we would call it "waiting money".'

'Waiting money, an excellent name! Here it is.' He took an envelope from the drawer of his desk. It was already addressed to her, and underneath he now wrote 'waiting money' in his meticulous handwriting, and 'To be renewed monthly while waiting'.

He got up, dropped it into her lap, sat down again and beamed at her with intense satisfaction. He felt he had successfully transacted a very difficult piece of business. Her immediate reaction, however, surprised him. She jumped up, bent towards him and for a moment he thought she was going to kiss him. But suddenly her face puckered, she turned and ran swiftly from the room. Mr Barlow looked at the hastily closing door. 'She is going to cry,' he thought, 'but she has taken the envelope with her!'

Upstairs Anita threw herself into an armchair and abandoned herself to her upwelling tears. They had come upon her so suddenly, so unexpectedly, that she had been

quite unable to control them. Now she was alone she attempted no defence, but allowed herself to weep long and abundantly. There was no pain, she was not racked with sobs, her face was not twisted in anguish; they were easy tears, and as they came something was released within her that she had hardly known had been there. She had not cried for years; not when her father had been killed, not when she discovered what kind of a man her husband really was, not – no, least of all – when her boy had been taken away. They had been so monstrous, these things, she had only stared at them in horror, stony-eyed, unable to believe that they were actually happening to her. They were outside the compass and measure of her humanity, of what in her heart and mind she could feel and understand. Violence and treachery evoked no emotions in her: not hatred nor anger, hardly even recognisable pain. They bludgeoned and stunned her into insensibility, she was conscious only of nausea and a dull, diffuse kind of suffering. She could not weep. To have wept, then, would have been to acknowledge these things, and her mind would have given way. She had not broken down. Some animal courage had kept her going, protecting her sanity by an instinctive refusal to feel. It was not an act of her will, it just happened that way, and she wondered at herself that she could behave as she did. As time went by, she came to realise that only in such numbness and rigidity could she face the continuity of her days. So she kept herself on the surface, steadfastly refusing to look inwards, disregarding herself, and working to the limit of her physical endurance, in self-defence.

And now Mr Barlow had broken through her armour; broken through it with a few words which were not just kindness and courtesy, such as he had shown her ever since she came to his house. They had pierced the general anonymity of their relationship. He had shown that he cared for her, for her personally, he had made her be herself again. And then this present of his, his thoughtfulness and consideration for her needs, his so touchingly contrived manner of giving. Feelings welled up in her that had lain dormant for years: tenderness, gratitude and – pleasure, plain unaffected pleasure at the prospect of getting some things she had missed for so long, trivial things to possess but so depressing to be without.

At last she dried her eyes and went to look at herself in the glass. 'What a fright I look!' she laughed. She picked up her broken comb to smooth her hair, looked at the gaps in its teeth, at its tarnished spine with affectionate disgust – (how long I have made do with it!) – and tossed it into the waste-paper basket.

'Tomorrow I'll go shopping,' she told herself, 'life still holds the ridiculously exciting promise of a new comb!'

CHAPTER ELEVEN

Emily decided she would talk to Mrs Peacock about Milton Place. Mrs Peacock was not an intimate friend of hers, and that was one good reason for choosing her as a confidante. Mrs Peacock knew very little about her and her family and nothing of the circumstances which made the disposal of Milton Place desirable to her, therefore she could be told just as much or as little as she, Emily, liked. But Mrs Peacock was also the wife of a county councillor. Mr Peacock was a builder and contractor of considerable local importance, a public-spirited man who took an active interest in the administration of that part of the country in which he carried on his business. Mrs Mannering had taken the trouble to find out which department of the county's government particularly engaged Mr Peacock's attention. It seemed that he sat on the Welfare Committee. Nothing could have been more perfect.

Mrs Peacock, it is understood, did not belong to Mrs Mannering's inner circle of friends. They were not, so to speak, in the same set. True, they had a great deal in common. As regards income, there was possibly not very much to choose between them. There may have been more money in the

Mannering household, but that is not certain. The Peacocks were sure it was so, while the Mannerings, if they had been consulted, would have come to the opposite conclusion. Of course, money was of longer standing with the Mannerings, but that didn't make it buy any more. If anything, it bought less, because they had more commitments.

The ladies used to meet on several occasions. Mrs Mannering and Mrs Peacock were both members of a number of women's organisations. In one of them they co-operated regularly in the sorting and distributing of clothing; together, with a few others, they ran a girls' club; and together they organised many a bazaar. The men met rarely, but thought highly of each other. They were both conservative in their politics, but Mr Mannering thought of these chiefly in a national context and did nothing active about them. He talked and voted. Mr Peacock, on the other hand, rarely discussed general opinions, but took a lot of trouble to get things done which he thought right and necessary in local affairs.

It happened sometimes that the Mannerings and their friends would be dining, of a summer evening, at the same country hotel as the Peacocks with theirs. Then there would be amicable greetings in the bar and remarks about the weather, enquiries about the family and talk about cricket – all the general, common denominators. And then they would each go their separate ways. The Mannerings did not invite the Peacocks to the house, and the Peacocks did not expect to be asked. There would have been some awkwardness in returning the invitation. The Mannerings had dinner, but the Peacocks – with the exception of an occasional outing – had tea.

Therefore, wishing to talk quite especially to Mrs Peacock privately, but not too privately, Emily rang her up and invited her to coffee at the Tudor Rose. This, the town's most fashionable confectioner's, with its spacious Georgian-style dining rooms and trim, uniformed waitresses, was always packed around eleven o'clock with ladies reviving their spirits in the midst of their morning's shopping with coffee, gossip and buns. Emily took the precaution of reserving a table in a corner of the glazed verandah. What a lovely day it was! Crisp and bright, with the sun almost too hot on the window-panes and positively dazzling.

'Do come and sit on this side, Mrs Peacock, so you don't have it in your eyes. Who would have expected such a sudden change in the weather after yesterday's gales!'

Mrs Peacock changed her place. Mrs Mannering was being very affable and Mrs Peacock wondered what it was all about.

Emily soon decided to come to the point. There were rumours, she said, of a new enterprise in welfare work. She had heard that there was to be a home for girls who had had babies, a place they could go to when they left hospital, and stay until they were fit for work again, while in the meantime they could be advised what to do with the children and arrangements could be made for them according to the circumstances of the case. She thought this was an excellent idea. So many of these poor little illegitimate mites were being born these days, their problems could not be dealt with haphazardly and individually, especially as the girls, by becoming mothers so inadvisedly, had shown that they were ill-prepared to be responsible for their own lives, let alone for their helpless babies. It was a social problem and should be dealt with by a social institution.

Mrs Peacock nodded. That was exactly, she said, what her husband thought. He had been thinking, and saying it, for a long time. It was, in fact, one of his pet schemes. She must say that she herself did not agree with him. She had been brought up to believe in morality, and it was not at her time of life that she was going to turn her back on her beliefs. For her, sin still had a meaning, it was not just an old-fashioned word as it seemed to be for so many people now. She thought that things were being made much too easy for the feckless, and that this was just another device to encourage more irresponsibility.

Mrs Mannering said that, morally, Mrs Peacock was certainly right. She wouldn't go into that. One had to be practical. Mr Peacock was a practical man, that was what gave him his standing in public affairs. Her husband thought very highly of Mr Peacock for that very reason and wished we had more men like him. She, too, was a practical woman and that was why, she supposed, her way of looking at things was very much like Mr Peacock's. Though, of course, from a different point of view, Mrs Peacock was right too. However, if some such plan was being discussed, it would be necessary to find a suitable house for this purpose. It would have to be a country house, of course, with sufficient grounds, not too far from town, for it had to be accessible. But not too near, otherwise they would have the girls running off to the pictures or the public houses instead of looking after their babies and making up their minds what to do with them. Well, all she wanted to say was that in case this idea should take definite shape, she would probably be able to suggest the very house that would be required.

'Really?' said Mrs Peacock who felt that now they were getting to the heart of the matter.

'Yes,' said Mrs Mannering. She realised that these were early days to talk about it, but she thought it right to mention it because her own proposal was also only tentative and she could not commit herself at all definitely. But she did think that her father would not be staying much longer at Milton Place. He was an old gentleman who lived there alone with two old servants who were quite unable to cope with the work. They would have to be taken care of in some suitable way. The house was large and structurally in good condition – one of those big, solid Victorian buildings that would last for ever if properly maintained. She admitted that it was not being properly maintained now, except for the gardens – her father was quite crazy about those. But so far the house had suffered no serious damage, and it would not cost very much to adapt. A coat of paint, inside, and perhaps a couple of additional bathrooms would be all that was needed, she thought. 'Naturally,' she added with a sigh, 'I grew up there and am attached to the place. I should be happy if it could take on a new lease of life and serve a useful purpose, instead of falling into disrepair and becoming derelict.'

'Well,' said Mrs Peacock, 'I'll tell my husband about it, if that's what you want me to do. I'm sure he doesn't know that Milton Place is on the market.'

'Oh, but it isn't,' Mrs Mannering interposed in some alarm. 'You mustn't jump to conclusions. I am speaking to you in the greatest confidence. You see, my father will make no move to sell, he will never take the initiative. You know how old people are, they come to dislike even the thought of change. My father would have to be approached from the other side. He would have to be persuaded. Then I should do my part, of course, and so would my sister, I know. We are his only near relatives, he has no one else to consider, and we should be all for it. Neither of us would want to live there, or could afford to do so. And it would be entirely for his own good. Life is impossible for him there. He could be so much better looked after in a flat near to one of us.'

Mrs Peacock looked non-committal. 'I see what you mean,' she said slowly. Was this meant literally? It didn't seem so. Mrs Peacock's thoughts were taking another direction. 'Milton Place, indeed!' she went on. 'It's quite a name in the county. I don't think Reg even knows what it looks like, it's always been kept so private.'

It was time to change the subject, Emily felt. Quite enough had been said for the moment. The little seed had been sown; she would now wait and see whether it took root, whether the shoot would come up. It would be wiser not to force it. But she would have to cultivate the soil in which it was planted. So she now mentioned the regional meeting of an organisation to which both she and Mrs Peacock belonged and which was going to be held in another county town. Would Mrs Peacock be going? If so, would she care to come with her in her car? Mrs Peacock, she believed, did not drive herself? Yes, Mrs

Peacock would, indeed, like that very much, it was an awkward journey by train, cross-country, with two changes. Mrs Mannering would be only too delighted to be helpful.

Mrs Peacock purred inwardly. She knew she was being wooed by Mrs Mannering – an unlooked-for and very pleasurable situation. She would allow herself to be wooed. It would look very well for her to arrive at that meeting in Mrs Mannering's car. 'I went with my friend, Mrs Mannering,' she would be saying, afterwards. Then the question arose in her mind: what would Mrs Mannering be wearing on that occasion? Probably one of those devastatingly simple, tailored suits. Mrs Peacock's rapid mental survey of her own wardrobe convinced her that she had nothing to match it. Not that she liked that type of clothes very much, she fancied something a little more dressy herself. Still, if she was going to see more of Mrs Mannering in future, she had better take her cue from her. She would have a suit made to measure at the earliest opportunity – using her influence she might even get it in time for the meeting.

Anita, too, was thinking of clothes, or, rather, looking at them in the shop windows, as she wandered up and down the High Street, round the Market Square, and into all the quaint little side-streets that branched off from it. She had come into Waterington early, by bus, having firmly refused Mr Barlow's offer to have Nichols drive her to town in the old Bentley. She would so much prefer to be on her own, she had assured him, even if it was a quarter of an hour's walk to the bus stop. She had a timetable, and she enjoyed walking. She had, however, been obliged to agree that Nichols should meet her in the afternoon at the War Memorial and take her home; he would be going into town anyway to fetch some tools and various things Alice had asked for.

But that was a long way off – Anita had several hours in front of her. She felt light-hearted and free, with the freedom that comes from being alone in a strange town where no one knows you, no one cares where you go or what you do, nothing reminds you of your past or makes demands on your future. And what a beautiful morning! What an enchanting old town! Some of it, at least, was old; small windows with leaded panes looking down out of half-timbered, black and white houses, though in the main thoroughfare the shop-fronts were modern, with wide plate-glass displays. It was good to be free and anonymous and to merge with the crowd, to be a stranger, but not a castaway, unknown but not excluded; to be one of these busy, purposeful women – they were mostly women – who, with baskets or bags on their arms, went in and out of the shops, or stood, as she did, looking appraisingly at the windows. She pressed her handbag to her side with her elbow, where she could feel its reassuring presence, for this contained the magic that made her belong here and be no different from all these other friendly people with whom she mingled unnoticed. There was money in her bag, not a great deal of money, but the first she had possessed in this country, and she, too, would be able to walk into a shop when she wanted to, and buy. But she was not in a hurry. She would first try to see all the shops to make sure which looked the most inviting; she studied and compared the prices, and all

95

the time she was drawing up and recasting her budget. What did she want most? And if she bought this, would she still be able to afford the other?

She had looked at most of the shops a dozen times before she made up her mind. Several times, too, she had passed the Tudor Rose where Mrs Mannering and Mrs Peacock were having their conference, and once she stopped and studied the luncheon menu displayed in a frame by the door. She might easily have met the two ladies as they came out. But by that time she had moved on. The place attracted her, but it seemed expensive, and she did not want to waste money on her lunch. At last, fairly exhausted and encumbered with paper bags and parcels, she decided on a small, rustic-looking tea-room in one of the old houses off the square. There were red-and-white check curtains and when she peered in, past an uninspiring green plant in the window, she discerned tiny varnished tables set with rubber doilies. A notice on the door advertised light lunches. There were three old ladies, a woman with a little girl, and a rather dreary-looking man in the place, and as she pushed open the door, a smell of cabbage hit her in the face and she almost turned tail. But suddenly she felt more tired than she thought she was – she had walked for nearly four hours – and she thought she would go no further, cabbage or no cabbage. After all, she need not eat it. So she ordered baked beans on toast, stodgy but satisfying, cheese and biscuits and tea. The tea was good, and she felt better drinking it.

Then she unpacked and examined her purchases, one by one. Her greatest extravagance had been a pair of shoes, brogues for country walks to which she was looking forward.

She stroked them with her finger – lovely, smooth, brown leather which smelled so good, strong and yet shapely. Her legs would look well even under an old skirt if her feet were neat in those. The other things were small and almost all of them were cosmetics: soap, shampoo, a comb of course, face-powder, eau-de-cologne, two different creams and a lipstick in a new, fashionable shade. How smoothly it wound up and down in its black-and-gilt case! She looked at it doubtfully. The woman in the shop had assured her it was just right for her colouring, but she hadn't used one for years, and it made her feel self-conscious. She looked round. Nobody was taking any notice of her, so she searched her handbag for the little square piece of looking-glass that always hid itself some-where in its depths, and applied the lipstick. The result quite startled her. Somehow, it made her eyes shine. Her face seemed to come to life and glow, even her hair showed high-lights which she had not seen in it before – The peace and inward restfulness of Milton Place, the moisture of the atmosphere and the gently filtered light had done their soothing, smoothing work on her mind and muscles, on her soul and her skin. She had felt it happening without conscious awareness of it, and now when she heightened the colour of her lips, her new-made face and the life that lived in it suddenly came into focus. She looked at herself and almost laughed out loud. 'Is that really me?' she thought, 'Is it *still* me? How ridiculous!' But she was pleased.

Meanwhile Mr Barlow had eaten his luncheon alone, as he had done for years. Towards one o'clock Sims came into the study, removed the books which had inadvertently piled up on the little oak table which he used for meals, and began to lay it as he had always done before. 'You won't want your luncheon in the dining room today, Sir,' he had murmured in a tone between a query and an affirmation, the latter, however, predominating.

Mr Barlow, who had been deep in a book and had not noticed these familiar ministrations, looked up when Sims spoke. 'No, that's all right, Sims, carry on,' he said and put down his book. He looked at his solitary plate and glass, and then out of the window, across the lawn to the great cedar spreading its branches against the sky. It was the well-loved view, the familiar room, but for the moment some of the comfort had gone out of it. 'I should never have believed I could miss her so,' he thought, 'she is actually making me feel lonely, just by not being here. I should never have believed it!' he repeated. He tried to cast his mind back to that other figure, the young girl of his early and so persistent infatuation, but he found he could no longer form a clear picture of her. Her face had become shadowy, undefined, and the whole incident of that brief, passionate meeting of so many years ago when he had been young, now seemed to him to be purely fictional, like something he might have read in a book. But Anita was real. He thought of the day when she had arrived in her nondescript fur coat with the bunch of violets pinned under her chin, tired and drawn, with big, dark circles under her eyes. Even then there had been her magnificent carriage and graceful movements, her soft voice and slightly foreign intonation which gave such a peculiar and attractive colour to her otherwise correct speech. Yes, he had liked her at first sight. She was nothing like the girl he had been trying to remember; she was not a girl but a mature woman, and it was obvious that life had not used her kindly. Yet there was still a look of innocence about her, something of an essence that could not be sullied – and that was the one thing she had in common with that early love of his, and who so unaccountably, it seemed, had been her mother.

She was looking much better now than she had on that first night. She always repeated that Milton Place was doing her good. Undoubtedly it was, he could see that for himself. The haunted expression had disappeared, she looked rested in spite of all that 'spring-cleaning' she insisted on doing. Mr Barlow, as he finished his biscuits and cheese, thought with gleeful self-satisfaction of how he had contrived to persuade her to prolong her stay. She was a very pleasant woman and comfortable to have about the house.

After luncheon he went out to find Nichols to remind him to meet Mrs Seiler at the War Memorial, and to emphasise that he must wait for her however late she might be, for she might have lost her way, being a stranger in the town, or have been delayed in a shop. She was sure to be tired and he did not want her to come back by bus, with the long walk from the bus stop at the end. Nichols had been told this before and he assured Mr Barlow that there should be no question of his returning without Mrs Seiler. Even if she had lost herself in the town he would find her and on no account leave without her. But Mr Barlow felt he had been right to make sure this was understood.

In fact, Anita, having no more shopping to do, was early at the War Memorial and stood there quite a while studying the list of names inscribed on the slabs of grey stone on each side of the high stone cross; a very long list for the men of 1914–18, and a shorter one for those of 1939-45. A wreath of red poppies, placed there last Remembrance Day, and rather bedraggled from having spent the winter out in the open, was hung above each of them. 'Many or few,' she thought, 'they had all been young and dearly loved, and for each one the heartache had been the same.' One cannot do arithmetic with pain – neither add nor multiply nor divide it. It is always one and indivisible, and everyone carries the whole of it.

As she waited, a gipsy woman passed, selling primroses. Anita emptied the last shillings out of her purse and bought the basketful. She put them at the foot of the cross, and added under her breath a name that was not inscribed – for Martin. . . .

Nichols drew up just as she had finished. If he had seen it, he said nothing, and after a short silence, sitting beside him on their drive out to Milton Place, she told him about her purchases, her lunch and her window-shopping, and how much she had enjoyed it all.

CHAPTER TWELVE

A few days later Tony arrived for the Easter holidays. He would be eighteen next month and the summer term would be his last one at school. He was, in fact, only putting in time now, for he had already passed all his examinations and won a scholarship for a Cambridge College last December. But his father who, during Tony's school years, had taken little notice of his education, now insisted that he do his National Service before he went up to the university. That would force him, he said, to rub shoulders with all kinds of people he had never had a chance to meet at his public school. It would do him good and broaden his outlook to see life a bit in the raw, to find out what 'ordinary chaps' were made of. There was, no doubt, a core of sound judgement in Dr Crawfurd's view of the matter, but he did not put forward any reasonable arguments for his command which Tony would have understood and accepted. Instead, he made it sound as unwelcome and opposed to Tony's inclinations as he could, for Tony's behaviour at home, sensitive, aloof and withdrawn, had always infuriated him. He now told him sarcastically that he thought far too much of himself, that he had been pampered and flattered by his mother and grandfather and taught to look down on 'common fellows' like his father. Tony went very white when Dr Crawfurd said these things, but he never answered, and the doctor really got more enjoyment from stressing, when his wife was present, all the physical discomforts that would be in store for her darling and which he, being made of so much finer stuff than ordinary young men, would find it so much harder to endure.

But Tony's headmaster, when told of Dr Crawfurd's wishes, had concurred, and for reasons not so very dissimilar in substance, but which, by a shift of emphasis, were made to look very different indeed. He thought that Tony had developed intellectually beyond his years and that it might even be to his ultimate advantage if he were obliged to let his brain lie fallow for a while, especially as the kind of thinking in which Tony excelled – mathematical thinking – demands the most concentrated effort of abstraction and imagination. Military service would set him a different kind of problem, and allow his physical and moral fibre to mature and toughen, thus providing a better balance and more substantial support for his mind. He therefore said to Tony that it would be not only dutiful but wise to defer to his father's wishes, because he would find it much more tiresome to be a soldier *after* he had spent three or four years enjoying the delights of Cambridge. So Tony agreed that he might as well get the thing over and done with, and was simply waiting for his call-up and trying, for the present, not to think beyond his holidays at Milton Place which he considered the one bright spot in his life.

Mr Barlow, too, was looking forward to his grandson's arrival with pleasurable anticipation. This was now heightened by his having Anita to talk to, and during the last few days he spoke of almost nothing else but Tony. Nevertheless, he always broached the subject apologetically as it were, in a deprecatory tone of voice and in falsely disparaging terms, though the substance of what he said was always to Tony's credit and in praise of him. The accompanying smile which lit up the old gentleman's face, though meant to be ironical, did not disguise the pride he took in the boy and the tenderness he felt for him. Anita was half amazed and half amused at all these precautions to conceal what was, after all, such a natural affection, but she felt, in the end, that they were meant as a protective shield for feelings that were too vulnerable to be shown bare. There was, however, one melancholy note which recurred several times in Mr Barlow's conversation during these days. It saddened him, he said, that Tony would never be able to own Milton Place and to live there. He knew how deeply the boy loved it, but even if he were to disregard his daughters and leave it to him, death-duties would force him to part with it. He would not have the means to keep it up. Tony knew this, although they never spoke about it now, but he sometimes felt, when Tony stood still to gaze at some particular vista or went off for one of his long walks through the woods, that he was consciously trying to take possession of it all in his mind, as if he might be seeing it for the last time.

When the day came, Nichols took the old Bentley into the town to fetch 'Mr Tony' at the station, and Anita went with him to get a few things for the house before the arrival of the train. Sitting next to him, Anita soon got him talking and Tony was the first and most obvious topic. It seemed that Nichols, too, was very fond of him; he had spent much time at Milton Place as a small boy before the war and had been his, Nichols', constant companion and assistant at whatever he was doing in the garden or the greenhouses. He had also been great friends with Dick, Mr Tollhurst's son, down on the farm, and Nichols had often taken him there to play with Dick, or had fetched Dick up to Milton Place for tea. And Mr Tony was still friends with Dick, in spite of their both being as good as grown-up now, and Mr Tony being so clever, so he was told, and soon going to college. This was all the more remarkable, Nichols thought, as the boys hadn't seen each other during the war years, for Mr Barlow had then come out of his retirement and gone to live in London. Yes, he had deliberately gone to live in London, in spite of the bombs, and he had offered his services and had an important job in the Ministry of Transport, because Mr Barlow had been an engineer of a very special kind and his knowledge and experience had been very valuable. But Milton Place had been taken over by some secret department of the Air Ministry and had been out of bounds to civilians and very closely guarded. So Tony had not been able to come there for his holidays during all that time, and they had missed him very much. 'And you should have seen, Ma'am, how pleased he was when he did come back, how he went all over the place and looked at every nook and corner. It was all very much the worse for wear by then, the house and the grounds, but we've pulled the grounds round a bit since Mr Barlow came back, though not much was done to restore the house, as well you know yourself, Ma'am.'

'And what did *you* do, Nichols, while the place was taken over?' Anita asked.

Nichols said he had stayed on, he and Mr and Mrs Sims; they to look after the officers, and he to do as best he could with the vegetables with the help of two little girls, his grand-daughters. He and Sims had been too old for the army, so they had been Home Guards and had gone out, in turn, on night exercises, but they were never seriously needed – which was perhaps just as well. At the time, though, he had felt that it was rather a pity they hadn't had an invasion. 'We'd 'ave liked to 'ave a go at them!' he said, adding one or two epithets which were not in Anita's vocabulary.

They then drove in silence, and Anita turned her face to the green, undulating countryside, studded with the great century-old trees that were so much a feature of the landscape and never failed to impress her with their beauty, all looking so peaceful and gentle in the soft spring sunshine. Her mind went back to those terrifyingly intoxicated summer days which she had lived through over there, when it had seemed that nothing could stop those marching feet, those rumbling tanks, those tearing bombers. 'For today we are masters of Germany, and tomorrow the world is ours. . . .' Would she ever be able to forget that song? But because these people here had been prepared 'to fight in the fields' – these fields, these people going quietly about their business, it had all passed away, and even those who had been most exuberant and power-drunk at the time were now pretending that it had never happened. She looked at Nichols' gnarled, brown hands on the steering-wheel: he would have liked 'to have a go at them', he had said. She thought of Mr Barlow, his old-fashioned courtesy, his grand manner, his reticence and almost humble modesty, 'going to live up in London in spite of the bombs'. . . And suddenly there was a lump in her throat.

Tony came up the stairs of the station to the barrier and waved to Nichols, who had placed himself next to the ticket collector. Tall and lanky, his hair rather too long round his ears and over his forehead, dressed in a worn tweed jacket and shapeless grey flannels, his fine features and grace of movement dominated his slovenly appearance like the sun shining through ragged clouds. His skin was very white, his brow broad, the nose finely chiselled and slightly arched. His light-grey eyes looked out from under very straight eyebrows, the mouth was thin and rather hard which gave him a severe look, an impression enhanced by the very strong line of the jaw which joined to form a prominent, slightly cleft chin. His hair was wavy and dark. Seeing him there for the first time, being greeted by Nichols, and while he was still unaware of her presence, Anita had a sudden, hallucinatory vision of him wearing tight, light-grey trousers with straps under his boots, a yellow waistcoat and blue frockcoat with a wide collar and high cambric stock. The vision flashed across her mind, she was never able to account for it, but it left a photographic impression on her inner eye and she remembered it always as something seen.

'Hullo, Nichols!' Tony called out, waving a brown paper parcel in his right hand, the string of which was threatening to come undone. Laundry showed where the edges of the paper were coming apart. In the other hand he lugged a battered and obviously heavy suitcase.

'Nice to see you home again, Mr Tony,' said Nichols, bending to take the suitcase from him. But Tony was having none of that. 'Too heavy for you, Nichols,' he said, 'books, you know. Here, take the shirts, please, before I scatter them all over the station. I forgot to pack them, so Ma had to tie them up at the last minute. How's Grandpa?'

Nichols had secured the parcel just in time to prevent its total disintegration, and Tony, having reached the top of the stairs, was searching his pockets with his free hand for his ticket. Having found it and given it up, he repeated the question, adding: 'How are things?'

'Mr Barlow is keeping well and looking forward to seeing you, Mr Tony. There is a lady –'

'I know, Nichols, Ma told me. Someone from Grandpa's dim past, I gather. Rather a bore.'

'I mean to say,' said Nichols quickly, 'that the lady is here – here, Mr Tony.' He nodded towards Anita.

'Good Lord!' exclaimed Tony, 'I mean, how-do-you-do. Sorry, and all that. I didn't mean to be rude, Mrs . . .?'

'"Seiler", said Anita, 'pronounced like a cockney "sailor", so I have been told. I didn't know when I came what "cockney" meant, but it seems to work.'

'Sylor?' said Tony, and laughed.

'Yes, that's right.'

They had been moving towards the car; Nichols opened the boot into which Tony heaved his suitcase. Then he opened the rear door for Anita and was about to follow her.

'I expect you would prefer to sit with Nichols and hear all the news of Milton Place,' she said. 'Please do.'

'Thanks, I will.' He slammed the door and slipped in next to Nichols with whom conversation, conducted in blurred tones and fragmentary sentences, started up immediately and never flagged until they turned into the drive at Milton Place.

Mr Barlow was on the terrace when they arrived and Tony was out of the car and round the corner of the house to meet his grandfather before the old gentleman had come many steps towards him. Anita, not very sure what to do with herself, had followed from force of habit. She was used to telling Mr Barlow she had returned whenever she had been out walking or driving. So she saw the meeting between grandfather and grandson.

'Hullo, Grandfather!'

'Hullo, my boy!'

That was all. Tony grinned, and Mr Barlow smiled, and they turned to go into the house together. Mr Barlow gripped Tony's arm, and Tony squeezed the old man's hand. They seemed to move in unison.

Anita turned and went indoors quickly before them, going straight up to her room. She was glad she had witnessed the meeting, for that brief minute had told her much. She had needed no confirmation of Mr Barlow's love for his grandson, the tender and self-tormenting love of the old for the young, love that would be protective and knows itself helpless, delight with an edge of pain. She knew that this was the living nerve by which Mr Barlow, so serene and passionless in the face of distasteful change, was still involved with fate's vicissitudes and vulnerable to suffering. Now she had seen it in his face and in the gesture of his fine, blue-veined hand which had gripped the boy's arm with convulsive intensity. But she had also seen Tony's expression and movement, the warmth in it and the spontaneous flow of affection that went out from him, and had nothing in it of duty or deference as conventionally due from a grandson to a grandfather. It leaped the gap of years and generations with a fine flourish, as if no such gap existed. If Mr Barlow loved Tony with an edge of pain, at least it was not the pain of being unrequited. She was glad. Nice boy, Tony, she thought, and the sense of some innate grace which had shown him to her fleetingly in the dress of a more polished age again passed through her mind.

Nevertheless, there was no denying that for the next couple of weeks life at Milton Place was less comfortable for Anita. They were three at meals now, at the little round table in the far corner of the dining room. Conversation was not always easy. Mr Barlow and Anita had mostly spoken of small day-to-day occurrences, or had been silent without any feeling of constraint. Now Mr Barlow was too intent on watching Tony to make desultory remarks to her. Nor did talk between him and Tony flow as naturally as it would have done, Anita felt, if she had not been there. Surely, Tony would have been more forthcoming? If Mr Barlow questioned him, not searchingly but in the manner of plain friendly interest, about his parents or the latest events at school, he answered in monosyllables or in entirely non-committal, stereotype phrases. His father was always very busy; his mother was all right; nothing much had happened at school; things had gone on as usual.

This did not seem to disturb Mr Barlow who just went on with his lunch or dinner, smiling quietly as if to convey to Tony: I'm not pressing you for information, you know; I'm quite content with anything you care to say or not to say. But Anita was sure that Tony was putting up his defences against *her*. It made her feel shy, and she even felt obliged to avoid looking too often in his direction because his appraising gaze seemed to be fixed upon her, embarrassingly, most of the time. But he certainly had no intention of being ill-mannered, for in all other respects he was studiously polite to her, opening doors for her or moving her chair when she sat down or got up. For the rest of the day, however, he seemed to keep carefully out of her way. If she came into Mr Barlow's study and he was there, he was always just on the point of going out; and so strongly did she feel this avoidance that in the evening she now tried to invent some excuse – a headache, the need to wash her hair, or some imaginary letter to write – so that she could go to her room and leave them alone.

Throughout the day, though, he kept himself busy and one never felt with him, as one does so often with young people on holiday when there are no games to play, that he didn't know what to do with his time. He got up early and set out on a bicycle in riding-boots and breeches for the farm where his horse was stabled. He was away for two or three hours and came back to a late breakfast, wet, tousled and ravenously hungry. Alice said he took a hunk of bread with him when he went out, but never allowed her to get up and make tea for him. She had eggs and bacon and stacks of toast ready for him in the kitchen when he came in, and Anita would hear his cheerful voice, laughing and talking to her and making her laugh too, while he ate. Anita wished she could join in, but dared not intrude. Then Tony would change into an old pair of flannels and go and say good morning to his grandfather, after which he would install himself in a corner of the walled garden, if the sun was there, or at a rickety old table in the conservatory where he sat hidden from view by a shelf of potted ferns and last year's azaleas. Later in the day he often went off for long walks or down to the farm again if there was a job of work on hand with which he was able to help.

Mr Barlow did not seem to notice any unease between Tony and Anita. He was aware that they were not very much in each other's company, for he told Anita after a few days that Tony always kept very much to himself when he was at Milton Place; that he had a craving for being alone, which was not strange if one remembered the community-life he was obliged to lead at school – classes and games by day, dormitory at night. Only during this last year had he had a study of his own which he did not have to share. Mr Barlow explained this during one of their habitual morning walks and, as usual, they came to rest, at the end of it, on a bench in the walled garden where the massed wallflowers were now exhaling clouds of honey-sweet scent, and innumerable bees, their brown velvety bodies hardly distinguishable from the brown velvety petals to which they clung, filled the air with the sound of their ceaselessly vibrating wings. They found Tony ensconced in their favourite corner, with a stack of books beside him, though he was not reading. His head was thrown back, his eyes half-closed to the sun; he seemed to be dreaming or intently listening. Seeing him so, Mr Barlow did not go towards him, but led Anita to an opposite corner, as if to emphasise what he had just been telling her: that Tony, when he wished to be alone, should not be disturbed, even by him.

Anita knew, however, that Tony and his grandfather had plenty to say to each other if she were not present. In the afternoons Mr Barlow would now go for another stroll, this time with Tony; and as they mostly walked on the terrace, Anita could watch them from her window. Though she felt excluded, she loved to watch them. She could see how carefully Tony restrained his steps to match them with Mr Barlow's slower movements, and from the animation of his face and gestures it was clear that he was talking volubly, while Mr Barlow listened and stopped from time to time to reply or to argue. For surely they were arguing, if in the most friendly manner, when they stood facing each other and Mr Barlow tapped with his stick on the ground, while Tony jerked his head back and then bent forward again to hold forth in full spate. If the day was wet and Mr Barlow did not go out, the sound of these lively conversations would drift up from the study.

At last she ventured to ask Mr Barlow: 'What kind of things do you and Tony discuss between you?' – saying it lightly and as if in jest, so that if he chose to answer 'Oh, just one thing and another', she would not have appeared to be really curious, and he would not feel he had reproved her. But he answered her very seriously: 'Mathematics, my dear.'

'Mathematics?' She would not have been surprised if Mr Barlow had said 'Politics', as Tony always seemed to talk so passionately, but now she could only say, helplessly: 'I don't understand!'

Mr Barlow laughed. 'No, my dear, and nor do I, some of the time. I was never what is called a "pure mathematician" myself, and the discipline has advanced so considerably since my young days that I have some difficulty in following my Tony's arguments, though I do my best. And then there is a new science called cybernetics which has to do with machines designed to reproduce the functions of thought – or some of its functions, its selecting and combining capacities, for instance – electrical devices to take over what Tony calls the drudgery of brain-work. It's all very exciting to him and, I'll admit, a bit over my old head. But Tony is very patient with me, he is determined to make me understand.'

This information, Anita felt, was, in a way, comforting because it now appeared that if Tony did not talk much in her presence it was not because he was hostile to her, but because he wanted to talk about things she could not understand. But it also made him seem even more unapproachably remote, as if – living in the same house, sitting at the same table – speaking the same language – they belonged to entirely different worlds. What does it matter? she asked herself, Why should I care? But she did.

CHAPTER THIRTEEN

When Mrs Mannering and Mrs Peacock parted from each other after their interesting coffee party at the Tudor Rose, they were both feeling very pleased with themselves. Emily congratulated herself on having taken the first step towards her ultimate objective, the disposal of Milton Place. If this plan succeeded and the County acquired it as a home, she would have achieved a double purpose: to rid the family of a useless burden and turn it from a private liability into a social asset. This was how she liked to deal with a problem – no loose ends left lying about. Quite apart from the personal interest involved in it, the neatness of the solution delighted her. There was a long way to go yet, of course, but with ingenuity and determination almost anything can be achieved. She had plenty of both, and she never enjoyed herself more than when she had something on hand which gave her scope for the exercise of these gifts.

Mrs Peacock's satisfaction with her morning was of a different complexion and her motives were possibly less mixed than Emily's. She did not pretend, even to herself, to be particularly interested in the progress of social institutions.

If she thought about them at all, she would have said, as she had already half-hinted during coffee, that they were being overdone. It was not the fashionable thing to say so, and she had not quite said it, but in her heart of hearts she didn't think that people ought to be relieved of so much of their responsibilities. It somehow offended her sense of her own value and dignity. She was as benevolent as the next person, she hoped, and as ready to help a neighbour in difficulties, within reason, as anybody else. But welfare occupations now belonged to the pattern of life and she took them in her stride as something a woman with leisure on her hands was expected to do. And there were advantages connected with such work. One met people, desirable people, on easy and friendly terms of equality, and it was up to oneself to make what use one could of such opportunities. It was not easy, of course, for this mixing at a common task seemed to get itself very quickly unmixed as soon as the task was performed. The more 'desirable' elements then withdrew with a smile and a nod into their own inaccessible world until the next meeting when they would come and mix again and disappear again as before. Mrs Mannering was one of these desirable elements and she behaved most characteristically in the way described. But now a new filament had been spun between them; it was a tenuous filament as yet, but with care it might be strengthened and eventually draw them together into a degree of intimacy that would be very gratifying. Several imaginary conversations went through Mrs Peacock's head as she peeled the potatoes and carefully placed the steak-and-kidney pudding in the steamer for their midday dinner: 'I'm sorry I can't go to the dress-show with you, my dear, I have promised to go with Mrs Mannering. She asked me a week ago.' Or else: 'We are meeting the Mannerings at The Hare and Hounds, that place on the road to Framley. It's under new management, and the Mannerings have quite taken it up. My Reg and John Mannering always like to talk to each other, and of course Emily Mannering and I are *great* friends.' – That daydream, too, was quite as far from realisation as Emily's plans for the disposal of Milton Place, but after this morning's coffee party it no longer seemed quite out of reach.

Husbands, however, are dense creatures and their minds seem to work so differently from those of their wives. Neither Mr Mannering nor Mr Peacock gave much encouragement to the schemes so nicely conceived by the ladies when, by each in her own way, they were mentioned to them.

'I have had an idea, John,' Emily said that evening after dinner, 'about what to do with Milton Place. I have just put out a feeler in that direction. I don't know whether anything will come of it, but it might work. I think it's worth trying.'

'Nobody's ever going to do anything with that deadweight of masonry, my dear. Too inconvenient. Chap from the Air Ministry, who lived there when his department had it during the war, said he'd never been so cold in his life. As for the plumbing –'

'Yes, I daresay, something would have to be done to the place, I know that.'

'Something? I should say: everything! Why, it would cost thousands! Cheaper to pull it down, I should have thought.'

'But *have* you thought, John? It's such a very solid, sound construction, built at a time when everything had to be of the best, materials *and* workmanship. Nothing was skimped or done on the cheap in those days. Yes, I suppose the plumbing and all that would have to be modernised, and the rooms could be partitioned.'

'Partitioned?'

'Yes, I mean if it were used for a home or institution. Because, you see, I think the County Council might be interested. That's what I'm trying to find out.'

'The County Council? Well, they have the money, no doubt, with all we have to pay in rates. But what would they *do* with it, if they bought it? Besides, it isn't yours to sell!'

'I know that, John, but sooner or later Father will have to see reason. He simply can't go on living out there at his age, and I'm sure he can't afford it, not really. He must be digging into his capital with both hands, keeping up those grounds, though he won't do anything to the house.'

'Maybe he is, but what can you do about it? He is in his right mind, if it is an obstinate one, and I don't think you'll persuade him to sell if he doesn't want to. If he wants to go on living there, you ought not to bully him about it. I'm very fond of your father, Emily, and I sympathise with him. He wants to keep his own roof over his head, and I don't blame him. I'd feel the same way myself.'

'I've always said men were more sentimental than women,' Emily laughed. Good humour seemed to accentuate her features, rather than soften them. 'I often think only women have common sense. You're as incurably romantic as Father is. By the way, you know about that Austrian woman he invited over – the daughter of a girl he was once infatuated with as a young man – have I told you that she is still there? I didn't see her the last times I went out there. Father said she was busy cleaning out some of the rooms, and didn't think herself presentable. *I* think she was keeping out of my way. It seems she is recuperating from some kind of unpleasant war-experience and is rather shy, so Father says. I shouldn't want her to entrench herself too much there, though. She's already made several changes in the house, and Father seems delighted with them.'

'Really? I should have thought he'd have resented any change or interference with his settled habits.'

'So should I, but no, anything Mrs Seiler does is all right. But you had better see for yourself. Can you drive out with me one Saturday or Sunday?'

'I can, if I cut golf. What's more, I'd like to. I haven't been to see your father for ages, I'm sorry to say. But I'll tell you one thing, my dear. I'm not going to have anything to do with moving him out of Milton Place. That is entirely between you and him. I know you Barlows, and I'm not going to be caught between an irresistible force and an immovable object, if I know what's good for me!'

* * *

Mrs Peacock broached the subject to her husband equally casually as they were retiring to bed that night.

'I heard a piece of news this morning that you might like to know about,' she said.

118

'And what may that be?' he asked.

'I've heard of a place that might be suitable for that pet-scheme of yours, that home for girls and their babies that you want to set up.'

'That *I* want to set up! You talk as if it were all my own idea, and a bad one at that! What do you know about it anyway? It's in committee stage as yet, being privately discussed between members – nothing has been laid before the Council. And there you go gossiping about it to all and sundry. I wish I'd never mentioned it to you, you're so indiscreet.'

Mr Peacock was seriously annoyed. There was nothing particularly secret about this plan for a home for unmarried mothers, but he did not want it to appear as if he discussed public business in his private life. He felt that it would be contrary to his duty and impair his dignity as a public servant, if he did so. The two things must be kept separate. It was a matter of principle.

His wife thought this was just queer, masculine prejudice. 'What a fuss you make, Reg,' she said. 'It wasn't me at all that started the conversation. Other people seem to know about it all, so other people must have talked. These things get about somehow. And if you want to know, it was Mrs Mannering who mentioned it this morning over coffee.'

'Who's Mrs Mannering?'

'Oh, come now, Reg! Mrs John Mannering – you know who John Mannering is.'

'Very well. I didn't know you and Mrs Mannering were such buddies.'

'I daresay you didn't. Do you want to know what she told me?'

There was silence in the darkened bedroom, it seemed for ages. A beam of light from a passing car slid between the curtains and wavered across the wall. Mrs Peacock feared that her Reg would refuse to hear her news by pretending to be asleep. Then, at last: 'Well, let's have it, what did she tell you?'

'She said that Milton Place might soon be coming on to the market. Old Mr Barlow is Mrs Mannering's father, you know.' Mrs Peacock sighed. The news had been imparted.

Mr Peacock grunted. 'You can tell your bosom-friend Mrs Mannering that as far as my plans are concerned, Milton Place is too far, and too grand, and no use at all. Good night.'

So that, it seemed, was that.

But Mrs Peacock continued to think of Emily Mannering and Mr Peacock could not help thinking of Milton Place as a possible site for his projected home. He had turned down the suggestion gruffly enough when he had first heard of it, for his wife's slightly derisive reference to his 'pet-scheme' had annoyed him, all the more so because he really had it very much at heart. It was for him, though all unconsciously, a symbol of his own emancipation, of his spiritual emergence from the narrowness and the prejudices of his early environment from which his success in business had liberated him materially. In devoting so much of his energies to the service of the community – to his honour, be it said – he had brought to his endeavours a private and personal slant. Because he had come from a moral background in which severity had been more stressed than charity, he was inclined to assist and protect the 'undeserving' rather than the deserving, the 'fallen' rather than the merely unfortunate. The needs of the young, the old and the sick were acknowledged by all, but the care for 'sinners' – and as such Mr Peacock thought of them, just as his wife did, though he did not, like her, condemn them – to care for them was to him a token of broad-mindedness and enlightenment.

* * *

It appears therefore that Emily's soundings had met with more response than she herself knew at the time.

She was certainly not in the best of tempers when she and her husband drove out to Milton Place for lunch on a Sunday later in the month. A tiny incident had occurred when she was making the arrangements for this expedition, negligible in itself, but it had annoyed her out of all proportion to its importance.

Mr Barlow himself had answered the telephone when she had rung up to announce herself and John, and Mr Barlow had said 'Very well', in his usual even voice, 'that will be very nice. I haven't seen John for a long time.' And then he had added: 'Hold on a minute, I'll just ask Mrs Seiler whether it's all right.' Mrs Seiler was evidently in the room, as it had hardly taken a moment to obtain her consent which, of course, she had graciously given.

'Ask Mrs Seiler whether it's all right!', Emily repeated to herself. 'What next, I wonder!' John was driving. Emily did not like that very much either. She felt irritated and on edge, but John never noticed such things, or maybe took no notice. It was more comfortable for him.

He always enjoyed the drive to Milton Place, up to the moment when he came upon the house. He enjoyed driving in at the gates which Nichols, who had been told to expect them, came out of the lodge to open for him. Very slowly he drove up the lime avenue which now formed a pale-green openwork canopy overhead. Glancing to the left, between the tree-trunks he caught sight of a strip of scarlet tulips against a background of dark rhododendron bushes. Then came the turning where, to the right, both the house and the wide sweep of country which it commanded came into view. The terrace was edged with yellow tulips and wallflowers. 'Look,' he said, 'no wonder your father loves the place. When I see this, I wish I could live here myself – only the house is so depressing.' There it stood, massive and uncompromising, without a smile on its face, in the sullen light of the grey day, the paint peeling off the window frames. All the loveliness it looked out upon seemed unable to cheer it up. The glazed porch still had its broken panes and the big door's brown paint was greying with age. 'As soon as I get indoors,' John said, 'I know I shall be glad to get out again.'

But today the atmosphere in the house was different. The chilly, vault-like stillness that usually filled the hall and the well of the staircase and from which one hurried to take refuge in Mr Barlow's dingy but habitable study, had some-how changed its quality. It was quiet but alive. One's steps no longer rang cold and hard on the stone-flagged floor. One large and two smaller Persian rugs had been spread on them, softening the footfall and muting the bleak, white light with the wealth of their deep-toned, multicoloured patterns.

'Hullo!' John exclaimed, but Emily only stared at them. 'They must have been put away in the attic,' she said, 'I seem to remember them, though they were never down here.'

There were also two large stone urns with azaleas in them just coming into flower, at each side of the stairs.

'Goodness knows where they come from!' she added.

They went into the study. There was nothing changed here: the same tall windows, wine-coloured walls and shabby, brown curtains, the dark carpet and ponderous armchairs, the high bookcases – and yet there was a difference here too. In spite of the grey sky, it was lighter, the windows looked clearer and there was a flower-table in front of one of them. Mr Barlow himself, though always so careful of his appearance, looked particularly spruce, as if he, too, had been spring-cleaned: he looked so cheerful.

John Mannering was just telling him how pleased he was to see him so well, when Anita came in. Mr Barlow introduced John who had been meaning to make a little complimentary speech to Mrs Seiler when he met her, about the improvements in the hall, but he suddenly seemed taken aback and only mumbled a rather lame how-do-you-do. This was glossed over by Mr Barlow asking after Tony. 'Why isn't he in? I reminded him not to be late.'

Anita said she was sure he would be down in a moment, she had heard him come in and go upstairs. '*Perhaps*,' and she stressed it, 'he is washing his hands,' she added, which made John grin. They went across to the dining room and at that moment Tony came dashing downstairs. Apart from, perhaps, washing his hands, he had made no concession to the presence of his uncle and aunt; he was wearing the same old tweed coat and shapeless trousers, but he had put on a tie – in a great hurry, it seemed, for its knot was already half-hiding bashfully under one curled-up wing of his soft collar.

'So sorry, Mrs Seiler,' he panted, charging at the dining room door to open it for her, while his eyes lit up with such a devastating smile that it made his untidiness look like specially contrived romantic negligence. Then the smile vanished. 'Hullo, Aunt Emily, Uncle John!'

'Hullo, Tony, my boy!' John Mannering slapped him on the shoulder, all affability and heartiness. 'How's life?'

In the dining room the large table in the centre had been laid with a damask cloth as of old, for Mr Barlow's linen-cupboard had not contained any place-mats. White narcissi and blue iris mingled in a silver bowl in the middle. There was some shifting and changing around the table because Anita, on a last-minute impulse, was urging Tony to take the place opposite his grandfather, so that she need not appear to be acting as hostess. Emily's critical looks suddenly seemed to make this imperative and Anita longed to make herself as inconspicuous as possible. But with John Mannering observing her relentlessly, albeit with approval, she felt embarrassingly self-conscious.

When they had at last sat down and Sims had begun to serve the excellent luncheon, largely prepared by herself,

Anita hoped, for Mr Barlow's sake, that all would now be easy and pleasant. He certainly looked very happy. His eyes wandered with dreamy contentment round the table, but he seemed to be contemplating the soft reflections of the sky on silver and glass rather than the faces of his family. Then his gaze came to rest on the iris. From which bed, he wanted to know, had they been cut? Ah yes, he remembered, there were two kinds there and he repeated their names, under his breath, quite absorbed in recalling them. Meanwhile John Mannering had continued addressing himself to Tony, in an over-jovial manner as if to a schoolboy, with facetious digs at his need of a haircut. To this, Tony, who had simply begrudged the time to go into town and have it done, answered stiffly: 'I happen to like it like this.'

John Mannering looked a little hurt – at the tone, not the words. Like a big dog, Anita thought, who has been rebuffed when meaning to be friendly. But Emily said: 'I'm not surprised. A certain set, I'm told, make a point of looking disreputable. It's artistic, or highbrow, or something.' John said, sheepishly: 'Oh, I didn't know!', which made Tony relent towards him: 'It's not that, Uncle John. I don't belong to any set, anyhow.'

All the while John Mannering had been trying to find some way to open a conversation with Anita from whom he had scarcely averted his eyes since the moment he had been introduced. Reverting to Mr Barlow's enquiries about the iris, he remarked how well they looked with the old china and silver and how nice it was for Mr Barlow to have them back on his table. Then, turning to Anita with a smile and a little gesture of

the hand that was meant to do duty for a bow, he compli-
mented her on having brought this about, as well as all the
other things she had done. Anita smiled back at him and was
just beginning to say how glad she was that he liked it and how
much she had enjoyed doing it, when Emily intervened with
the opinion that it was all very nice, but that, personally, she
saw no point in trying to put the clock back; this kind of thing
was bound to make more work for the old couple who would
not be able to keep it up once Mrs Seiler had left.

Whether or not Mr Barlow heard this remark and changed
the subject on purpose, or whether he just happened, at that
moment, to come out of his daydream, his voice suddenly
sounded rather louder than usual as he enquired from John
about some business-friends with whose firm he had himself
had dealings many years ago. John was forced to give his
attention to his father-in-law and his talk from now on
alternated between accounts of current transactions and the
personal histories and habits of the men engaged in them.
Snippets of this conversation came across the table whenever
he turned his head to watch Anita, which he did at every
movement she made either to help Sims change the plates or
to hand round a dish.

'Old Digby? He died last year, shortly after his son had
come into the firm. He is still finding his feet, but I think he will
do very well after a bit. Old Digby was very able, you know, but
he was getting very difficult, with all his prejudices. They were
impairing the firm's efficiency towards the end. It would have
been better if he had retired immediately after the war. You
have no idea, sir, how things have changed!'

'I daresay you're right, John. Nobody will reproach me with hanging on too long, though it's difficult to know when to go, especially when one feels fit. You'll find that out yourself some day.'

'The war has changed everything so much more quickly – the old methods are out of date. Now take Johnson's. . . .'

Anita wished she could talk to Emily. John Mannering's glances were becoming distinctly embarrassing, but Emily kept her eyes averted, bringing down an invisible shutter between herself and Anita. Seeing that Anita was, in spite of this, going to speak to her, she turned abruptly to Tony.

'How's your poor mother?' she asked and, without expecting an answer, went on to tell him how sorry she always felt for her sister, for the dullness and monotony of her life, her lack of energy and vitality. 'One thing accounts for the other, of course. Each in turn is cause and effect, but we know it's not altogether your poor mother's fault. It's your father who. . .'

But here Tony, who had been listening in silence, his mouth set in the thinnest of lines, interrupted forcefully: 'I don't discuss my parents, Aunt Emily, never, on principle.'

Emily said: 'Well! In the family, you know. . .'

'Especially in the family, Aunt Emily, on principle.'

'More and more like your father, aren't you!' Emily retorted. 'Just as unbearable. Poor Cecilia! And she complains that she sees so little of you. Why, it may be a blessing in disguise. Fancy having to live with two of you! I shall have to point it out to her.'

'Do, Aunt Emily, that would be kind!'

Emily stared at him, sensing some outrageous impertinence behind the conversational phrase, but unable at the moment to determine its nature. She was even glad of the diversion Anita made by passing her the fruit-basket with a comment on the unusual keeping-quality of apples this year. Then Mr Barlow indicated gently that he was ready to rise, and with a pushing and scuffing of chairs the party broke up. The weather had brightened during the meal and John Mannering announced that if they left directly after coffee he would still be able to get a round of golf. He had whole-heartedly enjoyed his lunch.

'Attractive woman, that Mrs Seiler, don't you think?' he said to Emily as soon as they had got into the car. 'And your father's looking better than I've seen him look for a long time. Excellent meal and general improvement in the whole set-up. A stroke of luck for the old man to have found her, eh? He'd better try to make her stay!'

'You think so?' said Emily. 'That's as may be. *I* think the situation will have to be watched – very carefully watched.'

CHAPTER FOURTEEN

Anita had gone back into the dining room to start clearing away. She was alone there, as Sims and Alice were now having their own meal in the kitchen, when, to her surprise, she was joined by Tony. He had never deliberately sought her company before. He came in hesitatingly, shut the door behind him, walked round the room and stood first by the sideboard, then by the window, watching her while she collected the glasses on a tray.

'Oh! do stop for a minute!' he blurted out.

She stopped and looked at him enquiringly. 'Yes, Tony?'

'I want to tell you how sorry I am – about my aunt and uncle – they behaved abominably to you. You shouldn't be treated like that. I feel the least I can do is to apologise. Perhaps Grandpa will, but, bless him, I'm not sure he even noticed, he seemed so wrapped up in his own thoughts. But you saw that I did – and I don't want you to think I didn't mind.'

'That's very nice of you, Tony, and makes me feel a lot better. I'm afraid, though, that your aunt objects to me.'

'Aunt Emily's an old cat. I never could bear her. You must try not to mind her. She's always like that. But Uncle John –

I would have thought better of him. He's not a bad sort, really, only that he's never quite grown up. I've always regarded him as emotionally retarded. He's that type of man, you see,' Tony explained with all the seriousness of his eighteen years. 'But today he made me really angry. I wished I could have hit him. The way he looked at you! All smarmy and messy, as if he were trying to feel you all over with his eyes. I know it can't be much fun being married to Aunt Emily – but that's no reason. . . I mean, not with *you*.'

'Oh, Tony, you mustn't say things like that! Such things should not be said!'

'I'm sorry. But I hated it. I suppose he doesn't have many opportunities – but *you*'re not the kind of person he *can* make free to look at in that way. I couldn't stop him though, without making a row.'

'I'm very thankful you didn't make a row. It would have made it much worse. Don't be upset, Tony. No harm has been done. In such a case it's always best to take no notice.'

'All right then.' He went to the door, stopped and turned back again. 'You're not angry with me?'

'No, Tony, of course not. Thank you – I'm grateful.'

He went, and a few minutes later she saw him striding past the windows, swinging a stick. Sims came in and together they finished clearing the table. Her mood had quite changed; gone were the doubt and discomfort the Mannerings had left in their wake. Surprise and amusement, and a little dash of tenderness, suffused her feelings. 'And I thought that to him I was just a domestic appliance!' she exclaimed inwardly, and repeatedly, like a recurring refrain, while chatting soberly and appropriately to Sims.

There was no opportunity for further talk with Tony that day, but next morning she kept on the lookout for him. She saw him come home from riding, waited for him to have his breakfast, and then saw him with an armful of books make for the little green door leading to the walled garden. She took off her overall, took a quick look at her face and hair and went down after him.

It was early yet, there would be plenty of time for a chat before Mr Barlow came out for his walk. She shut the little green door behind her, and there was Tony – stretched out on the grass, his back propped up against a bench, his books beside him, but making no pretence at reading. He saw her come, but evidently not believing that she intended to join him, he did not move. She, however, went straight towards him and only when she was within a couple of steps from him, did he realise her intention and start to scramble to his feet. But, putting her hand on his shoulder, she gently pushed him back onto the grass and sat down on the bench. He leaned back against it as before, his head now at the height of her knees. It was a glorious morning. The old brick wall shimmered in the sunshine, its colours indistinguishable in a haze of light; the shadows of the branches and twigs that fell upon it were sharp and strong. Anita stretched her arms above her head, leaned back and closed her eyes.

'What a lovely morning!'

Tony looked up at her, uneasily.

'I am not disturbing you by coming to sit here, am I?' It was a statement rather than a question. 'You were not reading.'

'No, I was not reading.' There was a silence. Tony shifted his position so that he could more easily look up. 'You are sure you are not angry with me, about what I said yesterday – about Uncle John, I mean?'

He had felt terribly embarrassed over his outburst as soon as it had happened, and not at all sure how Mrs Seiler had received it, in spite of her saying she was grateful. One's feelings, he thought, always get one into trouble just as soon as one allows them to be seen. Give yourself away, and you lay yourself open to every misunderstanding, worst of all, to possible ridicule. The only safe thing was to keep oneself always under lock and key. Here was Mrs Seiler now – he wondered what she wanted of him. He liked her so much – it might have been better if he had kept himself at a safe distance. Now, perhaps, he had offended her.

But: 'Oh, let's forget about that,' Anita said. 'I just came out to have a chat with you. Don't you want to talk to me?'

'Talk about what?'

'Oh, just talk. It needn't be about anything in particular. If one thinks someone is nice, it's a pleasant way of spending a little time with them. I like talking just for its own sake. One doesn't always want to be alone. At least, I don't. Why are you so much alone, Tony? Haven't you got any friends around here?'

'Dick, down on the farm, is a great friend of mine. We were boys together. I see him nearly every day. Not that we talk a lot. We don't have to. It's not that kind of friendship.'

'I understand. But of course you have friends at school, and at home where your parents live.'

He skipped the mention of home. 'There are some very decent chaps at school. I don't know whether I'd call them *friends*. One does things together, one discusses things – that's talking, I suppose.'

'In a way it is. It's rather impersonal. You discuss things with your grandfather, he tells me, very difficult and clever things which you work on. It would be no use trying to talk about them to me. I shouldn't understand the first word. So there we are – at an end even before we have started. It doesn't matter. It's companionable just to sit here for a while and be silent. As long as I know that you have no objection to me.'

She clasped her hands behind her head, making a rest for them to lean against. Looking down at him through half-closed eyelids, she contemplated the dark, smooth head, the wide forehead and finely pencilled eyebrows. Just a shadow of a moustache lay on his long upper lip. Would she ever know what went on inside that head? What a strange boy he was, closed as tight as the rugged shell of an oyster, with only a smile now and again to betray the nacreous luminosity within.

Meanwhile he, too, was looking at her; and what he saw was that her hair was tawny in the sun, and that the skin over her cheekbones and her jaw had the texture of very fine silk, smooth and yet grained with infinitesimal crinkles, which held a softness and a sweetness different from the glossy, polished surface of a young girl's face. He saw it, all uncon-scious of what he was seeing, for it went through his eyes straight to some secret inner place in his heart and turned his defences.

'What a strange person you are,' he said. 'I've never met anyone like you before. But I ought not to say "strange", because I mean just the opposite. I mean that you fit into this place as if you'd always belonged here. To tell you the truth, I was rather upset at the idea of your being here with Grandpa. It means such a terrible lot to me to be here, and to be with him – and you might have made a mess of it all. But you know, from the moment I saw you at the station, I knew that you wouldn't. It's funny the way one sometimes knows things without having anything to go on, quite unscientific. Of course, I didn't know then what a difference you'd make here; a wonderful difference, I mean, not a disastrous one. It's as if you'd got right into the heart of the old place and put new life into it. Not changing it from outside – I'd have hated that – but making it more like itself again, as it ought to be.'

'I'm glad you approve of my efforts.'

'I do. So does Grandpa. But it's not only what you've *done*. It's something about the way you *are* that makes you different from other people, that makes you belong here. I say!' – he suddenly pulled himself up – 'do you mind my going on like this?'

'No, Tony, please go on. Why am I different?'

'Well. . .' He hesitated, and then, suddenly, a surge of self-confidence swept away his doubts. It was as if he had thrown himself, reluctantly, into an unknown sea, and found its waters buoyant and exhilarating to swim in. 'It's really very easy to talk to you,' he said.

134

'Then tell me why you think I am different.'

'You seem to me to be just "there", like a tree is "there", being yourself, not always hankering after something, or resenting something else, like most people do. That's what makes you fit in here so well. Because Grandpa is like that, too. He's like his beloved old cedar, stately and grand, but without any kind of pomposity or pretence. Just himself; and by being himself, setting a standard.'

'You love him very much, don't you? So do I.'

'I rather thought you did.'

'What kind of a tree am I like?'

'Not a cedar, of course. You're not old and dignified. A birch, I should say, with a silvery trunk.'

'Thank you, that's very nice. And what tree are you, yourself?'

'Oh, I'm not a tree at all, or if I am, it must be a monkey-puzzle, prickly all over!'

'Oh, Tony, why do you say that? There isn't one in the whole place. I'm sure Mr Barlow doesn't like them, and I think they're horrid. They wouldn't belong here at all.'

'That's it. I'm not supposed to, you know.' He made a queer grimace; his lips twisted, not in a smile, but a grin of irony and disgust.

'But you *do* belong here. It's your home, isn't it?'

'So I like to think. But my father tells me – and has always told me every since I could understand him – that I only *want* to be here because I'm a stuck-up, self-important, arrogant little snob!'

'Oh Tony! But that's not true! You don't believe that.'

'No, I don't. I'm not stuck-up. I don't feel a bit arrogant. I'm just different, and I can't help it. But I do hate everything at home. I suppose I always have, though I haven't always consciously known it. It's a sickening aversion, I can't reason about it. I hate the flashy seafront, canvas chairs, palms and all, the sprawling hotels, the flower beds laid out in circles and squares, the gardens with their lawns and shrubs all beautifully combed and curled – a glossy magazine addict's dream. That's the outside. And inside the shabbiness, the second-rate, the dinginess of the mind. The house smells of disinfectant and wax polish. Lace curtains and green plush in the front room – it's also the waiting room – carved oak and looking-glass in the dining room, bare, makeshift bedrooms. Please don't think I mind the lack of luxury, or even comfort. It's not that at all. Besides, we're not poor, it doesn't *have* to be like that. Father doesn't see and doesn't know, and Mother, poor dear, has no initiative of her own, and just leaves things as they are. I got some paint and brushes once and thought I'd do a bit of decorating, upstairs at least, but Mother said I was upsetting the household and making a mess, and the char was sure to give notice. And Father, when he heard about it, wanted to know how I'd paid for the paint. Grandpa gives me my pocket money – it had come out of that – so Father said he'd had to allow his son to be educated by his grandfather, but he wasn't going to have Mr Barlow's money making so-called improvements in his own house. He always speaks of Grandpa as Mr Barlow, so Grandpa calls Father "Dr Crawfurd" – not exactly what you would call "intimate", is it?'

'It certainly doesn't sound very friendly. But you know, Tony, it often happens in families, especially between in-laws, that they are not very congenial to each other.'

Automatically Anita had groped for that most common panacea that lies ready to the hand of anyone trying to console and soothe mental distress: one loosens the constricting knot of singularity as one loosens a collar, one places the actual predicament against the perspective of general experience, thereby reducing its impact. But she had hardly spoken the words when she felt how misplaced they were. General experience means nothing to the young, they know only their own, in all the intensity of its uniqueness, and which, with its unrepeatable anguish or delight, suffuses and colours the whole world. What did Tony care how other in-laws might behave! He brushed Anita's remark aside and she felt grateful that he had not taken her up on it. He was now pulling out little blades of grass and rubbing them between his fingers, intent on his own thoughts.

'I know I said to Aunt Emily,' he continued, 'that I never discuss my parents. Not with her, at any rate, nor with anyone else, so far. How could I, things being what they are? I don't want to discuss them now, but I do want you to understand. Father's a doctor. He was a very clever boy, he won scholarships. He thought he was brilliant, and that he was going to be a specialist, a consultant, or do some fine piece of original research. That is what he wanted. And then, after he had qualified, somehow something went wrong. Two of his friends, the ones to whom he had felt closest, succeeded. He didn't. He lost touch with them and all that they stood for.

He went into general practice, and the years went by, and he lost interest in his work. Now it's just a job, just routine that gives him no satisfaction. He just grinds away, so many patients a day with their dreary complaints – labels them, gives them their pills and their mixtures. He could do it in his sleep. He says so himself.'

'He must be a very unhappy man.'

'I suppose he is. But why does he have to be like that? What was it that went wrong with him? He blames it all on his bad luck, on everything always being against him, on not having had a fair chance because he hadn't got the right kind of voice or the smooth manners the other two happened to have. Somehow I can't believe that's true. If he had really been so able – the best man of his year, he says – surely that would have outweighed any such superficial disadvantages. They seem so unimportant. It couldn't have been only those things that stood in his way.'

'I think maybe it is easier to put the blame on something superficial than to look deeper into oneself for one's own shortcomings.'

'Well, it puzzles me. I don't know what he really believes because he taunts me with those very things the lack of which – so he says – prevented him from having the career he wanted. That's why he calls me stuck-up, and arrogant, and a snob. It doesn't make sense. I can't believe he's right about himself. I know he's wrong about me.'

'What does your mother say to all this?'

'Poor Ma – she just says nothing. Father jeers at her even more than he does at me. Of course I don't answer, but I wish *she* would stand up to him sometimes. She hasn't got it in her, she's just the opposite of Aunt Emily. She cringes to Father and that makes him worse. And she's always fussing, always in a dither, every little thing turns into a crisis. All she can do if that happens, is cry. So, of course, if only for her sake, I keep my mouth shut and stay away as much as I can. Thank God! Grandpa insists on having me here for most of the holidays. *He* knows, though we never talk about it. So now I've told you. And, please, let us not talk about it any more either.'

'Yes, Tony, I quite understand. But thank you for your confidence.'

Tony scrambled to his feet. 'Here is Grandpa coming to look for you.'

Mr Barlow, wearing a soft straw hat and carrying a stout stick, had just come through the little green door. Anita, too, rose to meet him.

'So you two have made friends at last,' he said with a twinkle and, nodding to Tony, he put his arm through Anita's. 'Come along, we will go and see how Nichols is getting on with the bedding-out.'

CHAPTER FIFTEEN

It was Mr Barlow who suggested, at lunch, that Tony should take Anita with him when he went for his long walks in the afternoon. He felt that Mrs Seiler would like some rather more rigorous exercise than the measured strolls she took with him in the garden could provide. He had seen her devote her energies to rejuvenating the house and of that, he thought, she had done more than enough. Now that the fine weather had come she ought to be out enjoying the country-side. He himself had been a great walker in his day and he was glad that Tony shared his predilection. The only way to get to know a stretch of country intimately was to walk in it. Dashing about in cars along metalled roads, skimming a view here, glimpsing one there, was like going to those short-lived parties that were now so much in vogue, making desultory conversation with people one had never met before and might never see again. But walking was living with a place and making friends with it. It needed time and patience and the measured rhythm of your own pace to put you in touch with the things that are near, while the distant prospects shift very slowly and you take them in from imperceptibly changing angles. Both Tony and Anita agreed, but Tony added that riding was even more enjoyable. You can go faster and further, without losing touch with the earth, and if you are in mutual confidence and understanding with your horse, his strength and life-force flows into you and enhances your own.

'Tony preferred a horse to a motorcycle when I offered him one or the other on his sixteenth birthday,' said Mr Barlow. 'I must say I was pleased when he chose a horse.'

'It was not a difficult choice. I never hesitated.'

'Now that I know you a little better, I am not surprised,' said Anita, 'but on the face of it I should have thought it unusual for a young man of today.'

'Tony is not machine-minded, although he is a scientist,' said Mr Barlow.

'I am not a scientist, Grandpa, I'm a mathematician, a pure mathematician,' said Tony. He stressed the word 'pure'. 'And you didn't mean "scientist" just now, Grandpa. You meant "technician" when you spoke of being machine-minded, and I'm *not* a technician, though I may try to go in for pure science when I go up to Cambridge.' Again he put emphasis on the word 'pure'.

'What is "pure" science?' Anita asked.

'Knowledge,' he said, 'knowledge for its own sake – and nothing else.' It sounded almost like a challenge.

Mr Barlow smiled at him. 'It is a point we often discuss,' he explained to Anita. 'I think what Tony aspires to is wholly admirable. Of course I myself, as an engineer, have had to move on a more humble plane – a mere technician.'

'Oh, Grandpa, you are laughing at me!'

'I am teasing you a bit, my boy, but I am not laughing at you. That's not quite the same thing. I know how serious you are.'

'I *am* serious, and I think this is important, at least for me. Machines are important, too. They're useful, they serve a purpose. What I mean is that I should decide the purpose, not the machine. They can help me live the life I want to live, but they must not force upon me the kind of life they are constructed to produce. I should have liked a motor-cycle if I wanted to get away from here – fast and far. As, when I am here, I want to *stay* here and *be* here, I preferred a horse.'

Mr Barlow nodded and, turning to Anita, added: 'You see?' as if concluding Tony's argument.

Anita saw. Although she did not quite grasp the scope of the distinction, she understood that Tony was saying something that appealed to her own inner sense of values, and he was saying it with the insight and authority of a grown man, rather than with the enthusiasm of a boy. For an instant she glimpsed, though unconsciously, the power and stature of his personality behind his boyish looks, and felt his presence. The next moment he had changed back to a lighter vein and to the subject they had started from.

It would be very jolly, Tony said, if Mrs Seiler would come walking with him, only he must warn her that where he went was often very rough going: long, wet grass, muddy tracks or no tracks at all, gates to climb over, barbed wire to negotiate. At all this Anita laughed. Such things, she said, held no terror for her and she would love to come if he would let her. So when Mr Barlow had retired to his study to read and rest they set off together; she in her sturdy shoes and her old skirt, carrying a knobbly stick which Tony had dug up for her from some old chest where such things were kept, to help her deal with slippery banks and tangled undergrowth. But he soon found that she matched him easily in speed and agility and that she could climb and jump as readily as he did.

Not that the country around Milton Place demanded any strenuous efforts. The woods Anita walked through with Tony were never very extensive, nor the hills they climbed very high. From spinney to copse they skirted ploughed fields or crossed meadows where placid cows were grazing, and then, for a while, there would be a stretch of road or a lane between hedges. If then they came to a white barred gate behind which, on a sloping pasture, there was a scattering of sheep with tiny white lambs tripping and stumbling beside the staid, heavily-coated ewes, Anita would beg Tony to wait a little because she could hardly tear herself away from the sight. Another thing that entranced her were the little tight-rolled fronds of young bracken, like miniature shepherd's crooks, which she found so extraordinarily tough to pick, but could never resist adding to the bunches of wild flowers she invariably took home to her room. At such moments Tony would walk on a little way, indifferently swinging a sapling he had cut and peeling it, or whistling to himself under his breath. But when she was not looking, he would turn and watch her intently, noticing the curve of her back as she bent down, or her slender ankles when she lifted her feet; but what he liked best were the silky wisps of fair hair that worked themselves loose from their pins and were blown by the breeze round the nape of her neck like down. These little secret observations he kept carefully to himself like hidden sweets which no one should know he possessed; and so, also, when he waited for her at a stile to climb over or a boggy patch to cross, he would pretend that she needed his help so that, for an instant, he could hold her hand or feel her weight on his arm.

There were not so very many of these afternoons, for Tony's holidays were drawing to a close, but as they followed each other, day by day, in an unbroken spell of sunny weather, they seemed to form one long, continuous and luminous avenue of pale green leaves and glancing golden light, leading always, at the end, to the big grey house with the great dark cedar by its side, and Mr Barlow's welcoming smile within.

Lying in her bed at night, Anita asked herself what was happening to her. Was it just the spring? She had lived through more springs than she liked to think, but none had been quite like this one. Was it just that now, for the first time after what she called 'the desert years', she was alive again? In those years spring had been nothing but a season in the calendar, almost unnoticed by her stony eyes and indifferent heart. If then, in an unguarded moment, in early morning the song of a bird, or at dusk a remembered scent had pierced her consciousness, they had had in them a stab of pain, like a deliberate taunt to the world of staring horror and creeping fear in which she had dragged out her days.

Then she tried to recall the springs of her girlhood, but they, too, had not been like this one. On Sunday mornings she had walked with her father in the Vienna woods. There had been violets and anemones in the undergrowth, and the sunlight had glanced and glittered through lacy foliage on carpets of brown pine-needles and beech-leaves. Or she had sat with her governess on little painted chairs in the park and the air had been heavy with the scent of lilac and horse-chestnut and lime-blossom. In those days a cloud of warm scent seemed always to be billowing over the city, making one's limbs languorous, bringing longings to the heart and disturbing cravings to the senses – an enervating delight, an exhausting enchantment. . . . This spring, now, was clearer and cooler; instead of languishing, it sparkled. The smell of the earth and the new green shoots was different, too, from anything she remembered; fainter, but more exquisite, subtler and less heady. The ghost of a smile on a serious face, she thought, is more entrancing than the wide parted lips of too much laughter.

The ghost of a smile on a serious face – that was Tony's smile. He was the spring that was surging in her blood, thrilling her heart and quickening her pulse. He was the surge of life in her, her rebirth and reawakening, her praise and her rejoicing. Never, as a girl, had she felt like this. Then, it seemed to her, she had been dreamy and half-asleep; now she was fully conscious and wide-awake. For a moment, and to test herself, she fixed her mind on Martin and saw before her his thin, anxious, fear-haunted face. Would he have been like Tony if he had been allowed to grow up to manhood? It was unimaginable. Did she feel for Tony what she would have felt for her son? A thousand times NO! Tenderness and pity and helpless anguish she had felt for the poor boy whom she had tried, and been unable, to protect. My poor darling, she murmured to him – she would gladly have given her life for him – but now. . . . She was taking nothing from him by being alive, magnificently and rejoicingly alive – through Tony.

On the last day of his holidays Tony had chosen for their walk a circuit she was particularly fond of because it took them along a crest of land from which there was a wide view over lower-lying meadows, orchards and fields. The apple-trees in the middle distance were clothed in pink, and further away a blue haze hung between sky and earth like a gauzy veil. To the left was a farm, flanked by an oast-house whose twin blunted conical hats gave to the landscape an intimate human focus. They sat down on a large log at the edge of a copse and looked into the distance. Anita realised suddenly, with a shiver in her heart, that tomorrow he would not be there beside her. But it was Tony who spoke.

'I always hate going away from here,' he said. 'This time it seems quite unbearable.'

Be quiet, be calm, she told herself. Speak with an even, natural voice. 'I shall miss you terribly, Tony. These lovely walks! I've enjoyed them so much.'

'This last term,' he went on, 'I've been thinking about it a lot these last few days. It's such a shocking waste. I shan't be able to work, I'd accepted that. I'll play a lot of cricket – that looked quite promising, a little while ago. Now it's different. If I could have foreseen – this, I might have arranged not to go back.'

'Foreseen – what?' Her voice now sounded strange in her own ears.

He kept his face averted, looking into the distance, as he replied: 'That there would be you.'

'It was something we neither of us could foresee. It was so improbable.'

'And now I have to go away.'

'But you'll be coming back – in the summer.'

'Of course, but meanwhile. . . One can't afford to waste one's life, especially when one has just discovered what it means to "live" it. I seem merely to have "existed" somehow up till now.'

'Ten weeks is not a very long time.'

'What's length got to do with it? You can't measure life by lengths. My life – it's immeasurable, unique, unrepeatable, it's *now*. I'm eighteen. I shall never be eighteen again. If I don't live now, when am I going to live? I shall grow old and settle down and get blunt, and I probably shan't even care!'

'But not in ten weeks, Tony.'

'Ten weeks – or ten years! What's the difference? Neither of them is now! Don't you know what I mean? I've thought about this so often. Don't you know what it feels like when the day, a day like this, is full to bursting with something that has *got* to happen, something just at the edge of one's reach but never quite within it; and then evening comes, and the colours fade and all goes flat and grey, and nothing has happened. It's just been another day.'

'Perhaps, this evening, we could light a candle.'

He looked round at her sharply, troubled, questioningly, and his eyes clouded. It was she who now looked away. Would he kiss her now? But no. 'I must tell you a silly story,' he said.

'One summer, before Grandpa came back to Milton Place, and I was spending the holidays at home, Ma was always at me for shutting myself up with books or else going off alone, and she said I needed companionship and asked "Why wasn't I more sociable?" So, in the end, she made me go on a horrible expedition called a "hike" with a number of people from the grammar school and some girls from the High School – rucksacks, you know, and sleeping in youth hostels. I hardly knew anyone in the party, who all knew each other, so I was a bit out of it from the start. I didn't want to be "in it" anyway, and I didn't mind about that. I'd agreed to go, and I just went along. Then I noticed, on the first evening, that all the girls went into a huddle together, whispering and giggling like the silly brainless creatures they are, but they kept looking round at me, so I knew they were talking about me. On the second day one of them sort of attached herself to me, walking beside me and making some silly little remark now and again. Well, to tell you the truth, I was thinking about differential equations which I was working on at the time, and it was rather boring to have all this chatter going on next to me. In a kind of hollow we were walking through she managed to get us left behind a bit and, all of a sudden, she threw her arms round my neck!'

'And kissed you?' Anita asked.

'Yes. Her teeth knocked against my mouth. Her face, seen close up, looked all shiny, and she smelled unpleasant. It was most disgusting. "At least I've kissed you," she shouted, and ran off, to tell her friends, I suppose. It must have been a bet. Anyway, they left me in peace after that. Of course, that was a long time ago. Two years, in fact. I've kept clear since then.'

'Oh, Tony – darling!'

'You don't think me ridiculous?'

'Because, two years ago, you didn't care for a schoolgirl? – Come, we must go back now. It's getting late.'

They walked back in silence. On the terrace he turned to her, his eyes veiled and cloudy. She nodded. 'Tonight.' Then they both went in.

The night was mild and the curtains moved very gently when Anita drew them over the half-open window. They swelled and sank as the night air breathed in them like a child in its sleep. Anita turned out the light and lit a candle. It wavered and spluttered before it steadied itself: a tiny yellow flame with a blue edge, a little ghost of a light. She had found a packet of them in one of the cupboards of the pantry; they were the cheap, semi-translucent kind, probably bought during the war as a standby if the electricity failed. The wrapping had been torn and one or two had been used. She had also remembered seeing on the dressing table in one of the bedrooms a white china candlestick with a handle like a teapot, dating from the days when members of the household collected their candles in the hall before going up to bed. Now it stood on the little mahogany table next to her, throwing a pale silken sheen on the coils of her fair hair which she had left to fall loose round her neck and shoulders. The depths of the large room had turned mysterious, and the big, carved cupboard at the far end, shrouded in shadow, loomed like a fortress. It was very still. Then faint footsteps approached and Tony stood in the door which she had left ajar for fear he might not have the courage to unlatch it. His feet were bare and bony under his dressing-gown and he carried his slippers in his hand, anxious that even these might have made too much noise.

'Shut the door, Tony,' she said softly.

He did so and came across the room. He looked round as if for a chair, but there was none near, so he sat down on the edge of the bed. There was a moment's silence and in it she could hear his teeth chattering, though the night was warm.

'You are so cold, Tony, with your bare feet. You had better come and get warm.'

For an instant he hesitated, then dropped his dressing-gown and came beside her, obediently, like a little boy. She had moved over to make room for him and then, reaching out behind his head, she extinguished the candle between finger and thumb.

Now the dark was like black velvet. Neither of them moved nor spoke, and so they lay for quite a long while. Gradually Tony ceased to shiver, the warmth and exhalation of her body enfolded him. He felt for her hand. Then she turned to him and kissed him. 'My love,' she said, 'my dear, dear love.' And so, with infinite tenderness and then with increasing passion, Tony learnt to be a lover.

When the window paled in the dawn, she awoke and wakened him gently. 'You must go now, my darling, my heart's love. Keep our secret well. And when you come back –'

'Oh Anita! I'll be back soon, very soon. I'll find a way. Even if I have to break a leg or get myself expelled!'

'Nonsense, darling, you'll do nothing so foolish! You must

promise. I shall wait. We'll be together again. I'll see you before you go.'

But she didn't. He had got Nichols to take him to the early train, and when she came down to breakfast he was gone.

CHAPTER SIXTEEN

'He says it's too big and too grand and rather out of the way,' Mrs Peacock reported to Emily the next time these two ladies were together sorting and sizing the bundles of secondhand clothing that had arrived at the depot.

'Is that what he said?' Emily asked unnecessarily. 'Please check the sizes of those skirts so that I can enter them on the list.' Meanwhile, her mind had started to work on how this objection of Mr Peacock's could be overcome. Her brows were severely knit as she thought hard.

Mrs Peacock looked at her anxiously. Was Mrs Mannering going to take this as being the end of the matter? She certainly looked displeased. So, in order to avoid the subject being dismissed out of hand, Mrs Peacock embroidered a little on her conversation with her husband.

'So I said to him,' she continued, 'how do you know it's too big and too grand, seeing you've never been there? No more have I, neither. Of course, everybody knows it's a big place, I said, but very few people know what it's like, what with being kept so secret by the Government during the war, and Mr

Barlow keeping himself so much to himself since then. As for it's being a bit out of the way, well. . .'

'I shouldn't have thought that objection very relevant,' said Emily. 'There are roads, and there's transport.'

Mrs Peacock saw that the door which she had feared closed was, in fact, still open. It might be a good idea to insert a wedge.

'Mrs Mannering would hardly have made the suggestion, so I told Reg, if the place weren't suitable,' she went on. 'Mrs Mannering is not a person to mention anything lightly-like. I know her. You should talk to her yourself, I said, and you'd soon see.' She looked inquiringly at Emily.

'I don't think that will be necessary at this stage,' Emily replied. 'There is no immediate hurry.' She was not going to allow Mrs Peacock to rush her. What she had in mind was a difficult and delicate operation, and she must remain the sole judge of the nature and the timing of her moves. She could not dispose of Milton Place over her father's head, or behind his back. She could only create an opportunity which must appear to be unforeseen, and predispose him to take advantage of it. So Emily argued, as she went on sorting, counting and listing.

The door was shutting again, it seemed. Mrs Peacock made one more attempt to keep it open before it might be irrevocably closed.

'Well, I did what I could, didn't I? And I couldn't very well contradict Reg, as I had nothing to go on, never having had as much as a glimpse of the place myself.' This evoked no immediate response and, as far as Mrs Peacock could judge, Mrs Mannering hadn't even heard this last remark.

The job was finished for the day and some of the ladies working in other departments were repairing to the little kitchen-and-pantry place to make tea. Mrs Mannering never stayed when invited to spare a few minutes for what was inevitably described as a 'cuppa'. 'Terribly sorry, have to rush, wish the day had more than twenty-four hours – next time, I hope!' With some, or all, of these exclamations she was usually gone. Amazingly, however, this time proved to be the ever-elusive 'next time'. Mrs Mannering drew up her chair and accepted with an acidulated smile the thick mug of black tea with the dollop of condensed milk. She, too, did not want to close the door.

'I've been thinking, Mrs Peacock,' she said, 'of the objections your husband made about Milton Place and which you, of course, couldn't answer. I think it might be best if you came out with me one of these days and had a look round. Then you'd be able to tell your husband more about it.'

This was sweet music in Mrs Peacock's ears. She longed to go to Milton Place. But she was wary. It wouldn't do to look too keen. Like the young ladies in once-fashionable stories who, for many chapters, have been angling for a proposal and then, when it comes, exclaim, 'Oh, Mr Smith, this is so sudden!', Mrs Peacock pretended to consider the suggestion with care.

'That would be very nice,' she said, 'but not being acquainted with Mr Barlow, I certainly shouldn't want to intrude. He might not like strangers walking about the place without being invited.'

'Nonsense, Mrs Peacock,' Emily retorted sharply. 'You would be with me, of course. I should let my father know we were coming. What's more natural than that I should bring a friend out to tea with him.' Having said this, Emily realised that never in the past years had she ever taken a friend to have tea at Milton Place – the idea had never occurred to her. She had not even considered whether her father would enjoy meeting any of her friends; and if she had, she would have been sure that they, for their part, would have found the old gentleman a bore. And Mrs Peacock would certainly take some explaining as a friend. However, the invitation had been given and an explanation would have to be found.

Meanwhile Mrs Peacock had accepted it with the greatest alacrity. 'That's different, of course, Mrs Mannering. I shall be very pleased to come. Which day do you suggest?' She was not going to be content with the limbo of 'one of these days' which may never come. And so Emily understood.

'Now let me find my diary,' she said and started hunting for it with unnecessarily nervous fingers amongst the welter of objects in her handbag. It gave her a few moments to review the situation. 'Ah, here it is. Now let me see. Not this week, I'm afraid, nor next.' She flipped through the pages. 'All terribly, terribly full!'

At last a day was found about a fortnight hence and the hour fixed at which Mrs Peacock should be picked up. Mrs Peacock was a little disappointed at the delay, but produced her own diary, consulted it, and then agreed that fortunately the date happened to suit her also. And there, for the moment, the matter was left to rest.

But the thought of it did not rest either in Emily's or Mrs Peacock's mind. In Emily's, with her active and purposeful temperament, it called forth a lot of mental activity both conscious and subconscious. She must give her father some plausible reason for bringing Mrs Peacock to Milton Place, for it would be impossible to pass it off as just a social call. For the next few days the problem nagged at her unpleasantly, on and off, whatever she was doing, and at the end of the week she was almost of a mind to ring up Mrs Peacock and cancel the whole thing with some conventional excuse. But Emily hated going back on anything she had undertaken to do, were it even of the most trivial nature: that was too much like an admission of frailty and weak-mindedness in herself, and an offence to her self-esteem. Then, as the day drew near and it became a question of 'face it or shirk it', suddenly the subconscious took over and came to the rescue. In the middle of the night an idea sprang up, fully-fledged in every detail, the perfect solution. She couldn't imagine why she hadn't thought of it before.

And this was it: she would have a fête in the grounds of Milton Place this summer – on August Bank Holiday, perhaps. It should be the event of the season. The secret of success would lie in providing familiar entertainment in unfamiliar surroundings. Mrs Peacock herself had given her the cue: she had stressed that nobody knew Milton Place. She was curious to see it, and so would lots of people be curious if they were given the chance. Once they got there, they would, of course, have to find all the things they expected and enjoyed – all the usual stalls, donkey-rides for the children, a tea-tent and, if possible, a brass band. She could do even more. There should be a cricket match for the men to watch, for there was a field adjoining the road where Mr Barlow always allowed the neighbouring farms and villages to have a friendly game. He kept it specially for this purpose and had the pitch mown and rolled every summer, for it was one of the things he enjoyed and he always strolled down to watch whenever a game was in progress. Special buses should be run from the centre of the town to take the people there, and Mr Peacock would see that it was not really out of the way at all. The proceeds should be devoted to the Mother and Baby Home, the scheme he had so much at heart. He and the other councillors and aldermen with their wives should be specially invited, and Emily would entertain them in a separate tent and show them all over the place. This was obviously the reason why Mrs Peacock, as one of the committee ladies, had to come to Milton Place in the guise of an advance reconnaissance party, to investigate the lie of the land.

How would Mr Barlow feel about this massive assault on his privacy? He would object, of course, but she thought she could bring him to agree. He would not be able categorically to refuse if she spoke to him in Mrs Peacock's presence, and once he had become familiar with the idea, she would make him see it as a social duty. It was the accepted thing, nowadays, that private property should be open to the public. She could remind him that Lord Brackenbury was showing the famous staterooms at Anvil, and she believed that on those occasions Lady Brackenbury even dispensed tea in the gate-house.

In any case, Emily was now determined to go through with it. Ultimately, though he might not see it at once, it was going to be for her father's good, and there was for her a kind of grim satisfaction in the thought that this might break the shell of his seclusion once and for all.

By the time she set out to drive to Milton Place with Mrs Peacock, Emily was so full of her plans and their ever-proliferating details that she forgot that Mrs Peacock knew nothing about them. Much as Emily enjoyed minding other people's business, she was quite insensitive to other people's thoughts and feelings. In this case her disregard of Mrs Peacock's feelings very nearly wrecked her own scheme, for she did not realise that Mrs Peacock, when she heard of it, would consider herself to have been taken to Milton Place under false pretences. For this lady's thoughts were running on quite different lines. To her way of thinking she was about to make a social call on Mr Barlow on the strength of her growing intimacy with his daughter. For the past fortnight she had lived with this notion, and it had gradually become so familiar to her that it had lost a lot of the glamour and excitement it had held for her when it first arose. She was now prepared to be completely at her ease and to behave as if such calling was, with her, a daily occurrence and belonged to the usual pattern of her life. So successfully had she convinced herself of this, in the time that had elapsed between the prospect and its fulfilment, she no longer felt flattered by being invited, nor had she any sense of achievement in having obtained so easily what only a few weeks earlier was outside the scope of her desires. She was therefore determined not to show any undue admiration. The place was 'too grand', her Reg had said; she had decided that it probably wasn't as grand as all that after all.

As they turned in at the gate, Emily put on the manner of what she intended to be the amiable hostess, but which immediately struck Mrs Peacock as patronising. The lime avenue, Emily said as she drove along it very slowly, was considered to be exceptionally fine. Mrs Peacock just glanced up at the trees and pronounced primly that they were 'very nice'. She also scarcely looked at the house as they approached it, or at the view that it commanded, and she nodded stiffly to Sims who came to open the door. For one instant she conceived that he might be Mr Barlow, but fortunately Emily's calling him by his name halted her incipient gesture to shake hands. They were shown into what Emily knew as the 'small drawing room' – which was the latest of Anita's works of restoration – across the hall from Mr Barlow's study and of comparable size. Like the study, it had two tall windows looking out onto the terrace, but it was an essentially feminine room with a blue Chinese carpet and delicate furniture. Two glass-fronted cabinets containing porcelain figurines flanked the white marble chimney piece. It seemed that Mr Barlow's grandfather had conceded the frivolous grace of the eighteenth century to be permissible in his wife's boudoir, while preferring the more ponderous taste and style of his own time for the rest of the house. Unfortunately, some of the pieces, frail as they were, had been too long neglected and had suffered minor damage from chipping and cracking. The yellow damask of the curtains was broken in some places along the inner edge where the sun had eaten into them, and the matching silk of the chairs was worn and faded. The pictures on the walls in their dull golden frames were so darkened with old varnish that it was difficult to see what they represented. Nevertheless, the room, with the afternoon sun streaming in, looked bright and elegant in spite of its blemishes.

Emily had not been in it since her mother had left the house many years ago. When Mr Barlow came in almost immediately and had been introduced to Mrs Peacock, this proved to be the opening gambit of conversation. Mrs Peacock, having said that she was 'pleased to meet' Mr Barlow, looked round for a comfortable seat, but finding them all equally unpromising, sat down stiffly on the edge of the nearest one. 'You *are* spreading yourself, to be sure, Father,' Emily said. 'Mrs Seiler certainly excels herself as a housekeeper, though I don't see the point of opening up so many rooms.'

'Ah, here *is* Mrs Seiler,' Mr Barlow exclaimed, as Anita came in with the tea-things. Mrs Peacock said 'how-do-you-do', but, after her narrow escape with Sims, refrained from offering her hand. She noted with satisfaction that she was right, for Anita had not expected to shake hands with Emily either. She was obviously the housekeeper Mrs Mannering had just mentioned, and a foreign one at that, as was plain from her speech the moment she sailed into the conversation as bold as you please.

'I call this the afternoon room,' Anita said, turning to Emily, 'because of the sun, of course. If you have a morning-room in the east for breakfast, why shouldn't you have an afternoon room in the west for tea?' She began pouring it out. 'You like a lot of milk?' she asked Mrs Peacock, handing her a cup of pale-golden liquid with a flowery scent that was not much to her liking, and holding a silver milk jug poised over it with her other hand. 'The sugar is next to you.' Then Mrs Peacock was offered a tray of small squares of bread topped with chopped ham or chopped egg, or chopped other things not so easily recognisable. 'Will you have a sandwich?' the housekeeper said, though to call these queer little things sandwiches was quite preposterous. They did look pretty, though, and tasted all right.

Mr Barlow, observing Mrs Peacock sitting so stiffly on her chair and casting uneasy glances round the room, wondered what motive Emily had had in bringing her to Milton Place. That she had a motive, he was not in doubt, and he was to discover it very soon. Meanwhile he would make conversation.

'You heard my daughter remarking just now,' he said, sipping his tea, 'that we seemed to be using too many rooms in this house. You see, Mrs Peacock, I am an old man and have become something of a recluse. I very rarely leave the house and the grounds these days, so moving from one room to another takes the place of a change of scene and becomes something of an adventure, especially as it means rediscovering a number of things I have not seen for a long time. Although I was born and grew up here, I was away out East for a great part of my life, and when my wife went to live in Torquay for her health, so much of the house was shut up and so many things were stored away that I had almost forgotten them. So now, finding them again revives so many

161

memories.' Mr Barlow spoke dreamily, but then a glance at Mrs Peacock's face told him that she would probably not have many memories of her early life she would care to revive, nor any old furniture to attach them to. 'You must forgive me,' he said, 'for the way I am apt to lose myself in the past. You are much too young, of course, to dwell on early reminiscences. To do that is, I'm afraid, a concomitant of old age.'

Mrs Peacock relaxed and smiled at him. She didn't quite understand all the words he used, but she felt he was behaving in his own natural way and was not talking down to her. She liked him immediately for that and felt it safe to give him her own views and opinions. 'Of course,' she said, 'there are people who like what they've always been used to. My Reg – my husband, I mean – is a bit like that. I've had to fight him about it all along. I'm not that way myself. I don't hold with hanging on to a lot of old stuff. When a thing's had its day, it's best to get rid of it, I think. Not that one always can, of course,' she added hastily, glancing round the room. 'I've had to make do myself, time and again, and I know what it is. Only when things get broken and torn, they make me feel so depressed, and they do wear out so, don't they? It's one of the comforts of life, as I'm sure you'd agree, to be able to have something new when one wants it.'

'It depends what kind of new things,' Anita put in. 'A lot of new things are not nice at all.'

'If you mean contemporary,' Mrs Peacock went on with a jerk of her shoulder towards Anita, 'I don't like that either. It's too arty, and not really comfortable. Just now I'm trying to persuade Reg – my husband – to get rid of the front-room suite, because I've got my eye on one in Jones's that's really beautiful! I'm sure you must have seen it, Mrs Mannering, it was in the window last week. You haven't? Well, they've taken it out now because I went in and put down a deposit on it. I think Reg will agree to have it.'

'What is a suite?' Anita asked.

Really, that woman was always butting in! Mrs Peacock turned her shoulder a bit further and tossed her answer back over it: 'Settee and armchairs, of course, all to match. Perhaps you don't have them abroad.'

'I think Mrs Seiler was not familiar with the expression,' Mr Barlow remarked gently.

'Oh, I did see it!' Anita exclaimed, 'It was dark-green satin with golden chrysanthemums on it.'

'That's it,' Mrs Peacock acknowledged.

Anita bit her tongue. There was a pause, just slightly too prolonged. Mr Barlow ended it. 'I'm sure it's very attractive,' he said. Anita poured out more tea.

Then Emily, who had taken no part in this superfluous conversation, got down to business. She refused a second cup and looked rather impatiently at Mrs Peacock who had accepted one although she didn't want it. 'When you have quite finished, Mrs Peacock,' she said, 'we will go out and look at the grounds.'

'Oh, I would like Mr Barlow to show me the garden!' Mrs Peacock replied, 'I'll be ready in a minute.'

'My father has probably walked enough for today,' Emily said, 'but he need not come. I can show you all I want you to see by myself.'

Mrs Peacock's face fell. She did not want to be parted from her host to whom she found she could talk so easily, and to be marched about by Mrs Mannering. Besides, the shoes she was wearing were rather tight, being her best pair and almost new. 'I'd much rather see the garden some other time, then,' she suggested. 'It would not be nice to leave Mr Barlow alone when we've come here to see him.'

'Oh, he won't mind that at all, I know,' Emily retorted. She turned to her father with her brightest, cheeriest smile. 'Mrs Peacock and I are going prospecting, dear. I've got a little plan up my sleeve which I'll explain to you when we come back. We want to use part of the grounds for a garden fête this summer. I haven't organised anything of my own since the war, and I just have to do something at last to raise a little money – something really effective. One can't vary the attractions very much, but new surroundings will make all the difference, and we've never had a fête here before. Now you needn't look alarmed, dear,' she went on, though Mr Barlow had given no signs of alarm, but had continued to look straight in front of him with a steadfast, expressionless gaze. 'It needn't bother you in the least. There's plenty of room here, and you need have nothing to do with it. Just leave it all to Mrs Peacock and me. Come along, Mrs Peacock, and I'll show you where I think we can put the various tents and booths.'

Mrs Peacock cast a last despairing glance at Mr Barlow as if begging him to rescue her, but he sat on in stony silence. So she got up and obediently followed Mrs Mannering out of the room. When the door had closed on them, there was such a stillness that Anita heard herself drawing breath. Mr Barlow didn't seem to be breathing at all. Then, quietly he asked her for some more tea. As he took the cup he looked up at her and a flicker of amusement crossed his fine face, setting it in a thousand tiny crinkles.

'So that is the explanation for Mrs Peacock,' he said. 'One of Emily's satellites, and a most unwilling one, I should say, poor woman. And poor Emily, too! How indefatigable she is, and how astute she imagines herself to be. I wonder why she thinks it necessary to resort to such wiles. I knew there was something in the wind the moment I set eyes on that excellent Mrs Peacock. She was brought here to induce me to take the pill Emily had prepared for me and which she thought I might refuse to swallow. Mrs Peacock was to arouse my social conscience and make me see my duty to the community, in which respect Emily finds me so sadly lacking.' He paused for a moment, musing. 'But Mrs Peacock, I believe, is miscast for the part,' he went on. 'I feel sure that if I appealed to her when they come back, and said I would so much rather not have what they call a "fête" in my grounds – if I told her that I dreaded the noise and the inconvenience, and the disruption of my quiet habits, she would desert my daughter and rally to my side. If I asked her to come again, quietly, by herself, and let me "show her the garden", as she put it, I should make her my friend for life. What do you think, Anita?'

Anita burst out laughing. 'Oh, yes, please, Mr Barlow, please do that! I'm not sure what is meant by a "fête", but of course you would hate it. So why should you give your consent to it?'

165

'A fête, my dear, is a kind of amateur fair, and with Emily organising it with her customary energy and efficiency, we can look forward to having half the population of Waterington milling around here on the fatal day. Rather a grim prospect, I admit. As for my consent, I haven't actually been asked for it yet, have I?' Mr Barlow sighed. 'I would so much rather give her the comparatively insignificant sum of money she will raise, all expenses paid, for whatever is her present good cause, than have this affliction thrust upon me. But there it is.'

'But why, why?' Anita exclaimed, 'Why do you allow yourself to be tyrannised like this? Why should you bear *any* affliction? Do you find it difficult to say "no"? Let me go out, then, and tell Mrs Mannering that you have thought about it and have sent me to say you don't want it, before she takes it any further. As you have said, I, too, believe that the good Mrs Peacock will help me!'

'Thank you, my dear, but it wouldn't do. If I want to refuse, I am still capable of doing it myself. But Emily wants the commotion even more than she needs the proceeds. She wants the organising and the planning and the excitement of it, and the ordering about of the people who will do the work for her. That's her life. What would she do with herself if she didn't do things like this? So, if I oppose her, she will have a thousand arguments, and in the end I shall be tired and give in. Therefore it will be better if I agree now.'

Anita felt herself to be strangely moved. As she took his empty cup from him, she paused to stroke his hand. He looked at her affectionately.

'You know, my dear,' he said, 'I am giving myself more credit than I deserve. A little while ago, when I was alone, I should really have been so appalled and upset by this prospect, that I should have taken refuge in my most uncompromising obstinacy. But since you are here, and will be with me when it all happens, I shall face it with equanimity. And who knows,' he added with an unmistakable twinkle, 'you and I together might even derive a little entertainment from watching the revels.'

Then Anita bent down and kissed him lightly on the top of his head.

Meanwhile, Emily had been conducting Mrs Peacock over the terrace and the upper lawns, and had pointed out to her from a distance the lower field on which cricket could be played, for Mrs Peacock had positively refused to walk any further. She would have liked to have lingered in the walled garden, for that, she exclaimed, was 'a real treat', but Emily said that it wouldn't be of any use for the fête, and that her father was so very particular about it, it had better be kept closed to the general public. She had talked volubly all the time, pointing out where each prospective attraction could best be situated, and she never even noticed Mrs Peacock's compressed lips and the absence of all comment on her part. She simply took Mrs Peacock's silence for the unqualified approbation which, in any case, was all that was required of her. If anything worried Emily during this tour of inspection, it was only what Mr Barlow might be thinking in the drawing room where she had left him, and whether Mrs Seiler had been encouraging him to oppose her plan. She ought not to have left them together to discuss it, she thought; it would have been wiser to have brought Anita out with them, and to have got her father's consent before she could have her say. The way that Austrian woman cajoled and cosseted him was really beyond belief! Emily again resolved to keep a wary eye on the situation lest some real harm should be done.

But her mind was set at rest, for the time being at least, when they returned to the house to say goodbye, and she found her father smiling, unperturbed and acquiescent, or – as she put it to herself – unexpectedly reasonable. So she embraced him with a rather greater show of affection than was her wont, and told herself that he was really ageing now and becoming at last more amenable to her guidance and protection. Even Anita was given an amicable smile.

So the critical afternoon passed off satisfactorily for all concerned, except Mrs Peacock who was the only one who had really expected to enjoy herself. She was baffled and disgruntled. Things had not gone as she had wanted them to go, and yet she didn't quite know what had been wrong. But, certainly, she had not been happy, and it added to her distress that she was unable to explain to herself why. When she took her leave of Mr Barlow, shaking his hand so vigorously that he was left ruefully rubbing his fingers and stroking his arm for the rest of the day, she felt tears welling up in her eyes which, fortunately, nobody saw. Good gracious, whatever for? Could it be because she would probably never again sit drinking tea with that sweet old gentleman in that rather tattered, yet strangely imposing room? Perhaps, in part; but far more likely because she had been hurt and bruised in her own self-esteem. Uneducated as she was, her feelings were finer and more perceptive than Emily Mannering's, and she felt that on this occasion she who had thought she could be Mrs Mannering's friend, had simply been made use of for that lady's convenience – a thing to serve a purpose. What purpose, she didn't quite know, but that it had been so, she clearly understood.

Thus she reflected, sitting silently beside Emily in the car, and half-easing off her smart shoes from her hot and swollen feet. All that time she was resolving to do everything in her power to disoblige Mrs Mannering. She would tell her that she didn't think much of the idea of a fête at Milton Place, and that her husband had been right in believing it to be quite unsuitable for any public institution – Mother and Baby Home, or anything else.

But when Mrs Mannering deposited her at her neat little gate which led up a dainty brick path to the arched porch of her neat little semi-detached residence in the trim, tree-lined road where she lived, these words were still unspoken. She saw her husband a little way down the road returning home for tea. He waved to her, and before she knew it, she had let Mrs Mannering drive away without giving her any sign of her displeasure. She was glad she had not been hasty, for had she spoken in anger, it would have meant goodbye to the daydreams she had been cherishing so fondly; goodbye to the world of Mannerings and its glamour. Mrs Mannering might not be the nice person she had thought her to be, but that did not detract from her glamour. Who knows, it may even have enhanced it? No, she would not 'drop' Mrs Mannering because she had discovered she was just a string to her bow. If she did, Mrs Mannering would simply pick up another string, and no one would be the loser but herself. And here was Reg, expecting her to have enjoyed herself ever so much. She could see it in his face and hear it in his affectionately teasing voice:

'Well, well, dressed up to the nines, aren't you, love, you're that smart. And what was it like? Are you going to unlock the door, or shall I?' he added, fumbling for his key.

'I will,' she said, 'and, oh Reg, it's a lovely place! A real treat it is, and old Mr Barlow is ever so nice, the sweetest old gentleman you could wish to meet. Such a pity that he can't keep it up. It must be lonely for him, in that big house, one can see that Mrs Mannering doesn't think it good for him. There's a foreign housekeeper there now – temporary, Mrs Mannering says – I didn't take to her, and I don't think she's trustworthy. Pushing, I'd call her, always butting in to the conversation. I was surprised, really, that Mr Barlow had her in to sit with us, when Mrs Mannering and I was visiting. I didn't think it was done.'

Mr Peacock laughed: 'Listen to her!' he said, 'You who like to be all modern and up-to-date! But you don't approve of illegitimate babies – or foreign housekeepers. Never mind, Glad,' he said, giving her a kiss, 'I was only teasing. Now tell me some more about the place.'

This Mrs Peacock did with considerably more detail than she had appeared to notice and far more enthusiasm than she had felt at the time. She did not mention the fête.

CHAPTER SEVENTEEN

Nothing had been heard from Tony, or almost nothing. Mr Barlow had had a postcard which stated succinctly: 'Term begun as usual. Love and thanks.' Mr Barlow had shown it to Anita without comment. He obviously did not expect anything more. But she had hoped; not, perhaps, that he would write to her, though to have received a letter from him would have sent her blood and every nerve and fibre in her singing with joy, but that he would send her a message, if only a quite conventional one, through his grandfather: 'Remember me', or 'Give my regards to Mrs Seiler', he might have said. It would have given nothing away, but it would have meant he had been thinking of her and she would have cherished it. But there was nothing. She tried to put herself in his place: would he be contemptuous of the use of such trite words, and yet not trust himself to write what he really felt? She did not know enough about the kind of life he led at school – was there not enough privacy? But surely, in his last term and at his age, he would be able to write freely? And suddenly she would be seized with dismay. Had he had a revulsion of feeling against her? Had he begun to think how much older she was, and to be ashamed of his love? Yet he had assured her so passionately that he would come back, soon, and at all costs. Remembering his words and the look in his eyes as he left her, she felt reassured. Then she would reflect that at best a relationship such as this must, by its very nature, be precarious and short-lived, and this thought made her long for him more intensely, his attraction for her more beguiling, because already her delight in him was edged with pain.

In spite of herself, time now had begun to hang heavily on her hands. The regular duties she had assumed in the house were light, and the long walks she had had with Tony in the afternoons did not tempt her now she was alone. Mr Barlow continued the quiet rhythm of his days, content to stroll or sit with her at his usual hours, serene, secure in her company, and mostly silent. But he did not fail to notice her change of mood.

'You are both listless and restless, my dear,' he said to her one day, pulling her arm closer through his and patting her hand. 'I'm afraid this is a very dull life for you since Tony has left us. Perhaps you should go into the town more often and see things. There are several cinemas, I believe, or else Emily might –'

Anita interrupted him hastily and assured him that she wanted nothing of that kind. 'It's the spring,' she said, laughing, 'it's always an unsettling time of the year, isn't it? Though, all these last dreadful years I've never even noticed it. And now, I suppose, I am just silly, when all I ought to be thinking about is growing old!'

'You don't want to anticipate that for a very long time yet,' he said. 'Since you came here, you seem to have been going backwards in time and to have grown younger every day. I saw you the other day, from my window, racing Tony across the lower field and I thought then that you were a child like him.'

Dear Mr Barlow – what an exquisite thing to say! But of course he couldn't know; he was only being nice to her. He went on: 'Of course you are still hungry for life. But when the time does come, you must not be afraid of being old. Let me tell you about it. At my time of life every season, almost every day, is a grace, and the spring is not an ache, but a glory. It is true, one loses most of one's desires, but one also loses one's impatience, and there is given to one the only moment of life that is real – the moment that always had seemed to escape – the present. All your life you have been hurrying along, and at last you stand still. The days that used to stretch ahead, full of promise or of fear, lose both their hope and their terror. You find them circling around you while you only look – and watch. The light changes and the shadows move, the flowers open; and all you do is just – see. When the sun sets and the flowers fade, you still see, but you are not perturbed. The great circling wheel moves on to another phase and will come round again in its own time, and if you are still there, you will still be watching. And if you are not – well, what difference will it make? Believe me, none at all.

'But very soon now, in a day or two perhaps, I shall have something to show you which, I hope, will make you think it has been worth your while to have stayed here and kept company with an old man.'

For the time had now come for the blossoming of the rhododendron valley. In that deep ravine some little distance from the house, behind the kitchen garden, where the ground fell away so steeply and huge blocks of outcropping rock balanced precariously, so it seemed, along its upper rim, the azaleas and rhododendrons began to stage their yearly miraculous spectacle. To its dazzling splendour was added the mystery of almost complete secrecy, for this fold in the ground was so deep and so well-hidden from view that no one driving about the countryside outside the confines of the park would have suspected its existence. No public road or pathway came anywhere near it, from no outside vantage-point could it be overlooked, and even from the garden side one came upon it suddenly and, in a manner of speaking, unprepared. Anita had sometimes climbed down the slippery slope to where a narrow stream ran through lush grass to feed a small lake which lay, part-covered with a metallic green film and encircled by a dense, untended growth of dark trees, at its farthest end. In winter it was all desolation, the dark glossy foliage in which it abounded dripping and glistening with the night's rain, and the pearl-grey skies looking high and faraway when glimpsed through the tracery of bare and soaring branches. There had been primroses here on the opposite, gentler slope where the wood thinned out to merge gradually into the meadowland beyond, and she had come here to pick them for Mr Barlow's study and her own room. But now, almost over night, this darkish and secluded place burst into a blaze of such brilliant colour that Anita, who was seeing it in flower for the first time, could only liken it to a magic transformation scene in a fairy tale. Bud after bud opened in bright yellow and orange, scarlet and crimson, pale mauve and dazzling white, until there was such a profusion of them that they stood between the darker trees like the flames of a silent conflagration. These were the azaleas, and they were only the beginning. Even more astonishing were the rhododendrons as they put forth their large, multi-coloured flower heads in endless variety, mother-of-pearl with a dark eye in each corolla, shell-pink, crimson and violet. Some of the tall ones looked like mountains of flowers. And at the foot of them all the bluebells made big, shining pools like a mirror of the sky.

They came here now every morning, instead of to the walled garden. It was a longer walk for Mr Barlow and a more difficult one down one of the steep paths, but as he had her arm and his stick to lean on, he never missed a day. This, he told her, was what he had been waiting for; what, above all, he had wanted her to see, and he watched her intently as if her amazement and awe, her final complete surrender to the beauty of the scene could infuse into his own recurrent pleasure that unique quality of surprise and revelation of 'seeing for the first time'.

But he also loved to explain, at length, how it had all been done; how his grandfather, on discovering the slopes and irregular declivities of this hidden valley, had been struck by the thought of acclimatising here the exotic shrubs and trees he had seen in the Himalayas. The tall trees that grew in the valley, oak and beech and hornbeam, had been left standing, but all the undergrowth and lesser wood had been cut out to make room for the exotics. The soil and the climate had suited them, and many of them now rivalled their native neighbours in height and exuberance of foliage. Mr Barlow's father had added the azaleas, and he himself had collected a number of new and rare species. He remembered them all: their names and the time of their planting, and if some of the nameplates which identified them had been washed away or become illegible, he asked her to make a note of them so that they could be replaced.

Anita often came again, by herself, in the afternoons. She brought a camp-stool and sat, first in one place, then in another, for long periods, looking at one particular vista either down towards the lake or along one of the grassy cuttings which made narrow avenues between the flower-laden trees. If the sun shone for a while and filtered down between the leaves to light a white or coloured jewel-flame, it burnt with such visual intensity, but without motion or heat, that her eyes were almost overpowered by having to apprehend it alone, without help from the other senses. A profound silence reigned over all, for in the afternoon even the birds were quiet, and if one of them uttered a call, that rare voice made the stillness even more tangible. She was almost glad if the sky was overcast, for though on such days the colours were muted and the splendour more gentle, it seemed somehow more bearable, more approachable than the almost terrifying glory of the spectacle in sunlight.

There she would sit or walk, and it came to her that this secret and undreamed-of flowering of a hidden valley was like the enchantment of her love for Tony: unforeseeable, unsuspected, doomed to be transient – but equally unforgettable and without compare.

Anita's response to the flowering of the rhododendron valley was all that Mr Barlow had anticipated; it gave him an even greater satisfaction to know that she spent some time there alone and for her own pleasure, though he could not guess the thoughts that occupied her in the solitude of that enchanted wilderness. Nevertheless, the feeling that she was restless disturbed him, and he began to cast about in his mind what he might do to vary what he conceived as the monotony of her life. He dismissed the idea that Emily might be helpful. Even if Anita had not so promptly waived aside that very tentative suggestion of his, he felt sure that she would not be at her ease among Emily's friends. But why should not he himself take her out? There were at not too great a distance from Milton Place two or three of the great historic houses whose owners had recently opened them to the sightseeing public, thereby providing for their upkeep. He would take Anita to see them and it would give him pleasure to do so. That he should even think of undertaking, for her sake, something so contrary to his confirmed habits showed even more conspicuously than his acquiescence in Emily's plans for a fête, the influence her presence was having on him – an energising, rejuvenating influence which he acknowledged to himself with ironical surprise.

Anvil Castle was the first and obvious choice because it could be visited within an afternoon and because he knew the family. Old Lord Brackenbury, who had died shortly before the war, had been a friend of his, and young John (as he called him in spite of his being now in his forties) was a very likeable, if rather eccentric, fellow who had always had a craze for the stage. Nevertheless, he had gone into the Navy, had had a very fine career and had married a very attractive wife. After the war John had left the Navy and they had come to live at Anvil again, where they had put the majestic staterooms, the famous Long Gallery, and the probably priceless collection of old china, the late Lord Brackenbury's special hobby, on view to the public. Mr Barlow hoped that this could be seen, as he had noticed that Anita had a special predilection for porcelain and more expert knowledge of it than she would admit.

Mr Barlow had not been to see the Brackenburys of recent years, for much as he liked them both they were, after all, of a younger generation, and he had felt shy of imposing on them the duty of entertaining their father's old friend. There would be no harm, however, in going to see what everybody was now entitled to see for the price of half-a-crown. When, however, Sims was instructed to telephone to the castle to enquire on which days it could be visited, as Mr Barlow wished to bring a lady to see it, he brought back the message that Lady Brackenbury would like them both to come to tea on the following Friday, which was *not* a visiting day, so that the lady could be shown round the staterooms in peace. A little note reiterating the invitation came next day, and in it Lady Brackenbury said how delighted she and John would be to see Mr Barlow again. She had not known that he was again living at Milton Place, or they would have got in touch with him before.

Mr Barlow thought this very pleasant and spent the evening looking up various books on local history in his library and reading to Anita the paragraphs concerning the castle and the families to whom it had belonged. He did not intend to tell Emily of the proposed expedition until it was safely over, but that turned out to be unavoidable.

Emily was in and out of Milton Place more frequently now – on short business calls, as she explained, bringing with her an electrician or a carpenter or some other tradesman in connection with her fête, and it so happened that she was there when Nichols brought the car to the door. There was Mr Barlow in a light overcoat and carrying gloves, and Anita wearing a summer dress and a new hat. There was no escape – Emily had to be faced.

'Father! Wherever are you going? To Anvil? But that is fantastic! You'll be worn out! Don't you know there is nothing more tiring than trailing through all those rooms in a crowd of people behind one of those dreary guides, and standing about for ages listening to their rigmarole? They won't even let you sit down. Really, you can't do it! Why, for goodness sake, didn't you tell me Mrs Seiler wanted to go sightseeing? I would have taken her myself.'

She looked disapprovingly at Anita whose hat was decidedly too smart for – well, for *her*.

'Put it off, dear,' she went on in a voice of gentle remonstrance to her father, 'it won't do you any good. If you want me to, I'll make a point of taking Mrs Seiler next week, I'm sure she won't mind waiting a few days. What did you say? You're both going to *tea* with Laura Brackenbury! I see. That's different. But I do think you might have told me before making all these arrangements. It does seem rather an imposition on Laura Brackenbury to have to take a complete stranger round the place for a private view. I might have come with you and taken that part of it off her hands. It really is tiresome of you, Father.'

'Lady Brackenbury invited us,' Mr Barlow said gently, 'and she didn't seem to require your assistance. Don't worry, dear, I shall be all right, and we really ought to be going now.' He stood back for Anita to get into the car. Emily shrugged her shoulders and stalked away.

CHAPTER EIGHTEEN

****

The stately old car rolled at a measured pace through the countryside, conforming in its progress rather to the traditional carriage-shape of its body than to the invisible horsepower hidden away under its bonnet. But Anita was glad of this leisurely journeying. There was so much to see and almost all of it was lovely. More than any other landscape she knew, this undulating country seemed attuned in scale and variation to the measure of human life at its most civilised, being at the same time natural without wildness, and cultivated without artificiality. The road wound its way up and down and around through alternate farmland, pasture and woodland, with farmhouses and barns tucked away in the folds, many of them flanked by the round towers of the oasthouses surmounted by their slightly asymmetrical cone-shaped 'hats'; with sheep or black-and-white cows in the fields and the white waving frills of lacy cow-parsley along the side of the road. And it was all so green and so golden in innumerable shades and intensities, with here and there the dark burnished copper of a beech or maple and the thick white clusters of hawthorn. They drove through two or three small townships where, in the High Street, a few old Elizabethan houses or a graceful Georgian portico rubbed shoulders uneasily with modern shopfronts gleaming with plate-glass windows and bright paint; and on the edge of one of them they passed a new housing estate in process of being built: interconnecting roads and crescents of raw brick houses, finished, half-finished and barely begun, with the naked earth churned up around them or slapped down out of sight under great slabs of concrete. Only a large tree stump here and there showed where not long ago a great oak had stood in its majesty.

More open country and then, for several minutes, they skirted a long, high wall above which only the tops of the highest trees were visible, while creepers hung down from its crown and moss and lichen clung to its crevices. A few cottages appeared on the left and suddenly Nichols slowed down and turned sharply to the right through a wide gate let into the wall. Crossing an open space, they drove almost immediately through a vaulted archway under a long, low building which stretched away for a considerable length on each side of this entrance. As they emerged from it, there was Anvil Castle before them. It was not a house, but a concrescence of many houses and it seemed not to have been built, but to have accumulated. The oldest part had been a fortress with its windows very narrow and far between, and a thick, round tower at one angle crowned with heavy crenellations. Adjoining these cumbersome defences the carapace of walls had thinned and become more lacy in texture. Large, tall windows interlaced with gracefully carved ribs of stone framed a multitude of small, leaded panes, and were themselves set off by carved stonework from the face of the brick walls. They stood forward and retreated in three wings from the main building, forming two courtyards: the smaller one immediately facing the car was gravelled, the other, further to the left, covered with grass. The main aspect of the castle, which was round the corner, was not visible from this approach. They drew up at a short flight of steps in the gravelled courtyard at the head of which was a door – it seemed an incongruously small entrance to so vast a mansion. The door stood open, and while Mr Barlow was hesitating whether to search for a bell or simply to enter, the problem was solved by the approach of a loud patter of feet and several high-pitched voices. Four children, between the ages of twelve and two, came down the broad staircase, the two older ones in a rush, and the smallest step by step, clutching the banisters, but all in a hurry to find out who had arrived. They advanced across the large empty stone-flagged hall whose only furniture consisted of two small bicycles, a tricycle, a wheelbarrow and various spades and buckets.

'How do you do?', the eldest little girl said politely, advancing towards the visitors, while the others came to a halt in the middle distance. 'Are you coming to visit? That would be the other entrance. But it's not open today, I'm afraid.'

'No, we've not come to "visit",' Mr Barlow explained, 'only to see your parents.'

Meanwhile, a man, hastily divesting himself of a baize apron and buttoning up a black coat, had emerged from a door in the background and said: 'Mr Barlow? Her ladyship is expecting you, sir.'

'Oh, that's all right then,' said the little girl, 'I'll take them upstairs, Barker, you needn't bother.' Then turning to Mr Barlow again, she went on: 'Our friends always come this way. These are the backstairs, only they aren't really, because there are lots more which are far more "back" than these, only we don't use them except for playing robbers. Daddy calls these the backstairs, and where we live he calls 'backstage', and where you came in is the stage door.'

Anita said: 'What a very nice name.' Mr Barlow said: 'It is such a very long time since I was here last that you and your sister must have been babies – and these two were not here at all.'

'It must have been a long time ago,' said the official guide, 'because I don't remember you. I'm Jane,' she said, now thinking it time to introduce herself formally. 'I'm twelve, Liz is ten. This is John,' she added, taking hold of his hand to help him remount the stairs he had so laboriously come down, 'he's two. He's John, because the eldest son is always called John.'

'He's not eldest, he's youngest,' said another little voice, 'I'm older than him.'

'That's Sally,' said Jane, 'she's four. Of course you're older, duffer, but you're not a son, see! We come in two batches,' she went on talking to Mr Barlow, 'because of the war.' They were proceeding very slowly, to suit Mr Barlow's and John's pace, up the broad, oaken 'back' stairs.

Anita said: 'I suppose your Papa was away all the time during the war.'

'Not all the time,' Jane replied, 'he came to see us sometimes in Scotland where we lived with Granny. But

Mummy was in Singapore. It would not have been convenient to have babies. Mummy was a Wren.'

'Women's Naval Service,' explained Mr Barlow.

'Didn't you know what a Wren is?' Liz burst out laughing. 'I thought everybody knew *that*.'

Suddenly John, who had now reached the landing, found his voice. 'Onable John Vine, that's my name,' he said.

'Oh, shut up,' said Jane, 'he says that every five minutes now since someone taught him the other day!'

Somewhere in the depth of Anita's memory that little voice rang a bell; it was only a faint tinkle and was gone before she could seize it.

Across the landing on the left, where it was open towards a wide gallery, a velvet rope was slung. On the right it led to a panelled corridor along which Jane now guided her party. At the sound of their voices a door opened at the far end and Lady Brackenbury came out to meet them.

'Do come in, Mr Barlow. I'm sorry you've had such a long walk. These are our new quarters. John's idea, of course. And this is Mrs Seiler? I see the whole pack has got hold of you. Now children, tea in the playroom today. Nanny is waiting for you. Mr Barlow and Mrs Seiler want a little peace. You can come back later, but quite a lot later,' she added. She closed the door on four rather crestfallen faces.

'Jane has already entertained us admirably,' said Mr Barlow. The room they came into was long and low with four windows, each set in a shallow bay over which the ceiling sloped a little. The walls were washed a very pale blue and they as well as the ceiling showed the ancient oak beams both as uprights and as rafters. There were some lovely Persian rugs on the polished oak floor, a large carved Italian chest stood against the wall at the far end and smaller chests and tables between the windows. But the deep leather armchairs were modern and so were the lamps. Pink and deep-red azaleas were planted in what once must have been copper cauldrons on the floor. A few portraits in the dress of many periods hung on the walls. Lady Brackenbury installed Mr Barlow with great solicitude near the chimney piece where, in spite of the season, a log fire was burning.

'It is such ages since we've seen you,' she began, 'so you've never been up here, of course. These were three storerooms, that were dark and all cluttered up, knocked into one. I never could have believed they could be made so pleasant, but John "saw" it all in his mind before he started the alterations. He wanted to live where no one had lived before – not easy in a place like this – to be "free of ghosts", he says. Not that there are any ghosts about; I have never heard of any part of the castle being haunted. But he enjoyed the planning and the designing of it all. What *I* like best about it is the view. Here we are partly over the long gallery which looks onto the rose garden, and from up here we can see over and far beyond it. On the clear days we can see the Downs.'

'I have been telling Mrs Seiler that Lord Brackenbury has always been interested in decorating and in designing for the stage,' Mr Barlow said.

'Yes, and he intends to take it up professionally one of these days, only just now he has started a herd of pedigree cattle and I am trying to manage a market garden, so we are pretty well tied up out here at present and don't go up to London very much. The theatre plans will have to wait until the children go to school.'

Lord Brackenbury came in, and tea was brought, during which he and Mr Barlow talked farming and politics, while Anita asked Lady Brackenbury about the children. Then Lord Brackenbury got up and declared they must not be idle. Mr Barlow should stay and talk to Laura, 'but we,' he said, turning to Anita, 'will go on the set, for that is what you have come for.'

They walked back to the landing and he unfastened the velvet rope that cordoned off the gallery.

'Here is the book of words,' he said, 'which you can study, if you care to, later on. You will realise that we are starting the wrong way, as we ought to have come up the main staircase instead of going down it.'

Room after room of beautiful panelling, of pictures and tapestries, of silken hangings, inlaid cabinets, of marble and bronze and silver, collected for the use and splendour of many generations, the setting of many interconnected lives, and now frozen into stillness and immobility as if at the touch of a witch's wand; all so lifelike as if the mistress of the house, her children and servants, the master and his guests had only this instant left the room and would return forthwith – the image of life, and yet quite, quite dead. Involuntarily one looks for a trace of the incision which betrays this semblance of life for what it now has become: an embalmed and painted death. It is inconspicuous, but it is there. A thin silken cord extends the length of each room from door to door, a narrow strip of drugget stretches along the floor to preserve it from the tread of a thousand feet. No one will sit on those chairs again, or make a fire in the chimney; no house-party will sit down to dinner at that long table permanently laid with silver and china and cut crystal; no one will look up at that familiar picture by candlelight before going to bed, or forget a piece of embroidery on that table, or listen to a proposal on that window seat. It is all as remote, as immutable as if cast in some invisible medium of perfect transparency, for the very air that fills the space in these rooms is neutral, sterilised of all emanation and reduced to the pure function of breathability, while the curator-care expended on them, paid for by the admission fees of the public, constitutes the preserving-agent.

Anita walked slowly and silently at Lord Brackenbury's side. Occasionally she looked round at him, at his young-old face which in spite of its fine bone structure had something slightly undefined about it, as if it were a late impression from a die that had been used many times before. The colours, too, and possibly for the same reason, were a little faded: the hair very fair and the eyes too pale a blue. But there was a lot of lively amusement in his eyes, and irony round the mouth which showed his individual personality asserting itself with an undoubted purposefulness and definition. As they walked through the rooms, he made only the very tersest comments on what he was showing, not feeling very sure which of the standard treatments would be appropriate to her case. Neither the learned historical exposé, nor the more flippant 'isn't it all rather quaint and ridiculous' tone seemed to fit, and he did not attempt either of them. By the way she looked he couldn't make out what she felt about it all, and she herself found it impossible to put it immediately into words.

All she could bring herself to say when they came to the end of the last room was: 'Do you mind?'

It took him a few seconds to grasp her meaning and then, suddenly, he understood; understood the reason for her look of sadness and embarrassment which she had been feeling on seeing all this in his company.

'Oh no,' he said, 'not at all. You mustn't imagine anything like that! I don't mind a scrap, on the contrary, I think it's fun. I am quite, quite detached from it all; it seems to me to have no connection whatever with the world we live in today. It would, in fact, be an intolerable burden were it not that I have been able to transform it, for myself and for others, into a stage. As a stage, of course, it is wonderful and most exciting; I get an endless variety of enjoyment from it. You see, in my imagination I have turned it into an illusion, as if it were all made of cardboard and plywood, simulating the real thing without any of the implications, the weight and responsibility of real life. You know what it's like in the theatre: all the emotions, heightened and distilled, coming at one from behind the footlights, and then the curtain comes down and you return to your own, probably humdrum, concerns. Of course, you could never get stage-properties as perfect as these. Here you can go close up, touch or look at things from all angles without, so to speak, discovering the canvas and the slats behind them, but that only adds spice to your secret knowledge that they are all an illusion all the same. And then there are the reactions, the attitudes of other people to enjoy. There are the specialists and the experts who come to study, to classify and compare. I usually keep out of the way on their particular visiting day, unless they have a personal introduction, but in the course of time I have picked their brains and I can hold my own in discussing style, provenance and workmanship! The general public is much more fun, because for them, too, the whole thing is a show, but a show at which they are admitted onto the stage and can feel themselves as actors moving about on it. Their illusion is the obverse of mine – they think they are escaping, for half an hour, into a more thrilling real life, while *I* tell myself I am watching a play. And I feel very much in sympathy with my audience and rather proud of putting on such a fine production. The box office is gratifying, too!'

She said nothing, but gave a deep sigh as if relieved of some intolerable perplexity. Her face brightened and she gave him a long, grateful smile.

'You don't think I'm quite mad?' he asked her, but he knew that she didn't. He knew that she understood. He had never so explicitly spoken his thoughts to anyone, however often he was used to referring, in banter, to 'the stage'. His family and friends accepted it as a joke. But this woman understood his inner need of this make-believe with all the subtleties of its elaboration he had been explaining to her, by simple sympathetic intuition. She communicated it to him completely by her look and her nod of assent. It needed no words.

While he was speaking, they had left behind them the long suite of furnished rooms and had come into a gallery with a marble floor and stuccoed walls in which the famous collection of china was displayed in glass cases. Anita gave a little gasp of pleasure. Looking at china was quite a different matter from wandering through the corridors of past lives; china was meant to be looked at, admired and enjoyed for the exquisiteness of its substance and craftsmanship. She walked from case to case, asking questions, and Lord Brackenbury, in spite of his light-hearted disclaimers, had a lot to say about dates and places and master potters, as well as about texture and glaze. Almost all of it was English of which Anita had seen very little except in illustrations, and which she found especially interesting and delightful. Then, in front of a case of Dresden figurines, she exclaimed at a set of painted coffee cups: 'These, surely, are Old Vienna!'

'They certainly are. My father bought them when he was at the Embassy there before the first war.'

Suddenly the little bell in Anita's memory which she had heard fleetingly earlier in the afternoon, rang again.

'Were you in Vienna too? And were you then called John Vine?'

'I was, and still am. It's my family name.'

'And did you go to a dancing class taught by the master of the opera ballet, Mr de Hamel?'

'What sinister reminiscences you are conjuring up!' He laughed. 'Yes, it was the winter before the war, the year before I went to school. How I hated that dancing class!'

'Oh, what a pity you hated it! Because, you see, if you were John Vine and wore a white sailor-suit with long white trousers – I was so very much in love with you!'

She had forgotten about the porcelain. She looked dream-ily at Lord Brackenbury without seeing him. She was looking into a distant childhood when, in a white-and-gold ballroom, she had been a little girl in a blue sash, and there had been a much taller, very fair-haired little boy.

'Do you mean to say,' he asked laughing, recalling her from her dream, 'that we have been dancing partners?'

'Oh no, you wouldn't dance with me because you said I was too small. I remember hearing you say so. I think you were eight, which seemed quite grown-up to me – I was only four. I was very unhappy about it. I thought you were so wonderful. Of course,' she concluded, 'it may have been the trousers. All the other boys wore shorts.'

'It must have been. I'm so sorry I don't remember you.'

'But you do remember Mr de Hamel? How big and stout he was, and yet so light on his feet! And how he held up his coat-tails with the tips of his fingers to show the little girls how to make a court-curtsey?'

'Oh, yes, I remember *him*. He was like a big, floating balloon. The only dance I liked was the Washington Post. It had a jolly tune, and it always came at the end.'

'That was the only one you ever danced with me, and only once. I remember how happy I was that afternoon, being taken home in the carriage. Ah well – *tempi passati*. This kind of thing seems to run in my family.'

'What kind of thing?'

She laughed. 'Falling in love with Englishmen at the wrong age, at the wrong time. It happened to my mother.'

'When *she* was a child?'

'No, she was a little older. But nothing came of it, all the same.'

192

For an instant they faced each other in silence, which seemed heavy with all the might-have-beens of past lives. Then: 'Shall we go back now?' she said. 'Can one go a different way? I would rather, if you don't mind. Out here and up these stairs? Very good!'

He would have liked to ask her more about herself, but she went on ahead of him, walking very fast, and the chance was missed.

They found Lady Brackenbury and Mr Barlow deep in conversation about delphiniums.

'Do you know that Mrs Seiler and I are old friends?' said Lord Brackenbury. 'It seems we met, well, I won't say how long ago, in Vienna.'

'At a dancing class,' Anita said. 'I should have remembered at once if it were not for the disconcerting habit Englishmen have of suddenly changing their names. It makes English history so difficult to learn, one never knows who's who. It was your little son who reminded me by telling me his name.'

It was time to go.

'Goodbye, Mr Barlow. We will come over and see you one day. And you, too, I hope, Mrs Seiler, since you are such an old friend of John's. How long will you be staying in this country?'

Lady Brackenbury had asked a perfectly natural question, but Anita did not know how to answer it. Her difficulty was made worse by the look of alarm and expectancy on Mr Barlow's face as he, too, waited for her reply.

'I – I don't know, Lady Brackenbury,' Anita stammered a little. 'I came here to find a job, you know. I felt then that I needed to drown myself in work – as a kind of anaesthetic one might say. But it's not like that any more. Mr Barlow has been so kind to me.' She smiled at him. 'So now,' she concluded, 'I am just abusing his hospitality and his patience.'

'I'm sure they are both inexhaustible,' said Lady Brackenbury, as she watched Mr Barlow take Anita's arm to go down the wide stairs.

These words, exchanged in conventional courtesy, hung between them during their drive home. They had brought out into the open a thought which neither of them had yet cared to face, let alone to express. How long could Anita be induced to stay at Milton Place? How long would she be allowed to stay?

CHAPTER NINETEEN

These thoughts remained unuttered and were, for a while at least, relegated to the background of their minds by the surprise that awaited them as they drove up to Milton Place. For there, on the steps, with a wide grin on his face, was Tony! He opened the door of the car before Nichols could get round and helped his grandfather out.

'Why, Tony! How did you get here?'

'In a taxi. I hadn't got any money left, so Sims paid. I said I'd tell you at once and that it would be all right. Well – aren't you glad to see me?'

Mr Barlow overlooked that question. He was not smiling. 'I mean,' he said, 'why are you here? Why are you not at school?'

'Ah,' said Tony, still chuckling with the fun of having brought off a successful operation, 'it's an ill wind – and so on, you know – case of polio in the house.'

'And you were all sent away?'

'Well, no, not exactly. Mr Marriott notified all the parents and said that if any of them wished their son to leave, it was all right. The doctor didn't actually think it necessary, but he wouldn't oppose. They don't know much about this thing yet, so they don't want to take too much responsibility. But I got on to Ma and put the wind up her – that's not difficult – and in this case she played up splendidly and insisted that father should wire for me to come home. So I came here. Just had enough money for the fare – none for the taxi.'

Mr Barlow was still not smiling, and his tone was very dry when he said: 'I see, but you were supposed to go *home*, Tony.' Then he went into the house, adding over his shoulder: 'We will discuss this in the study, in half an hour.'

The laughter ebbed from Tony's face. Anita had got out of the car and they now stood facing each other, but found nothing to say. Then Anita blushed deeply and Tony also reddened, turned brusquely away and strode out into the garden. She went up to her room, leaving the door open to listen for Tony's return when he should go and speak to Mr Barlow.

Anita was filled with a confusion of emotions. For an instant her heart had leaped with joy at the sight of Tony and with pride that he had come back to her. But Mr Barlow's displeasure had been immediate and unmistakeable; she had never seen him displeased either with Tony or herself, and the sudden impact of it had chilled her. Tony, too, had not seemed to expect it; he had thought he would give his grandfather a pleasant surprise and had looked for a warm welcome from him. Why was Mr Barlow so angry? Didn't he believe Tony, and had he guessed what had really brought him back to Milton Place in the middle of term? It hardly seemed possible – and yet. . . . She took off her hat, changed her dress and kept listening till she heard Tony's footsteps in the hall and the study door open and close. Then she closed her own door and sat down by the window in a misery of uncertainty, looking out over the lawn and the meadows in the soft evening light.

Dinner time came. There was no sound in the house. Should she go down to the kitchen as she usually did when she had not herself been cooking, and help Alice with the dishing-up? It had always been such a matter of course that she should do so, the easy and unquestioned assumption of her place in the household, accepted and welcome. Now, suddenly, she felt like an interloper – in the way. She did not know what Mr Barlow was saying to Tony in the study, but she knew that Mr Barlow was angry and Tony was hurt. When she met them again they would both be strained and stiff in her presence, the presence of a stranger. But worse still, if she had herself been the cause of the disturbance, if she should discover in their looks or their behaviour some sign that this had indeed been so, then she would not know where to hide her face!

She went down, not to the kitchen, to avoid any comment by Alice or Sims, but straight to the dining room and waited there. Mr Barlow was never late for meals. Sims looked in once or twice, but Anita did not turn her head.

After ten endless-seeming minutes Mr Barlow came in, apologising for the delay. He seemed to have regained his composure, but not his genial smile. His manner towards Anita, however, showed no disapproval, not even by the slightest over-emphasis of politeness, and her apprehension was immediately relaxed. She glanced through her eyelashes at Tony. He looked crestfallen and subdued, and seemed to have had the worst of the argument, whatever the argument had been. Suddenly, at a moment when Mr Barlow was absorbed in helping himself from a dish which Sims was handing to him, Tony gave her a prodigious wink. She sighed so audibly that she had to cover it with a fit of coughing. Even if all was not well yet the crisis, she knew, was over and it had had nothing to do with her. Silently and fervently she thanked her propitious patron saint.

Tony came to her later that night, and when they had celebrated their reunion with all the tenderness and exultation that the occasion called for, Tony recounted his interview with his grandfather. 'Of course,' said Tony, 'Grandpa was really very pleased to see me, and in fact he was glad that I had come away and done my best to avoid even a remote risk of infection. He is really just as scared of my catching anything bad as my mother is. I think when I first mentioned polio, he had a fright. One keeps forgetting that old people don't take that kind of thing in their stride like we do. But what, it turned out, really upset him was my using Ma to make Father send for me, and then coming here instead. That, it seems, was very bad indeed – undutiful, irresponsible, unkind, and all the rest of it – in fact, thoroughly disgraceful. I've never heard Grandpa talk like that before. It really made me feel quite awful. And he threatened to send me home where, he said, I ought to have gone!'

'Oh, Tony, no, not that!' Anita exclaimed and then added thoughtfully, 'But I do see what he meant.'

'No, you don't darling, you don't know all the complications. Anyway, he can't send me home, I'm not a child. Only, if he wouldn't let me stay here, I should have to go away, and that's the last thing in the world I want to do now. Besides, I don't want to quarrel with the old man, I love him too much, and I'd do anything in the world he wants me to do – within reason – to make him happy.'

At this point there were more embraces. Then Tony continued his story. 'It's all got to do,' he said, 'with Grandpa having sent me to his old school and paid for my education, bless him. But somehow, goodness knows why, he feels guilty about it and that by doing this he has come between me and Father and made things the way they are between him and me. It's not Grandpa's fault, I can assure you, I should never have got on with Father, school or no school. But I can't make Grandpa believe that. Anyway, Grandpa has always tried to be nice to Father, without any kind of success because Father won't let anyone be nice to him, least of all Grandpa. And Grandpa has also always done his best not to offend him, although Father always takes offence whatever you do or don't do. But now it seems I've really done something that he has a right to be offended about – by getting him to have me sent home and coming here instead. I've "challenged his authority", "flouted his dignity" – Grandpa's words of course – and I've made it look as if Grandpa condoned it! Well, he doesn't condone and he won't condone it, and make no mistake about it!'

Tony snuggled down still closer to Anita and began to kiss her shoulder which was cool and silky to the butterfly touch of his lips. She stroked his hair. 'Well,' she said, 'what then?' She thought it must be very difficult to be angry with Tony for very long and that Mr Barlow must have found it so. Tony had a gift of turning away wrath which, if it had guile in it, concealed it under a look of the most innocent candour.

'I thought Grandpa was making very heavy weather of all this,' Tony went on, 'but I didn't say so. Instead, I agreed with him and admitted that I had not looked at the thing from that angle. I said I had only thought of seizing a golden opportunity to get back here and spend as much time as possible here with him before I have to join up, and to concentrate on some serious work before that same fateful date.'

'Oh, Tony, what a wicked fibber you are!'

'No, I'm not, Anita. Quite seriously, I really do mean to work, and Grandpa is going to order some special books I need down from London. After that, instead of arguing like antagonists about a point in dispute, we got down to discussing as allies how best to deal with an awkward situation we had got ourselves into.'

'So you and Mr Barlow have made it up? Thank God for that!'

'Oh yes, but I have had to submit to Grandpa's terms, and they're pretty stiff. Very hard for me to swallow indeed. In fact, I couldn't have done, if it weren't for you. Oh, Anita, I do love you!'

'I love *you*, my darling.'

The old, old words. Always the same from the beginning of love, and always rediscovered as something unprecedented by every new pair of lovers. Time passed, and time stood still.

That is the meaning of ecstasy. Then Tony went on.

'I must write to Father and apologise. I must say that Grandpa knew nothing of all this – of my intention to come here, that is – and that he entirely disapproves of what I have done. And I must offer to come home immediately if Father wishes me to. That's a great risk, Anita. It means I might really have to go. I tried very hard to get out of that bit, but Grandpa insisted, and I had to promise.'

'Do you think your father will order you to come home?'

'I'm sure he doesn't want me, but he might do it out of sheer cussedness.'

'But your mother will want you, of course.'

'Yes – and that's my main reason for hoping that Father won't insist. He'll say to her: This is the way you wanted it, and now you've got it. You have made your son ashamed of his home, and now he won't come near it, or near *you*!'

'Oh, Tony, but that's dreadful!'

'Not a bit dreadful, darling, if it means I don't have to go. As for Ma, she'll be coming here later on anyway.'

Mrs Crawfurd always came to Milton Place for a few weeks in the summer, whether Dr Crawfurd managed to have a holiday or not. He said, every year, that he could afford neither the time nor the money to have one, but he usually got away for a few days at a time while Cecilia was at Milton Place, fishing or sailing with friends she scarcely knew even by name. He had probably planned it several weeks in advance, but he always made it appear that the suggestion had been made to him unexpectedly and that he had allowed himself to be persuaded into going against his conscience and better judgment. Every year it was the same. Cecilia could never refrain from enquiring anxiously before she went away how he was going to manage in her absence, and the very tone of her voice, full of nervous worry, would goad him into giving her the answer she anticipated: that it would be a holiday in itself not to have her dithering about the place, and that he would enjoy having his meals out. She knew this was coming to her and yet she asked for it and winced when it came. She, too, had got into the habit of pretending that her visits to her father were not a matter of course and needed a special invitation from him which she could submit to her husband in justification of her having to neglect her duties to him for a short time. This pretence also infuriated him, but she would never abandon it.

This year Mr Barlow sent his invitation earlier than usual, including it in the letter he wrote to her the morning after Tony's sudden return, and in it he said soft words to her, explaining Tony's behaviour and inventing excuses for it which he thought would do more to console her than any strictures he might make on the boy's lack of consideration for her. But Mr Barlow did something more. He also wrote to Dr Crawfurd and after having stated categorically that he had had no knowledge of, or part in, Tony's escapade, he pressed his son-in-law very cordially to come himself to Milton Place with Cecilia so that they might all have the pleasure of seeing something of Tony during his last school holidays. 'This is the last of his boyhood,' Mr Barlow wrote, 'Let us now both establish a new relationship with the young man he is about to

become and of whom, I have no doubt, you will have every reason to be proud.'

Tony also wrote his letter and the replies were received by return of post. To Tony his father wrote that since he obviously felt no inducement or desire to come home, he, Dr Crawfurd, would not lay himself open to ridicule by attempting to enforce his paternal authority on a practically adult son. He realised, he said, that he had, long ago, mistakenly and to his great regret, abdicated this authority in favour of Mr Barlow when he had allowed him to assume the responsibility for Tony's education, and he knew that if his son was now estranged from him, he had only himself to blame. However, what was done could not now be undone, and he would not attempt anything so futile. He would make no demands on Tony, and Tony need make no demands on him. If he did not wish to come home he could stay away, but if, at some future time, he did come, he would not, indeed, find the door closed, unless he did something to disgrace himself, but he must *not* expect his welcome to be very warm – at least from his father. His mother could do as she pleased.

To Mr Barlow Dr Crawfurd wrote: 'Sir – I have received your letter and take note of your assurance that you had no knowledge of the correspondence which preceded my son's premature departure from school or of his intention of coming to Milton Place. Seeing that you have at all times encouraged him to regard your mansion as his home, it would hardly seem necessary for you to offer him any special inducement to come to you in this particular instance. I thank you for your invitation to join him, but you will no doubt appreciate that it is not incumbent upon me to go chasing after my son if he does not see fit to come to me. Moreover, I am not, as you know, a man of leisure who can employ his time as his fancy takes him, and I shall use the short vacation which I hope to be able to take away from my practice to attend a medical conference from which I expect to derive some professional profit. I shall not, of course, stand in the way of my wife, your daughter, making her annual visit to her paternal home.'

Both these letters were shown to Anita by their recipients, but it was the one to Mr Barlow which she saw first because he handed it to her immediately after breakfast.

'I want you to read this,' he said, 'because it will be a comfort to me to talk to you about it – because I can see how fond you are of young Tony. It will show you what he and I are up against.' And when she had read it in silence and given it back, he went on: 'What a misfortune it is that Dr Crawfurd is such a very awkward man! Poor Cecilia must have a very difficult life with him, but then she is not the kind of woman he ought to have had for a wife. He is a man of great integrity and, I believe, extremely able, but his humanity is so warped and twisted that one might sometimes think him both stupid and vicious. And Cecilia has not been able to help him. He would have needed a woman capable of appreciating his good qualities and of sympathising with his weaknesses, and she should also have had the courage to stand up to him when these weaknesses incite him to be a bully. Then he might have found his balance. Cecilia has none of these exceptional qualities – not many women have. So things have gone from

bad to worse. For my part, I have tried to do the right thing for Tony, to give him what I think a boy needs most: love, and stability. Perhaps I have acted mistakenly – but it is out of my hands now. I am old, and Tony is grown up.'

'It seems to me,' said Anita, 'that Dr Crawfurd is a thoroughly disagreeable man, and that Tony is very fortunate to have you to love and to look up to.' And in her heart she thought she now understood why Tony hated his father. Her own feelings flared up against Dr Crawfurd and she longed to tell Tony and to sympathise with him. She had no use for Mr Barlow's compassionate detachment.

But she did not see Tony alone until the evening, and then he came to her exultantly. 'All is well!' he exclaimed as soon as he had closed the door. 'Thank goodness, the danger is over and I can stay! I am not wanted by my outraged parent either now or perhaps even any more! Oh, darling, I don't know what I should have done if I had had to leave you now!'

Then he showed her the letter he had received. She read it slowly and then read it again. Something of what Mr Barlow had said that morning came back to her now and a nerve of pity began to quiver within her, pity not only for the boy to whom such a cruel letter had been written, but also for the man who wrote it, for she felt in it the secret suffering that had not been apparent in the stilted phrasing of the other letter. But Tony, it seemed, didn't care.

'What's the matter, darling?' he asked. 'You look all weepy. Aren't you glad I can stay?'

'Very, very glad, my dear one. But how sad this is. I'm

afraid your father must be terribly hurt. He must love you, Tony, or he couldn't write like that.'

But Tony drew away from her with an angry shrug. 'Oh, rot, Anita! How can you say such a thing? Father hurt? What about *me*? He as good as tells me he never wants to see me again, and it's with *him* you sympathise! He may sound very tragic to you on paper, but you don't *know* him. If you could hear his sarcastic voice and see that steely look in his eyes when he makes one of his cutting remarks, such as these,' – and Tony snatched the letter from Anita's fingers and tore it across – 'then you wouldn't talk such nonsense. Please don't say anything like that again!'

For a moment it was as if a chilly draught had passed through the room, causing the temperature suddenly to drop. Anita shivered slightly and drew her dressing-gown closer round her shoulders. That steely look in his eyes – she saw it now. Then Tony smiled and she relaxed. He threw himself on his knees and buried his face in her lap. Darling, darling Tony – she loved him so much. All she wanted was to love him – not to argue with him, only to love him.

CHAPTER TWENTY

Now began for the three of them at Milton Place a spell of exquisite attunement. At the height of a golden summer, for a period indefinable by calendar or clock, their separate entities blended and intertwined. As in a trio's *andante cantabile*, for a breathless moment of pure time the voices of three different instruments unite in a melody of predestined perfection and pursue it to its equally predestined end – so the discrepancies and contradictions inherent in three separate human destinies were, for a moment, held in suspense. They were not, and could not be, abolished or entirely suppressed as all three of them remained, in varying degrees, aware; but there seemed to be some tacit understanding between them that until the end of the movement no outside encroachment, no inner misgivings should be allowed to break in.

Anita was happy, and her happiness shone through her outward person like a concealed light in a translucent lamp. She looked really young now; her skin and hair had the lustre of youth, her eyes were bright and seemed always to be filled with laughter. Her heart sang and often, when she was brushing her hair or doing some job about the house, her lips sang too – a song of Schubert's or Hugo Wolf's in praise of her love or her lover, for she knew that no one would understand the words. It delighted her to be so exuberantly, so foolishly in love, to be alive again after so many years of physical and spiritual drought, and she never tired of repeating to herself the long list of enchantments she was discovering in Tony of which the fine grain of his skin, certain swift, unpremeditated gestures and some unconscious inflections of his voice were only the beginning. And when she recalled the look of intense concentration which he wore when lost in thought and which, when he smiled, would give way to such sudden illumination, she felt that she positively adored him. Thoughts of the future and of what was to be the outcome of their love scarcely crossed her mind, perhaps because from the outset she knew that it was, of its nature, ephemeral; and so its very transience added to the brightness and the intensity of the flame.

But if Anita was happy, the change in Tony's world was nothing short of revolutionary. For his whole nature and being was made to love and in this most profound need and impulse he had been frustrated since the dawn of consciousness. From his earliest childhood he had sensed the tension between his parents, and he had found it impossible to give his devotion to either of them. If his father's bitterness repelled him, his mother's sentimentality and cloying over-solicitude began to sicken him when he was still very young. Everything in his home jarred on his finer susceptibilities. He had found it difficult to make friends; among his contemporaries he had felt, at the same time, both superior and inferior, aware that he was vastly cleverer than most and yet unsure of himself and ill at ease. They, of course, thought him stuck-up because he kept himself so aloof, while he had only been at pains to conceal both his intellectual pre-eminence which seemed to single him out unfavourably, and what he felt as his inability to 'belong'. He strove with all his heart towards his grandfather and all he stood for, and towards Milton Place, as a plant seeded in a dark corner strives towards the sun, and he claimed them, fiercely, as his own; but he was conscious of the striving and the claim. There was always, also, this other 'home', the narrow, semi-detached villa in the unlovely street far back behind the sprawling hotels on the seafront, with its cramped, over-furnished rooms and the pervasive smell of disinfectant from the surgery. There was, on his mother's face, that eternal look of apprehension and on his father's, whenever he turned it away from his patients and towards his family – a sneer. It was not a place Tony cared to talk about or to which he could ever have asked a schoolfriend.

At Milton Place there was Dick, dear, inarticulate, unques-tioning Dick, who accepted him as belonging to Milton Place in the same way as he did himself and with whom he felt quite safe. There was his grandfather and the beloved countryside: his heart embraced them both. But still, all this was scarcely a sufficient outlet for the surging emotions of a passionate spirit, or for that indefinable, diffuse longing coursing through the blood and vibrating in the nerves which is the agony of youth. It is the agony of the pure and the fastidious for whom easy satisfactions are ruled out. Now the floodgates were suddenly opened. Tony had found love – love without inhibition or qualification, without question or doubt. He had never even dreamed that it could be as perfect as this, for dreams are tantalisingly unsubstantial, and Anita was real. She was beautiful, a goddess of ancient Greece, scarcely veiled in human shape. '*Incessu patuit dea*', 'In her gait she stands revealed' – old Virgil, he told himself, knew a thing or two after all. She was loving and kind, full of joy and laughter and warmth, and in her arms he felt himself enfolded and cherished. Every day he marvelled at the miracle that had happened to him. For through her the world had become a world in which he could *live*. No longer would he have to drag existence through unprofitable days with the fullness of life always out of his reach. Never again would he contemplate with dismay the endless stretch of years ahead in which the only alleviation for his burning heart would come from a dulling of his senses. Never again would he roam in spring through the awakening woods and feel all around him the sap rising hopefully towards its consummation in flower and fruit, while he saw himself heading for compromise, routine, resignation and, lastly, for indifference. Now he, too, like every living thing, like the trees and the grass and the birds, even like the sun dappling the sweep of fields and woods with light and shadow – he, too, was alive. He was no longer a mere spectator, doomed to watch as through a glass partition; he was himself part of it all, of the great, all-embracing, boundless scheme of things called Life.

Anita had pledged him to secrecy. No one, she told him, must know or even suspect what was between them. This needed little contrivance, they had only their own behaviour to watch, for Mr Barlow's room was in another wing of the house and the old couple had their quarters downstairs. There was nothing wrong, Anita said, nothing either of them need be ashamed of, in their relationship, but there was a sense of becomingness which decreed that a love such as theirs should be shielded from the eyes of the world. Discretion was always the duty of a lover, and secrecy the fine flower of love.

Tony hardly needed these warnings. They accorded only too well with his nature; the stronger his feelings, the less he was inclined to show them. Throughout the day he surpassed himself in aloofness and restraint. They had given up going for long walks, for the afternoons were sultry, but he continued to ride in the early mornings. From the depths of sleep at Anita's side he would go straight out into the awakening world – a quick kiss, a loving look, and he was gone – so silently, so carefully that sometimes she did not even hear him go. More often she did and pretended not to, just to catch under scarcely fluttering eyelids that gesture of tender consideration with which he folded back the bedclothes over her, that look of adoration which, thinking himself unobserved, he would bestow on her from the door before closing it with infinite care. Out of earshot, he would then sometimes start to sing and shout his exultation. But it was also on these early morning rides when he was alone with his horse in a solitude which encompassed the world, that he would dwell on this dispensation which had so suddenly come to him in a draught of such overwhelming strength and sweetness that he wished – and was shocked to find himself wishing – that it was all over, that he could put down the cup that was being held to his lips, and recollect himself in detachment and retrospect.

If Anita lived carelessly in the present and Tony was almost overwhelmed by its impact, Mr Barlow was the only one of the trio to be troubled, at times, by apprehensions of the future. He who had thought that for him the age of problems to be solved and decisions to be made was over, who had been content to continue in quietness and detachment from day to day, now found himself being drawn back, willingly or unwillingly – he hardly knew which – into the life-stream of difficulties and desires. They arose from the very pleasure he took in seeing Anita looking so well and so happy, but he realised that he was not only 'seeing', in the way he saw the changing hours and the revolving seasons, but that he was getting involved, that her buoyancy was acting upon him as if he had caught it from her like an infection, though in a subdued and muted form. For there was now something that emanated from her that had not been there before, some intangible effluvium that seemed to surround her and encompass him also as with the glow of an Indian summer. She was, he thought, having a ripening influence on Tony, too, who was suddenly much more grown-up and self-possessed in his whole bearing and demeanour. They were both giving Mr Barlow even more of their attention and affection than they had done before. He basked in their kindness, not dreaming that the tenderness they felt for each other, all demonstration of which they were bound to suppress, was being lavished as by tacit consent, in smiles and solicitude and a thousand small gestures upon himself.

Out of doors it was a variegated summer, not too set in its ways, dispensing a week or two of glorious sunshine and then a spell of grey days and rain. Anita, having given up her more strenuous labours in the house, had now begun to embroider tapestry-seats for the big drawing room's threadbare chairs. She seemed not to have given a thought to the time a task of this kind would take, but had come back from a shopping expedition to Waterington with yards of canvas and piles of wool. On rainy days she sat with her frame by the window of Mr Barlow's study, while he read or wrote letters at his desk, or, when it was fine, walked at his side in a shady corner of the walled garden. She strolled with him in the morning, and again in the evening light when the flowers in the borders shone so intensely and so clearly, as if the light itself had become incarnate in them, burning away their substance to appear as disembodied colour.

Tony was not much in evidence during the daytime. He spent some hours every day helping on the farm with Dick, and he studied intently the mathematical books Mr Barlow had had sent from London at his request. It seemed that his mental faculties had taken a leap forward, enhanced and illuminated by the surge of emotional life on which he rode as on the crest of a wave. He was experiencing at the same time a white-hot intellectual excitement which carried him over a threshold he had for some time been vainly striving to cross, and that now revealed to him a realm of more subtle and concentrated concepts than he had so far been able to grasp. Then, after dinner, half-exhausted, half-exhilarated by his mental adventures, he would endeavour to discuss his work with his grandfather, who would try his hardest to understand. Mr Barlow's training had been in applied rather than in pure mathematics, but he more or less succeeded in following what Tony was talking about, and was able to ask the right kind of questions Tony was so anxious to answer. Many sheets of paper covered with symbols passed between them, until Mr Barlow would sometimes confess with a sigh: 'I give up, my boy. You make my poor old brain creak!' But this Tony would never accept, and he would try again and again to explain, welcoming the discipline of having to make things clear to himself in order to be able to communicate them. And Anita, watching them with occasional glances between the stitches of her needlework, thought how enchanting they both were in their reversed roles, the boy as patient teacher, the old gentleman as painstaking pupil, and how they each persevered in them for the sake of pleasing the other.

On Saturday and Sunday afternoons, when it was fine, there was cricket on the lower field that bordered the road. The teams came from the neighbouring villages and surrounding farms, and Tony played in the 'home' side of which Dick was captain. It was Mr Barlow's great pleasure that he was able to provide this private cricket ground, and Nichols had standing instructions to hire sufficient help every year to mow, roll and keep the field in condition. It was not, of course, up to professional standards, nor was a first-class game expected, but Mr Barlow enjoyed nothing so much as the homeliness and neighbourliness of village cricket. A few benches stood around for the spectators, but they mostly sat on the grass, bringing with them their tea, their children and their dogs. Mr Barlow knew them all, at least by sight, and exchanged friendly remarks as he walked around, about the weather and the score, and enquired of closer acquaintances about the family or the harvest. No one ever did any damage or left any litter, for this was *their* field as well as Mr Barlow's, and they behaved, so it seemed to Anita, both with the care of ownership and the courtesy of guests. How nice, how really nice they all were! She had never liked people, just anonymous people, so much.

On one side of the field the ground rose in a bank, and here Nichols used to set up a few canvas chairs. From this vantage point Mr Barlow tried to introduce Anita to the game. Unfortunately he suffered from the handicap that frustrates high-ranking scholars in every field when they try to impart the first rudiments of their science: they cannot imagine the abysmal ignorance of their pupils. However elementary their explanations seem to themselves, they still presuppose too much non-existent knowledge. Anita watched and asked questions which Mr Barlow's answers never quite seemed to fit. 'In whose favour did it count that the man out there caught the ball?'

'If he hadn't caught it before it crossed the boundary, it would have counted six.'

'I see.' (But she didn't.)

'Do the two batsmen play on the same side or on opposite sides?'

'If they make only one run, they are at opposite ends of the wicket, but if there are two runs they are again at the same end.'

This, to her, made no sense at all, and until the end of her cricketing days she never grasped who was playing against whom nor what accounted for winning or losing, let alone what feat of skill was being applauded when Mr Barlow clapped his hands. So, after a while, she resigned herself and asked no more questions; what, after all, did it matter whether she knew what was going on or not? Was it not enough to lean back contentedly in her chair and watch the white figures moving to some hidden purpose on the green field, and especially one of them who moved with such a particular grace. It all put her in mind of a figure of ballet with a slow and stately rhythm that would suddenly quicken at the centre with an impetus that spread to some part of the circumference like a wave. Then the whole pattern would change and become set again. The accompanying music was made by the wind soughing through the trees behind them, the drowsy hum of insects, interspersed at intervals by the dry wooden sound as the bat hit the ball. It was pleasant, peaceful and pastoral – controlled and civilised: a game, though she did not understand it, after her own heart.

'Are you enjoying yourself?' Mr Barlow asked doubtfully, seeing her stretch her arms over her head and half-close her eyes.

'More than I can tell you,' she answered. 'I only wish this could go on for ever.'

Anita could say such words lightly, giving expression to a relaxed and happy mood on a sunny afternoon. But to Mr

Barlow they meant more than the condensation into speech of a sigh of contentment floating and dispersing on the summer air. To him, 'for ever' was not some unspecified, shapeless future with indefinite frontiers in time, but a limited period of years, probably few in number; and 'this' was the presence of Anita in what remained of his life.

In the three-part setting for that summer's melody, Mr Barlow alone found some disquieting, some threatening notes in his score. They were not, as yet, disrupting. In the mornings, with the prospect of another harmonious day before him; in the cheerful lamplight after dinner, with Anita and Tony in the room, all was well with him. But in the small hours of the night when sleep, at his age no longer a constant companion, had ebbed away, or in that always melancholy interval between day and evening after the sun has gone down and a chill comes up from the meadows – he was assailed by doubts and misgivings. He had thought when he gave up active life and retired to Milton Place that there would be no more problems to solve, no more decisions to take; that the sand in his hourglass would run out smoothly while in his spirit he watched the passing scene with unperturbed detachment. But now he realised that he was no longer indifferent. Once more his old heart had conceived a desire and, old though it was, had conceived it with all the intensity of his innate vigour. This was no passing whim that he might, with some self-admonition, shrug off as of no consequence. He had never been a man of whims, and he knew himself too well to indulge in such self-deception. This was a matter of life and death, and that, in his circumstances, was not an empty phrase or mere figure of speech, but a very literal and accurate rendering of the truth.

He wanted Anita, and if this 'wanting' was not the kind of physical desire as it is usually, and far too restrictively, understood, it was nevertheless a wanting of every fibre of his body, of his nerves and all his senses – sight and hearing and touch. He wanted the sound of her voice and her footsteps in the house, the sight of her face across the table, the feeling of her hand upon his arm. She had become part of Milton Place which, without her, would now seem to him, in the phrase John Mannering had used, nothing but a deadweight of brick and stone. She had become part of himself, too, and if she were taken from him, he would suffer the loss of a vital organ, a loss from which he would not recover.

But things could not drift along indefinitely as they were. He would have to speak to her and make clear what he wished. And what was he to say to her? There seemed to be only one suggestion he could make, one way only of giving her the position and security which was all he could offer her in return for the sacrifice he was asking her to make. For in his humility, and in his tenderness for her, he wondered whether it was fair to ask a woman still in the prime of her life to devote any part of it to the companionship of an old man. At present she might still be able to form, in her own country, a new and lasting attachment; in a few years it might be too late, even for her. Would she think him ridiculous if he asked her to marry him? No, she would never laugh at him, she had shown him too much affection for that. She would surely allow him to reason with her and to explain. And then the thought that she would be his wife, if in name only, brought a kind of throb into his throat. It struck him that he had never, since she came to Milton Place, been inside her room, had never set eyes on the intimate paraphernalia women keep on their dressing tables – had never seen her in a dressing gown or with her hair on her shoulders. Modest and decorous though they were, these thoughts troubled him more deeply than conscious reasoning could account for. It had something to do with what he obscurely called 'the dislocation of time', for if he had married Anita's mother, as he had so often and vividly dreamed, then Anita would have been his daughter – not, as he now intended, his wife.

These were his night thoughts. They moved uneasily in the depths of his mind like the looming shapes of fish in the darkness of an aquarium where the daylight of reason does not penetrate. By contrast, the practical implications of his remarriage, which he weighed and considered in the clear light of morning, caused him very little difficulty. They rather amused him. He had long intended to leave the bulk of his estate in trust for Tony; neither of his daughters were to have any say in the matter. They would have shared the income. Now he would settle it on his widow, and he would leave them legacies commensurate to the kindness they had shown him. He only wished he could be present when the will was read.

CHAPTER TWENTY-ONE

Two events brought the Milton Place idyll to a close. The first was spectacular and noisy, causing a mighty turmoil on the surface of the deep and silent-running waters of the life that was being lived there; the second, seemingly insignificant, made only a slight surface ripple, but sank to the depths and encompassed its final disruption.

All through the month of July, Mrs Mannering had been making preparations for the 'Milton Place Revels'. She herself thought the name unfortunate and would have much preferred 'fête', for she feared that 'revels' injected a threat of riotousness into what she had planned as a lively and popular, but nonetheless decorous, entertainment. She was also afraid that it would shock Mr Barlow. But when she showed him the draft of the poster that was going to be put up on the various noticeboards in the town, he merely raised an enquiring eyebrow and seemed amused. One item only of the announcement he insisted on having removed, and that was the mention of his own name. He would not have it said publicly that it was by his 'courtesy' that the Revels were to be had at Milton Place. 'Quite unnecessary, my dear,' he told his daughter. 'The thing is entirely your affair. Please leave me out of it altogether.'

Another thing he refused to do was to ask Lady Brackenbury to open the proceedings. 'She has more than sufficient duties, public and private, to perform without my soliciting her patronage for a thing that can't possibly interest her,' he said. 'All you want is to make use of her title.'

'Titles do attract people,' Emily sighed.

'Then you must find one among your own friends,' Mr Barlow replied, 'but I shall not impose on Lady Brackenbury.'

Emily's friends included the wife of an eminent, recently knighted surgeon and a dame, but she did not think either of them the right person to open her fête. So she decided to make do with the Mayoress, who would be pleased.

On the whole, Emily was agreeably surprised by her father's meekness and patience in the face of all the comings and goings which the preparations for the fête made necessary. She had expected him to raise any number of objections and difficulties when the sites for the tents and marquees were being marked out; and when she told him that the band would have to play on the terrace, and that the donkeys for the children would be using the grass walks between the shrubberies. But to none of these things did he demur. All he asked was that the walled garden might not be invaded, and that could easily be promised because it was useless for her purposes and the little green door leading to it could be locked.

It was all, she felt to her great satisfaction, going to be perfectly straightforward. As she went about Milton Place with her staff-officers and adjutants, it almost looked as if she had the place entirely to herself. To all intents and purposes it might have been uninhabited. She mostly came in the mornings, and then Mr Barlow was either in his study or in the walled garden; if by any chance they met him in the grounds, he would lift his hat silently and pass on with a look of complete detachment. Mrs Seiler was never in evidence; if they caught sight of her, she was always in the act of hurrying away, dressed in an overall and intent on some domestic occupation that could not be interrupted. Tony was out or in his room with his books. Even the kitchen, if Mrs Mannering went there to see Alice, was usually deserted. Mrs Jones, the char, who might be scrubbing or polishing somewhere, had no idea where she or Sims had gone; they had been here only a moment ago, she said, looking blank. The old couple, and Nichols too, strongly disapproved of all these 'goings-on'. They held that a gentleman's property was not a fairground, and that Mr Barlow was being shamefully 'put upon'. They could see well enough that he didn't like it, even if Mrs Mannering couldn't, but then she had never been one to take much notice of other people's feelings.

Everyone, it seemed, was aware of this, except Emily herself. So impervious was she to the subtleties of atmosphere that she moved about Milton Place as in a void. Even when its inhabitants were physically present, she perceived them physically only. They had their being in the same space but, as it were, on a different plane, so that the intense inner life and complex emotional relationship they were living remained invisible to her.

Nevertheless, she had to take account of them, if only to make sure that she knew what each one of them was going to do on 'the day'. She did not want anything to go wrong. Her father, she thought very thankfully, was going to solve his own problem by keeping altogether out of sight. She had hardly dared hope he would be so accommodating. Once or twice she remarked to John when discussing her arrangements, not exactly *with* him but in his presence, that her father seemed to her so 'withdrawn'. She would even go so far as to say that 'he was not quite conscious of what was going on around him'. And then John would reply that that was surely most unlike him, and he didn't believe it was true. In his opinion Mr Barlow was remarkably alert and alive to his surroundings, unless in the last few weeks he had changed out of all knowledge. But Emily was unshaken. 'He's getting on, you know,' she said, 'he's been holding his own for a long time, but these changes come suddenly.'

Mrs Seiler and Tony, she said, would both have to be spoken to. She had not really envisaged either of them being present at the fête, but now they would obviously be there. Tony, John said, ought to be an asset on such an occasion. A schoolboy nephew would surely be most useful in helping to organise the children's games. Had she but known it, Tony had already consulted Dick about running that part of the show between them, round-games, egg-and-spoon races, donkeys and all. But Mrs Mannering didn't like Tony; she thought him 'not the right type', 'too clever by half', and intolerably supercilious. She had a way of speaking to him, at once patronising and disapproving, that antagonised him from the first word she uttered and immediately killed all his good intentions. As soon as she tackled him on the subject of the games, he struck an attitude that he knew would annoy her and declared that 'he would rather be seen dead in a ditch than have anything to do with the town brats'. 'Anyhow, your whole ghastly show makes me sick,' he said.

Naturally, she flared up in anger. 'You're nothing but an ill-bred little guttersnipe,' she retorted, 'you'd better stay away altogether!'

'And so I shall, miles away,' he assured her, grinning, 'you won't see *me* at your bloody fête!'

'Tony! How dare you!'

Words failed her and would have been wasted anyway, for Tony had already made his escape, delighted with himself at having, for once, really got under his Aunt Emily's leathery skin.

Anita presented a different problem. She would, of course, be very useful in the tea tent and she, in contrast with Tony, was only too willing to be of assistance. Pushing, that's what she was, and far too talkative and at her ease with people, no matter who they were. Mrs Molesworth and Mrs Orpington-Brown, who were going to be in charge of the tea-tent, wouldn't like her – being so effusively amiable and wanting to take most of the work out of their hands; or perhaps they *would* like her, and that would be worse. And how should she be introduced? Not as Mr Barlow's housekeeper, for Mrs Seiler would neither look nor act the part. Mrs Peacock had already made adverse remarks about her on that score when she had met her at tea months ago. As a visitor and friend? Then Mrs Molesworth, who was *the* most inquisitive woman in town, would ask endless questions about her: how long had she been here? and why had they not met before? Emily thought she had not fully realised how equivocal Mrs Seiler's continued presence at Milton Place was becoming until she came up against it now. And there was certainly no point in inducting her into her own set at this late stage when, at long last, she would soon be leaving.

So when Anita asked point-blank what she could do to help Mrs Mannering on the day of the fête, Emily had not yet decided what to say. Therefore she feigned surprise at the question and said 'Well. . .' and 'Let me see. . .' several times over. Anita saw that she was causing embarrassment but pretended to ignore it. 'Could I take charge of the sweet stall, perhaps?'

'Oh, no, thank you very much, Mrs Seiler. Mrs Halliday *always* does the sweets at *all* the bazaars, and she brings her nieces. There would be too much of a crowd.'

'Then the white elephants? I have never sold white elephants before and I should so much like to try.'

Mrs Mannering declined to smile. Mrs Seiler, as usual, was being impertinent. So she replied icily that Miss Bulmer would be in charge of this particular stall, that she was very experienced in persuading people to buy, and that it was best not to interfere with her. And then Emily's face cleared: she had had a sudden happy inspiration. There was the band! Would Mrs Seiler please see to it that they got the necessary refreshments, and also the bus-drivers who would have parked by the gate, would she be responsible for their teas, too? It would be a load off her mind if she knew that was taken care of. Anita said she would be happy to oblige.

After these interviews, which occurred in the week preceding the Saturday on which the fête was to take place, Emily felt that everything was now organised and under control. The stalls, the games, the refreshments, the band, the equipment and the transport, everything was in competent hands and everybody would know what to do. Emily knew whom she could trust and how to delegate her responsibilities. Mrs Peacock she had retained close to her own person throughout, for Mrs Peacock's function would not be to do any of the menial chores but to tell her husband evening by evening about all that was going on. Mrs Orpington-Brown and Miss Blundell, two of Emily's more intimate friends, had been taken into her confidence, and so Mrs Peacock had basked in the sunshine of their frequent and friendly company. 'Quite at home with them now' she was, and 'they were ever so nice when you got to know them really well.' And what a lot of trouble they were all taking to raise money for the Mother and Baby Fund.

Of course she talked to her Reg about it, and about practically nothing else. And thus, gradually, the idea impressed itself on Mr Peacock's mind that not only must he acknowledge all these efforts by being present at the fête, but that Milton Place itself might be a suitable house for the home he had for so long had in mind. In that case it might be as well if his colleagues on the Welfare Committee and perhaps the chairman of the Finance Committee came along too. It

could do no harm to look at the place; the wives would enjoy the party, and they themselves would not need to commit themselves one way or the other on this purely social and charitable occasion.

So Mrs Peacock reported to Mrs Mannering, who duly wrote the gentlemen in question each a personal invitation. This, she felt, was the first step. Others would follow: an investigation and a survey, probably, and then, possibly, an offer. Mr Barlow would have to consider it, and she knew of several people who would strongly advise him to avail himself of an opportunity that would not easily recur. Things, she thought, were moving in the right direction.

Thus everything was settled except, of course, the weather, and on this count Emily was both hopeful and resigned. To plan such a large-scale outdoor entertainment in an unpredictable climate would seem the height of temerity, yet it is done year by year up and down the country and everybody finds it quite natural to take a chance. Ascot, Wimbledon, Henley, garden parties, all have their predestined dates, and none of these events would ever take place if they were going to depend on the weather. Its vagaries may possibly have some part in fostering the innate love of a good gamble so characteristic of these islanders, making them a nation of happy winners and philosophical losers. One might, on any of these occasions, have a glorious day, or get wet to the skin, or frozen to the bone – the uncertainty makes a fine day a matter of rejoicing and congratulation, and a wet one to be endured with a shrug.

On the Thursday the skies were heavy with rain, the trees

dripped and the grass was sodden. The lorries drove up with the tent poles and the men fixed them in the ground, but kept the canvas rolled. They laid the boards on wooden blocks on the terrace for the bandstand, but covered them with a tarpaulin to keep them dry. Trestle-tables and folding chairs were stacked in one of the disused greenhouses. But during the night the wind changed. On Friday the anti-cyclone hovering over the Azores began moving eastward across the Atlantic, rolling back the leaden shutters of rain, and the sky began to show blue between wisps and fistfuls of cloud. By the afternoon it seemed safe to erect the stalls and marquees and to set up the tables.

On the six o'clock news Emily heard with relief that the anti-cyclone was intensifying. The Saturday was undoubtedly going to be fine and not too hot. She had hastened to her car which was parked in front of the house to listen to the forecast and now, comforted and reassured, she decided to drive home early for a good night's rest before next day's labours. But at that moment Sims appeared in the doorway and asked her to come and see Mr Barlow before she left. Tired and nervy as she was, she got out of the car again and went into the study for a quick goodnight. But Mr Barlow asked her to sit down. He wanted to speak to her.

'What is it, Father?' Emily asked with a note of impatience in her voice. 'Can't it wait till after tomorrow? I've got a lot on my mind just now.'

'I'm sorry,' Mr Barlow replied, 'but what I have to say must be said now.'

'Very well, Father. Is there anything wrong?'

'No. . . not wrong, I would not wish to use such a strong term – an oversight, perhaps, on your part.'

Emily tried to think very fast what it was that she might have forgotten.

Mr Barlow continued. 'I understand,' he said, 'that this fête of yours is to have a kind of official blessing. I mean that not only is it to be opened by the Mayoress of Waterington – which she might do very fittingly in a semi-private capacity – but that the Mayor is coming too, and that several members of the County Council have also been invited. Don't you think this is something you ought to have told me?'

So he had found that out, had he? Emily decided to treat it lightly. 'Well, since you know about it, Father, I must have told you. Does it make any difference – their coming, I mean?'

'No, you did *not* tell me, Emily. Mrs Peacock told me. I believe that is her name? The lady you brought here to tea, if you remember.'

'Of course I remember. And when did she tell you this? Yes, her husband is coming, naturally, as she is on the committee. He is a county councillor, and there will be two or three others.'

'So Mrs Peacock said. I just wanted to tell you that I shall receive them when they arrive, and shall ask them to take tea with me in the drawing room.'

'Oh no, Father,' Emily exclaimed, 'there is no need for you to do that! They will not expect it at all. As it was I who invited them, I shall receive them, and there will be a special table for them in the tea tent. It is all arranged. You have said all along that you wanted no part in all this, and everybody knows and understands, so you need feel under no obligation whatever.'

'I don't know what you mean by obligation, my dear, but though the invitations were given by you, the fact is that these gentlemen – and ladies, I presume – are coming to *my* house; I am therefore their host and shall act as such.'

'Really, Father, this is most strange.' Emily recognised that he was speaking in what she called his 'obstinate' voice. 'It has always been understood that you were lending me the grounds for the fête and that you yourself would have nothing to do with it. You have said so repeatedly. And yet now. . .'

But Mr Barlow interrupted her. 'You asked me to lend you the grounds for a popular, charitable entertainment. You did *not* say that you were making this an occasion for inviting representatives of local government who will not be coming as members of the public, but in their official capacity as county councillors. Surely you can see that this makes a difference? I can permit the general public to enter my grounds and I need not receive it; I cannot allow persons of official standing to come by special invitation and not receive them. It was fortunate that Mrs Peacock informed me in time. I should have been most annoyed if I had not been prepared.'

So it was Mrs Peacock who had told him! Emily had seen them in conversation several days ago when they had met on the terrace; she herself had left them together for a few minutes while she attended to some other business. She could still hear Mrs Peacock's delighted greeting: 'Hello, Mr Barlow! Quite a stranger you are in your own place. Ever so nice to see you again, though, and looking so well, too.

Do you remember me?' Of course Mr Barlow had stopped politely when she addressed him in this way, and had stood talking to her.

'What else did Mrs Peacock tell you, Father?' Emily asked warily.

'What else should she have told me? Or was there something more to tell? I only wish to repeat, my dear, that this information ought to have come from you. I have been waiting all the week to hear it from you.'

And as Emily said nothing and compressed her lips which she always did when she was thwarted and displeased, Mr Barlow put out a hand and gently touched her sleeve.

'I realise, my dear,' he said, 'that you were actuated by kindness and wished to save me trouble. I appreciate that. But your solicitude was misdirected. I am not decrepit, and though I do not much care for company, I am still, I believe, quite presentable. And now I will not keep you any longer for I can see you are tired and you have a hard day in front of you. I will only add that if you are not too busy tomorrow, I shall of course be very glad if you will join us at tea.'

Emily almost gasped. She was actually being invited to attend her own party. 'Thank you, Father,' she said, 'good night.'

Well, of all the unforeseen developments! Was this Mrs Seiler's idea, she wondered. She should, after all, have employed her in the tea tent.

* * *

The next day dawned clear and cloudless. From early morning onwards Milton Place became the scene of intense activity. Stalls were being stocked, tables set up, chairs arranged on the bandstand, strips of bunting slung between the trees. By the time the committee-ladies and their helpers sat down in the seclusion of the tea-tent to enjoy their last undisturbed cup of tea and the sandwiches they had brought with them for their lunch, the lawns and walks around the grey, dignified old house really looked like a fairground. Then, for half an hour, all visible activity ceased and there was silence. It was as if the whole tawdry showpiece and everybody who had taken part in producing it, were holding their breath. One could hear the birds chirping in the shrubberies, and the red and purple pelargoniums cascading from the urns along the terrace balustrade suddenly caught the eye, asserting their quiet permanence against the jangle of colour of the invading decorations. A light breeze stirred the bunting like a sigh of apprehension: everything was ready. Would the people come? They came.

First the band arrived in a special coach, looking brightly gay in their fancy uniforms, and gayer still when they took their places on the bandstand and unswathed their shiny instruments. And hard on their heels came the public. They came from the town, from the surrounding villages, from the new housing estates, but chiefly from the town. They came in the buses which the bus company had been prevailed upon to deflect from their normal run to take in Milton Place and stop at the gates. They came by hired coaches, by car, by scooter, by bicycle and by delivery van turned family conveyance for the outing. It began with a trickle and grew to a stream. Emily had been right in believing that Milton Place itself would prove an attraction, and the publicity had been admirably managed. By the time the Mayoress arrived and was conducted by Mrs Mannering to the bandstand from which, in a high-pitched, almost inaudible voice, she declared the fête open, she could hardly have opened it more widely than it had already opened itself. But it was only after the Mayoress had moved her lips and smiled and received a bouquet from Mrs Orpington-Brown's youngest little girl that the band struck up.

Now everybody felt that they had really come to a fête. The band quickened every movement to its rhythm and inte-grated voices and laughter into its music. It even captured and juggled with the sunshine which, dazzling and glinting on trumpet and cymbals, was thrown back from them in bursts and showers of sound, scarlet and gold. People who had been drifting about rather aimlessly and had scattered into the depths of the park beyond the limits of the fair, turned and came back towards the front lawn and there formed knots and clusters round the various centres of attraction. Mrs Mannering observed them from her vantage point in front of the tea tent. She had been opposed in committee as to the need to hire a band, but she had carried her point, and how right she had been! True, it was going to be a considerable item on the debit side when the accounts came to be cast up, but see how much more cheerful everybody was, and therefore more willing to spend their money at the stalls and side-shows. Each one of these seemed to establish a little magnetic field of its own and to exercise its particular, selective drawing power to which the various affinities, jumbled up indiscriminately in the crowd, were specially and separately responsive. Thus the flower stall attracted on the one hand the friends and acquaintances of the committee who were patronising the fête for the sake of these personal ties, and on the other the more self-effacing and impecunious gentlewomen who lived in small hotels and boarding houses and were now seeking to combine their humble contribution to the good cause with the pleasure of adorning a treasured vase or bowl in their solitary rooms. The vegetable stall unexpectedly attracted the notice of the men who had been induced to come with their wives – though it is doubtful whether they intended to buy anything. They were interested in discussing and comparing the exhibits with the produce of their own allotments, but would leave it to their wives to buy up the lot in the last half hour before departure when prices would be drastically marked down to avoid having to take the things back again. But the most motley crowd of bargain-hunters with money to spend gathered round the 'white elephant' stall where a lavish collection of crockery, glass, mats, shawls, beads and ornaments of all kinds jostled each other higgledy-piggledy in colourful array. Here everything was critically examined and assessed in the hope of picking up something really valuable for the proverbial song, for to get something for nothing is the dream of every woman's heart. If only the article was glamorous and its price trivial, that dream was here fulfilled, and as everything on display had been thankfully got rid of by its previous owner and the salesmanship exercised in foisting it on a new one carried its

own reward, every shilling and penny that changed hands in the process was a clear profit and pleasure to all concerned.

While all this was going on, a couple of small donkeys in charge of schoolboys were meandering through the grass-walks with squealing infants on their backs, and a rubber play-pool with ping-pong balls floating on its shallow waters had become the hub of a wheel of which children, stretched out on their tummies, were the spokes: they were trying to capture a ball with their lips, and being rewarded for each success with a toffee apple. The older children were climbing the outcropping rocks and overhanging trees in the rhododendron valley which was now nothing but a leafy, disenchanted wilderness.

CHAPTER TWENTY-TWO

Mr Peacock arrived around half past three bringing with him Miss Carter, herself a county councillor and his fellow-member on the Welfare Committee. She it was who most closely shared his views and intentions and on whom he relied to support any proposals he made. Mrs Peacock, of course, had been on the premises all day, but she had promised to look out for her husband at that hour so that they might go in to Mr Barlow together. The other three gentlemen and their wives, who had come from different parts of the county, arrived at short intervals after him and were successively shown into the big drawing room by Sims, who had donned his black coat and striped trousers which he now rarely had occasion to wear. The big drawing room had been unswathed from its holland dust-covers on the previous evening, and a very imposing room it was, occupying all the centre front of the house between Mr Barlow's study and the yellow boudoir at the other end. Its four tall french windows, now unshuttered, looked out onto the terrace, and its many sofas, armchairs, and manifold tables were strewn in clusters like an irregular archipelago across a sea of carpet. Long looking-glasses in heavy gilt frames hung between the windows, two massive marble fireplaces faced them in the opposite wall. A carved Flemish cupboard and an Italian cabinet of ebony inlaid with mother-of-pearl occupied the spaces between these and the doors, and yet the room was not overcrowded: even the grand piano looked comfortably inconspicuous near one of the corner windows, sadly out of tune though it was, to Anita's sorrow, under its velvet drapery.

The truth is that even in the days of Anita's most arduous labours this room had presented her with too formidable a task to be tackled in detail. She had opened and aired it, dusted and swept it cursorily and then re-shrouded it in dustsheets and darkness. So when Mr Barlow had asked her, a few days ago, after Mrs Peacock had disclosed to him what invitations Emily had sent out, whether the room could be brought into use for the afternoon, Anita had hesitated. Were these people so important, she asked, and would there be so many of them that he wanted this big room to receive them in? 'No, it is not that,' Mr Barlow explained, 'it is not as if these people who are coming were friends. What friends I still have know how quietly I live and how circumscribed my household *now* is. They know that I do not live in the old manner, that I have practically no staff nor would wish to have it even if I could afford it. That is why I do not entertain. But now Emily has invited these people, some of them, I believe, from quite a distance: I do not know who they are or what walks of life they come from, but that is no matter. It is repugnant to me to receive them in a hole-and-corner fashion. The fact is that they have been invited to Milton

Place, and I should like Milton Place, if possible, to be itself to receive them.'

He might have added, if he had thought fit to express completely what he had in his mind, that Milton Place did not shelter a recluse, but that it still had a master and might soon, perhaps, have a mistress. But of this he said nothing at the moment.

Anita, excluded from any active participation in Mrs Mannering's fête, was only too eager to gratify the old gentleman's wish if at all possible. That she herself was not wanted had rather amused her; for she had accepted long ago that Mrs Mannering did not love her, but it was amusing that she should show her dislike so openly: it was heartily reciprocated. What did, however, rouse Anita's indignation was that Emily obviously wanted her father out of the way on that afternoon, as well as herself. She had been quite rough with him when he had insisted on being present to entertain *her* guests. How dare she try to relegate him to the background like that, in his own house! Petty self-importance, Anita thought, she wants *all* the limelight and all the prestige of the place for herself alone, as if it belonged to her. So if Mr Barlow wanted to assert himself against his daughter's encroachments, Anita would do all she could to help him. She investigated the big drawing room and decided that even at short notice it could be made presentable if not habitable, and that on a fine summer's day with the sun pouring in for a few hours through the open windows, it would neither look nor feel sepulchral.

It was in the big drawing room, therefore, that Mr Barlow received Mr and Mrs Peacock, the Mayor and Mayoress of

Waterington, Miss Carter and the other county councillors with their ladies. Anita had prepared tea and all its appurtenances, but had explained to him that she herself would not be present. Mrs Mannering, she said, would expect to be hostess, and she and Mrs Mannering would not run comfortably in double harness. Mr Barlow had to admit that that was true. Undoubtedly, this was Emily's day. But in future, he thought, Anita's position should be established unequivocally.

In the tea tent Emily noticed Mrs Peacock looking repeatedly at her watch and then steal hurriedly and, as she thought, unobtrusively away. She was unable to follow immediately because her instructions regarding the price of 'set teas' in relation to that of single cakes had been bungled, and she had to put them right. Coming up at last onto the terrace, she stopped for a moment to survey the scene, as in Napoleonic days a general would have surveyed a battlefield, and finding that everything was going according to plan, she hurried into the house. Several cars were already parked near the front door and Sims was in the hall. Seeing her take the wrong direction, he moved to open the centre door for her.

'Mr Barlow is in the big drawing room, Madam,' he said.

'In the big drawing room!'

It was unbelievable. But there they all were, standing in a little knot round Mr Barlow. Mrs Peacock must have taken charge of the introductions, for the buzz of talk was already quite lively, Miss Carter's deep alto and Mrs Peacock's nasal whine being audible above all the rest. Miss Carter was the retired matron of an important hospital in the county and was admirably cast for the part: a formidable and kindly person who exuded authority and benevolence. One could readily understand that she and Mr Peacock would be on excellent terms and that the two of them would see eye to eye on all matters of welfare business, for he struck one immediately as a man of great commonsense and high competence in his trade, on the strength of which he was at ease with himself and the world. In appearance, his clothes looked a bit too tight for his large frame, and his tie had something gloriously explosive about it, like a burst of fireworks – but what matter: he wanted it and liked it that way. From time to time he looked at Mr Barlow and smiled, and Mr Barlow smiled back at him; however dissimilar, they would not be at a loss with each other.

The other members of the company could not so easily be placed, for they did not disclose themselves at a glance, being content with walking-on parts and occupied with looking out of the window at the fête, making desultory remarks, while the Peacocks and Miss Carter carried the conversation. Mrs Peacock ought, on that afternoon, to have been endowed with the splendid feathers of her male namesake, for she was happily preening herself before the other ladies, the Mayoress of Waterington in particular, about her familiarity with the grounds and, to a limited extent, with the other rooms of the house: 'More cosy and intimate,' she said, 'than this big lounge which is more like a hotel, don't you think, than a room in a private house.'

Emily, who only knew the Peacocks personally, found herself being introduced to the others by her father. He was the centre of attraction and quite in control of the party as he invited the ladies to sit down, and sat down himself, saying apologetically that standing for lengthy periods made him tired. Emily looked about her nervously: this was not at all the situation she had anticipated and she was not sure how to deal with it. The phrase her father had used the night before: 'I am not decrepit and I am still, I believe, presentable,' recurred to her, for his manner of speaking and the animation of his face and gesture were anything but decrepit, while as for being presentable, there could be no doubt that everybody was admiring him. Mrs Peacock had described him as 'a dear', and Mr Peacock, who had the incorruptible sense of values that goes with self-knowledge and self-respect, thought him 'a real gentleman, the genuine article, and no mistake.' He was the right kind of man to own a place like this, and the place was the right setting for him. It was a shame, really, the two had to be parted, Mr Peacock thought as he watched him, and he was sorry that he was to be instrumental in the parting. Still – the family wished it, they had their reasons, no doubt, and the old gentleman seemed acquiescent. It was a big place, and lonely when everyone had gone away, for a solitary old man. Change was inevitable and, on the whole, for the better. It was only right that places like this should come into public ownership and be used for social purposes, Mr Peacock concluded, and accepted the cup of tea Emily was offering him with the brightest of her toothy smiles. She had quite recovered her self-possession and sense of purpose; for it was only Sims who had brought in the tea and when he had closed the door behind him she realised that Anita was not going to appear. Thank goodness the woman had at least had the good grace to make herself scarce and Emily was, as she ought to be, in sole command.

Meanwhile, and at the very moment Mrs Mannering had taken herself indoors, a new and somewhat unusual attraction had made its appearance amongst the holiday-makers in the grounds. A curious couple was seen threading its way through the crowd, stopping and glancing round from time to time to attract people's notice. And this they certainly succeeded in doing. They were an old woman and a young one, obviously gypsies, but of a much more colourful kind than those one is wont to see camping in the lanes or on pieces of waste ground in the neighbourhood of Waterington. The old woman was very old and of a rather horrible appearance, more like a fairy tale witch, with a brown wrinkled face, untidy wisps of grey hair and a black gaping mouth with only two or three surprisingly white teeth gleaming in it like fangs. The rags and patches of her shapeless dress were almost unbelievable in their many colours and textures; they looked as if they had been cobbled together out of a ragbag and had never been clothes in their own right. The old woman hobbled along leaning on a stick while with her other hand she clutched the arm of her companion. This girl was striking indeed, with a red handkerchief tied round her head, from under which locks of black hair curled over her forehead. Her skin was olive-brown except where a rosy blush coloured her cheeks, and it was as smooth and lustrous as satin. With this dark complexion her eyes were unexpectedly light under finely pencilled eyebrows, and she had painted her lips an outrageous geranium red. She was tall and high-bosomed, and wore a tinselled sleeveless jacket over a shirt or blouse with full sleeves gathered at her wrists, and a long wide skirt

242

which almost swept the ground. But when she walked, her brown bare feet with scarlet toenails parted its folds at every step. And how she walked! With swinging hips and swaying shoulders, pointing her breasts and turning her head this way and that with challenging looks and impudent smiles. The girl did not seem able to speak, but the old woman nudged people as she shuffled along and whispered in broken English that, if they followed her, she would tell their fortunes. She had come a long way, she said, over the sea from Spain, and she was camping with relations outside the town. In Spain, she whispered, they knew things much older and deeper than had ever been heard of in this country – and she pointed and beckoned.

There was a little octagonal summer house, the sides of which were made of a lattice of wooden slats, hidden behind a screen of laurel bushes. A twisting grassy walk, twice bending back on itself, gave access to it so that, although quite near the house, it was not easily discovered. Thither the old woman, when she saw she was being followed, led the way. Some thick red material had been stretched on the inside over the lattice-work, making the interior of the little pavilion impenetrable from without and filling it with a reddish murky darkness, for a heavy curtain hung also over the doorway. Into this secret retreat the old woman disappeared, not without leering and beckoning again to the dozen or so women and girls who had trailed after her. But her daughter – or granddaughter – remained outside the entrance, holding up a piece of silver between her fingers and then pressing it alternately to her lips and to her heart.

The first girls that went in one by one, came out after a short time tittering and blushing so that the curiosity of the others waiting outside was increasingly titillated, and the news of the fortune-teller, if such she was, soon spread from group to group. But what the old crone had actually told them, none would or could disclose. 'Oh – things. . .' they said when their friends asked them; and when they were pressed to say what kind of things, they just squirmed and giggled. It seems that she did not go in for the usual 'good news in a letter' or 'arrival of an unexpected stranger', but that with the aid of the mysterious, sensuous gloom surrounding her, and her own exotic appearance, she succeeded in touching the secret erotic nerve which gives rise, in young creatures hungry for the experience of love, to the private fantasies they indulge in and which they believe peculiar only to themselves. Finding herself so intimately discovered and understood, the customer's own imagination supplied the names, shapes and hopes of her desires, but the witch would answer no definite questions and with a mumbled incantation the girl was dismissed. With older women who soon, in their turn, decided to try their luck, the gypsy changed her tactics and struck the chord of nostalgia and regret, probing for longings that had been suppressed and romance almost forgotten. Some echo, however faint, was sure to respond to this heart-searching, and once or twice it even released some pent-up tears.

'What's the matter, ducks, she never made you cry, did she? She didn't give you bad news about your Ron? You don't want to take no notice of what an old gypsy woman says, so don't you be so upset!'

'I'm not upset, dear, and she didn't give me bad news, she only made my heart ache, making me remember things as I never thought I'd think of again. But she did so stir up my feelings.'

These sibylline murmurings in the summer house were quite sufficiently unusual and of a different nature from the jocular reading of palms or of tea leaves currently met with at fêtes and bazaars to create a certain amount of disturbance and unease among the female part of the public – but the girl standing at the entrance to the oracle's den very nearly caused a scandal. She had first been seen about the place supporting her mother, and had then been dragged by her, rather unwillingly it seemed, towards the summer house. So provocative and inviting had been her demeanour that a few men, who were in no way interested in having their fortunes told, went after her to get a closer look. There she stood, with one hand on the curtain and the other on her hip, rolling her eyes and flashing her teeth in so exaggerated a manner that had she not been so beautiful, she would have appeared grotesque. To those who spoke to her she gave no answer but only shrugged her shoulders and gestured to them to go inside. One bold man who tried to kiss her was given such a vigorous push that he almost fell through the curtain. Inside, the old woman, bending over a male customer's palm, whispered that his love life was about to be renewed and that a delectable adventure was just around the corner. Whether she actually made assignments for her daughter, no one definitely asserted, but when a man came out of the little house, the girl always cast down her eyes, pretending to look bashful, and then quickly looked up through her long dark lashes when they turned to look back at her.

Whatever had or had not been said in the darkness of the red-draped summer house, the fact is that on many an evening in the course of the next couple of weeks cars were seen to stop near the well-known gypsy camping-places, while their drivers got out and lingered around, looking at the sunset, perhaps, or the moon rising over a line of distant trees. But the lovely girl was not seen again, nor even the old woman.

No one saw them leave the grounds, just as no one had seen them entering, and that was not for lack of enquiries. Their disreputable behaviour had at last been reported to Mrs Orpington-Brown who, while Mrs Mannering was otherwise engaged, had been left in authority over the good conduct of the fête. As soon as she could be spared from the tea tent, she hurried down the winding path to the little pavilion to investigate what had been described to her as the 'goings-on' there. But she was too late. Both the old witch and her alluring companion had by then disappeared into limbo – much to Mrs Orpington-Brown's disappointment. All they had left behind was a trail of rumour and gossip which by frequent repetition from hearsay acquired more and more highly-coloured details, and it was by this incident of the exotic gypsies that the Milton Place Revels were long remembered as 'revels' indeed. One tangible token of their activities had, most surprisingly, also been left behind them. When the summer house was searched for any trace of their identity a knotted red cotton handkerchief was found containing a lot of silver coins and even a couple of pound notes, and these, when handed over to the committee, made a substantial contribution to the takings of the day.

Mrs Mannering did not hear about all this until the fête was practically over. She was in the big drawing room where the tea-party had become very animated and was lasting very much longer than she had anticipated. She was finding it increasingly difficult to break it up. It looked as if it was going to take all the afternoon. At last a moment came that seemed opportune for suggesting that Mr Peacock and his colleagues might like to have a look at the house and the grounds, and she rose resolutely to lead the way. Everybody trooped out after her, and Mr Barlow was left alone. He sat in a corner of the sofa he had been occupying with Miss Carter who had been talking to him volubly in her booming voice. Now there was silence, and suddenly he felt very tired and very desolate. Outside the crowds were still milling about the terrace and the lawn. The straggling row of tents and the strings of bunting were disfiguring the beloved prospect while the great cedar looked on, deploring its outraged dignity. How much longer was this dreadful invasion going to last? Then he heard Emily and all her party cross the hall and go upstairs. Surely there was no need for her to show them the bedrooms! He hoped most fervently that they would not go into his own – or Anita's. The thought of such an intrusion made him wince. Where *was* Anita? He wished, almost desperately, that she would come to him now. He half rose to ring for Sims, but remembered that the bell did not work – only the ones in his study and his bedroom had been put in order. At last Sims did come in to clear away the tea things. Did he know where Mrs

Seiler was? No, Sims had not seen Mrs Seiler or, for that matter, Mr Tony all the afternoon. They must be somewhere in the grounds, for they were not in the house. Not in the house? Then it was no use sending Sims to look for her. He would have to wait – to wait.

At last the tour of inspection seemed to be over and Emily's guests came to say goodbye. They all insisted on shaking him more or less vigorously by the hand and there was a profusion of 'Thank you very much', 'Such a lovely afternoon' and 'So glad to have met you'; but Mr Peacock waited until they had all moved towards the door and then, looking over his shoulder to make sure they were out of ear-shot, he drew Mr Barlow gently down onto the sofa again. He thought Mr Barlow looked tired and anxious and he wanted to give him a little comfort, for Mr Peacock was a kind man.

'I don't want to leave you, Sir, without saying just a word, privately, of course, and without making any promises. I'm only just one cog in the machine though not an unimportant one, I'll admit, and Miss Carter will agree with me, so that together we do carry some weight. Of course I've only been able to gather a very perfunctory impression of the whole place and there would have to be a very thorough investigation. But being what I am, I can tell even at a glance that it's a very well-built house and I don't think it would be very difficult to convert. So with all possible reservations, as no doubt you will understand, Sir, I think I may say there's a chance – a fair chance even – that the county would be interested. Naturally, there will be the question of price, but all that's for a later stage, and I daresay that if we decide to take the matter further, you won't want to deal with it yourself, but will put us in touch with your solicitors.'

Mr Peacock paused. Had Mr Barlow understood what he had been saying? He had such a vacant look in his eyes. He must be much woollier in his mind than he had thought, judging from the way he had been conversing at teatime. But after a moment Mr Barlow's eyes came into focus again. He looked Mr Peacock straight in the face.

'I'm sorry, Sir,' he said, 'I did not at first get the drift of what you were talking about, but I gather you have been suggesting that the county wants to acquire Milton Place?'

'I don't know about "wanting", Mr Barlow. It's true that we are looking for a country place for certain purposes we have in mind, and I think that if everything turned out to be satisfactory, this place might do, and we might be able to take it off your hands. But it's a big "if", Mr Barlow. I can't promise.'

'To take the place off my hands? But I have no intention of parting with it, Mr Peacock. If you came here today to see it with that purpose in view, I am very sorry indeed that you have been troubled. You must be under a misapprehension. Milton Place is not for sale – at least not during my lifetime. What my executors will do when I'm gone, I can't tell. You will have to wait and see. And now, goodday to you, Sir.'

Mr Barlow's face had become flushed and his voice shook a little with some suppressed emotion. It was anger. It had risen in him, unawares, like a wave, and it was flooding him though he tried to fight it down. He succeeded, and the wave subsided, for it was clear from Mr Peacock's startled expression that he was not to blame. Indeed, Mr Peacock had already begun to apologise. He was deeply sorry. There was obviously some misunderstanding. He did not know how it had come about. He hoped Mr Barlow would forgive him.

Mr Barlow had recovered his self-possession. He was able to smile at Mr Peacock. 'I'm afraid you have been misled,' he said. 'I think I can understand how it came about. It is not your fault. I regret that you have wasted your afternoon. Goodbye, Mr Peacock.' He held out his hand.

'Goodbye, Sir, please remain seated. I have enjoyed my afternoon, I can assure you. I will ask your daughter to come to you,' he added, for he thought Mr Barlow had gone very white and might be feeling faint.

'No, please don't do that, I am quite all right, quite all right. No need to call anyone. Goodbye.'

When Mr Peacock had left, Mr Barlow rose very carefully and walked very slowly, hunching his shoulders, to the door of the big drawing room, across the hall, and into his study.

CHAPTER TWENTY-THREE

For a long time Mr Barlow sat there alone, in his chair, with his eyes closed, trying to concentrate on breathing deeply and slowly, in order to quieten his disorderly pulse. From some dark depths waves of vertigo kept surging up within him, threatening to blot out his consciousness. When they ebbed away his spirit reasserted itself, fighting with tremendous courage not to give way. At last these waves diminished in intensity and, as he sat very still, they gradually subsided altogether. He felt calm and clear again, only very cold. He wondered what time it was, for the shadows had darkened in the room, and in the windows the sky had paled, but he dared not move yet to ring or call.

It was not really very late, though considerably past the usual dinner-hour. Things were a bit disorganised in the house that evening, and no wonder. No one seemed to know what to do next. Alice was wandering aimlessly round the kitchen, trying to think what to do about dinner, and Sims had not laid the table. They were both quite out of their depth and were asking each other why Mrs Seiler, who normally would have taken charge and put things to rights, was taking

such an unconscionable time in her room. From what they could hear, she must have been having a bath at this unusual and awkward hour. Mr Tony, too, was upstairs.

At last Anita came down. She went straight to look for Mr Barlow in the study. It was now almost dark there, and coming out of the lighted hall, she at first failed to see him. She had almost closed the door again when she heard him move slightly, and switching on the light, saw him in his chair. His face was very white and the skin around his nose seemed drawn downwards and taut. His hands were trembling a little on the armrests. He was quite calm now, his eyes were open and he smiled at her gently, but was too exhausted to speak. She went over to him quickly and, feeling how cold he was, said he must immediately go to bed and have something hot to drink. Calling urgently for Tony who came rushing down half-dressed, they helped him up and together supported him up the stairs and to his room. Anita would have stayed to undress him, but this Mr Barlow absolutely refused and would have no one but Sims. So she went to fetch him and get some hot-water bottles, telling Alice by the way that there would be no dinner in the dining room that evening. When Mr Barlow had had some soup and some fruit he felt better and said he would go to sleep. Anita and Tony had a snack at the kitchen table and helped Alice and Sims wash up and clear away. Though Mr Barlow could not possibly hear them, they all felt impelled to speak in undertones and move carefully to avoid making a noise. The old couple were much put out and gave it as their opinion that it had all been too much for the master. No wonder it had made him ill. The whole thing ought never to have been allowed.

But it was all over now, and to everyone's intense relief Mr Barlow was not ill. Anita had conferred with Alice on the advisability of sending for the doctor if he still felt unwell in the morning, and two or three times during the night she had tiptoed to his door and opened it a crack to see if he were in any distress, but he had been profoundly asleep, breathing deeply and regularly. When Sims came to him at the usual time, he told him he was quite all right, only tired and would have a day of rest in bed. Soon after Tony went in to see him, but to Anita he sent his thanks and his compliments. He did not want her to come to his bedroom. He owed it to his own self-respect to stand on a certain amount of ceremony with her and not to drift into intimacy, as it were, by negligence and the chance of a passing indisposition.

No one knew what had happened to him last night and no one should ever know. In any case, it was all over now. All he needed was a little rest. Tomorrow, or at the latest the day after, he would come downstairs again as usual and every-thing would be as before. Milton Place itself would be restored to its serene, unruffled self. The cars, the buses and the coaches had departed. Men had come and dismantled the tents, had taken up the boards of the bandstand and packed up the canvas chairs. The lorries carrying them away had lumbered down the drive and were gone. Their wheels had made ruts where the gravel was loose and had been ground into the earth beneath, and the coaches had churned up part of the lower field which had been used as a car-park.

The lawn below the terrace was the worse for the tramping of many feet. One of the urns on the balustrade had been chipped when it had been hit by a tent-pole and some of the pelargonia plants had fallen out. In the sunken valley where the children had been playing hide-and-seek, a few branches had been broken. But on the whole no serious damage had been done, and surprisingly little litter had been left about. What there was had been quickly collected and got rid of under Nichols' supervision. Nichols had also contrived some first-aid repairs to the urn so that the breakage hardly showed. And soon the grass would grow again on those bare patches on the lawn, a roller would repair the drive and a new urn could be ordered from the stone-cutters. Mr Barlow would not go down into the rhododendron valley until its flowering next spring, and then the scars where the broken branches had had to be removed would be hidden by blossom.

Thus Nichols reported to Mr Barlow that 'considering all that had happened, it might have been worse. There's no permanent harm, Sir, nothing that can't be put right.'

Mr Barlow smiled and thanked him, and silently repeated even more fervent thanks: it might have been very much worse indeed. Lying in his bed now, restful and relaxed, he began to ask himself what had caused him to be so unreasonably upset. Certainly, the disruption of his daily life had been annoying, the disfigurement of the grounds very distasteful to him – but was the peace and balance of his body and soul so precariously poised that they could be so violently overthrown by things like these? Then, suddenly, he remembered Mr Peacock. His thoughts had been groping around like fingers searching gingerly for the seat of the lesion which was causing a whole region of the body to ache. He found it. He had forgotten Mr Peacock, but now he remembered him and understood what had happened. Emily had been trying, by devious manoeuvres behind his back, to force him out of Milton Place. She had planned to make it appear that the council wanted the place urgently for some social purpose so that it would be difficult for him, a solitary, selfish old man, to refuse to sell. But Mr Peacock had been too straightforward – he was not the man to play such a subtle and complicated game – he had spoken out bluntly and given the show away.

He recalled Mr Peacock's look of astonishment when he told him that Milton Place was not for sale. Mr Peacock had been persuaded that he, Barlow, was anxious to sell, while he was to be coaxed, or driven, into accepting the council's bid to buy. 'Very neat, my dear,' Mr Barlow said, addressing Emily in his thoughts, 'or rather, no – very clumsy. It would never have come off.' Well, that was all over, too, now, and he would dismiss it from his mind.

But he could not dismiss it. For, however distasteful, he would have to speak to Emily about it, and when he thought of that, an uncomfortable fluttering which he could not locate but which was definitely somewhere inside him warned him that if he broached the subject to her, he would not be able to keep calm. And keep calm he must; he could not risk another uncontrollable upsurge of anger. At least, not yet. So any discussion with Emily on this subject would have to be postponed. Fortunately she and John would soon be going to Scotland, as they always did in August, and he could shelve the matter until her return. By then this treacherous physical weakness would have been overcome. By then, too, a great change might have occurred in his life, or rather a renewed assurance of its continuity, and then he would be able to laugh at Emily and tease her about her petty plotting and contriving.

Mr Barlow was right. The Mannerings were going to Scotland at the end of the week. Emily only came out to Milton Place once more and, as usual, she was in a tearing hurry. There were a thousand things to settle before she left. As usual, she noticed nothing and did all the talking, in staccato sentences to which she seemed neither to require nor to expect an answer.

'We're going to the Lennox's for the first week. I'll write and tell you where you can reach us after that.'

'There'll be a lot to discuss when I get back, but there isn't time now, and anyway, it had better wait.'

'By the way, the fête was a great success. We, I mean the committee, were very pleased with the result. We took almost a hundred pounds clear profit.'

Here Mr Barlow interposed mildly: 'It doesn't seem very much, seeing all the trouble you took.'

'The cash was a secondary consideration anyway. Of course we had a lot of expenses. But everybody enjoyed it so much. I've had a letter of thanks from the Mayor. He asks me to thank you, too. Here it is.' She tossed the letter onto the table. Mr Barlow did not pick it up.

'Well, I'll say goodbye. Cecilia will be here shortly, so she's told me. That's a great comfort to me. She can hold the fort while I'm away. These conflicting duties *are* such a problem. I *hate* leaving you, but I *must* go with John – he wouldn't enjoy his holiday half so much if I didn't go with him. Have you heard when Cecilia is coming?'

'Not yet. She always gives rather short notice.'

'I shall hope to find her here when I get back. Goodbye, Father.' In the door, Emily turned again suddenly. 'Hadn't I better say goodbye to Mrs Seiler? I might not see her again.'

'You wouldn't mind *that*, would you, my dear?' Mr Barlow said with a smile. 'But don't bother, I'll give her a message and tell her you couldn't wait.'

For a moment Emily hesitated; then she shrugged her shoulders and was gone.

* * *

Daily life at Milton Place now resumed the pattern and rhythm that had governed it before the interruption of the fête. It was the same, but not quite the same. The key had shifted, and every accent and tone was, ever so slightly, displaced. Nothing really tangible had occurred to alter the relationship between Mr Barlow, Anita and Tony, but there was a change of mood which the passage of time alone would, no doubt, have brought about, but which the interruption caused by the fête had served to hasten and accentuate. It was August and the days were sultry and heavy. The trees were dark and thick with leaf, the undergrowth saturated and lush.

At this time of the year this green, rich, rolling countryside is at a disadvantage from a surfeit of vegetation, which weighs on the senses and depresses the spirit.

Even in the walled garden where Mr Barlow now spent most of his time in preference to the terrace, because there, at least, there was no trace of the recent invasion, and not even the reverberation of strange voices had ruffled the flower beds – even here it was oppressive rather than sheltered. Mr Barlow's eyes rested on what he saw there with resignation, not with enjoyment. The roses were past their first flowering, the delphiniums had faded. Cactus, dahlias and Michaelmas daisies, which with their bright crispness would later herald the coming of autumn, had not yet appeared. The corner where the white broom had stood, like a May bride in a shower of lace, looked especially disconsolate with its tangle of grey-green filaments after its display had been dismantled. The beds were densely planted with antirrhinums, gloxinia and marigold, and Mr Barlow disliked them all: brash, grace-less flowers of glaring colours amidst their fleshy greenery, so he described them. He had often told Nichols to abstain from planting them – but what was there, Nichols always objected, to take their place?

Tony, by his youth and temperament the most mercurial of the three, was naturally the most sensitive to the disturbing electric currents lurking in the atmosphere. He was lan-guorous and unsettled. For more than six weeks he had been living at a high tension of intellectual and emotional excite-ment which could not be maintained indefinitely. When he tried to go back to his studies he suddenly found that they had gone stale and that he had, for the present, lost interest. Of course he attributed this to reasons completely outside himself, especially to the prospect that his call-up papers would be coming any day now and that it was not worth doing any more work while he waited. Time now hung heavily on his hands, there was nothing he really much cared to do, and when Dick came to ask him to help with the hay-making, he went rather reluctantly. He did not pretend that the next stage in his life was going to be much to his liking, but it would be 'something different' and he 'wished to goodness,' as he said, 'that it would begin.' He talked a lot about his going away, wondered what he would be doing in a month's, or in two months' time, spoke of 'going to have a last look' at a spot he was particularly fond of, and made Mr Barlow and Anita feel that he was impatient to be gone. Then, noticing one evening, after he had delivered himself of a string of remarks in that vein, that his grandfather was looking at him sadly, he thought it necessary to explain himself.

'You musn't think that I *want* to go away, Grandpa. But once you know you've got to go, it's like waiting for your train to start. You stand at the window saying goodbye and staring at the people you're leaving behind without really seeing them anymore. There you stand, yet what you want to do is to sit down in your corner, open your newspaper and get it over!'

On reflection Mr Barlow was inclined to agree with him. Tony's restlessness was becoming irksome and, loath as he was to admit it, it would be a relief when he was gone. For one thing, now that he could find nothing to do, he was engaging too much of Anita's attention. Mr Barlow thought that the two of them were behaving rather childishly together, evidently playing some silly game which made them laugh a lot and in which he had no part. They often threw allusions at each other across the table, causing more laughter, and once or twice he heard Anita address Tony as 'Esmeralda'; but when he asked what it all meant they refused to elucidate and put him off with 'Oh, nothing – just a joke.' Mr Barlow didn't care for these mystifications; he knew there was nothing in them, but it annoyed him to be excluded, not to be entirely in their confidence, or, to be precise, in Anita's confidence. These exchanges with Tony showed her to be in a frivolous mood, so Mr Barlow thought, and out of tune with what, one of these days, he would want to say to her.

He did not, of course, lack opportunities to speak to her quietly and alone. Every day she sat with him in the morning or after tea in the walled garden, sometimes with her needle-work, but more often with her hands in her lap and her eyes half-closed. 'I feel so terribly lazy,' she would say. 'I suppose it's the weather. I am always just on the point of going to sleep.'

So the days drifted by and Mr Barlow did not speak. There was really no immediate necessity to do so and it was much easier to put it off. When he thought of making his proposal at some unspecified future time, it seemed so right, so natural and reasonable all round that it could not fail to be accepted. There would be no argument about it at all, if he found the right words so that she would see it at once in its proper light. But faced with the immediacy of actually uttering these words, the whole undertaking would strike him as hazardous, almost as preposterous, and his decision would ebb away. Perhaps he also feared unconsciously the emotions which a conversation of this kind, on which so much depended, would arouse in himself, and felt it would be better if he waited a little longer till he could be surer of his self-possession.

Anita, in spite of her seeming abstraction, sensed on each of these occasions that Mr Barlow was on the point of saying something important to her. Under her outward immobility her attention was instantly aroused when, in the midst of a mutual silence, some slight movement on his part or a deeper intake of breath conveyed to her that he was tensing himself for some decision. But then, each time, the moment passed and he only made some inconsequential remark. At first she wondered whether he was going to speak to her about herself and Tony – and she prayed that it might not be so, not now when Tony was going away and 'all that' would in any case so soon be over. So she very deliberately made no move to encourage him and when it had happened two or three times without anything being said, she thought she must have been mistaken.

In these days her thoughts dwelt almost entirely on Tony.

He was going away and with his going this exuberant mid-summer intoxication which had given her such a burst of happiness would inevitably come to an end. There would be no renewal. His going would be the clean and definite severance of a relationship which was already beginning to show flaws and cracks which she clearly recognised, even if he did not. Some parts of her sensibility had already begun to ache, and a quick, sharp break imposed from without would, she felt, be more bearable than the gradual and hesitant tearing apart which she knew was in store for her if they remained together.

In what, almost imperceptible, manner was Tony treating her differently than he had at their first ecstatic falling-in-love? In what way had he changed? He was still her ardent lover, more ardent than ever, but he now seemed entirely obsessed by his own desire to the point of forgetting to love. Since he had so successfully impersonated a wanton gypsy-girl it seemed as if this play-acting had released in him some still lingering inhibitions. There was no more timidity, no trace of the initial reverence and 'goddess worship' in his caresses; he was demanding and sometimes far from gentle. Cradling him in her arms when he at last was still and had gone to sleep, she would be overwhelmed by a feeling of sadness and resignation, a helpless tenderness for his youth and beauty, more akin to a mother's than a mistress's love. But one night when she had called out to him: 'Darling, don't be so rough, you are hurting me,' he had laughed in reply, 'All right, grandma!' It was meant jokingly, of course, and as part of the game they had been playing together, but the words went through her like a shaft and the hurt was deeper than she cared to admit. In the morning the recollection of them lay in her chest like a stone. At her dressing table she looked searchingly in her glass at the tiny creases in the corner of her eyes and wondered whether the deep-brown wrinkles of grease-paint with which they had been covered had drawn his attention to them – whether her lips were less fine and shapely since the black sticking-plaster she had used in her disguise had made her mouth look toothless and deformed.

She wished Tony had not said those words, not even for fun. She did not really believe that he was callous or imperceptive and if, for a moment, she found herself reproaching him in her heart for being so, she would immediately add: But he is so young! Did that simply mean that she was so old? Perhaps it did. Perhaps it meant that the discrepancy between their ages was beginning to make itself felt through the thinning texture of their mutual infatuation?

For now there appeared another aspect of Tony's behaviour which had nothing to do with herself or their relationship with each other and which yet distressed her and grated on her almost in spite of herself. It concerned Tony's mother. Her coming was expected any day now, and Tony kept on complaining about it. He never said anything in his grandfather's hearing, but to Anita he was most outspoken. It caused her acute discomfort to listen to him and when she tried to answer it made him impatient and angry.

'I wish to goodness Ma weren't coming,' he would say, 'it's going to be such a bore. Spoil all the last part of my time here – and of our time together, for that matter.'

'But I had the impression,' Anita said, 'that your mother was such a quiet, mild person. Why do you expect her to make herself unpleasant? You say she's not like your Aunt Emily?'

'Oh, no, she isn't like her. She's quite different. There's nothing bossy about her. I suppose she's all right in herself, really. It's just. . . well, she gets on one's nerves.'

—◈—

'But don't you care for her at all? I'm sure she must love you very much. Even if she's perhaps not very clever – or interesting – you must surely have *some* affection for her? After all, she's your mother!'

'I do hate your saying things like that,' Tony retorted resentfully. 'It's just a cliché. And not like you at all. You've always been so *real*. I ought to love her because she's my mother, you say. Nobody ever loves anyone because they ought to. All this being maternal and filial is just a convention. But you have an indiscriminate sympathy for mothers in general – and for fathers, too – I've noticed that before. You have a bias in favour of parents. It's a question of generations, I suppose,' he added philosophically. 'But you, of all people, ought not to have prejudices like that. With real people, like you and me, age doesn't matter. Take Grandpa: I don't love him because he's my grandfather, but because he is what he is. And I love you, darling, because you're you, and I don't care two hoots that you're old enough to be my mother!'

They were, as so often before, sitting in the walled garden, Anita on a bench, and Tony stretched out on the grass, chewing a few long blades like a little boy. And talking like one, she thought. He looked up at her defiantly, challenging her to disagree with him. She smiled, but a little wistfully. His declaration of love engulfed her in a new wave of tenderness. He had not made one, articulately, for a long time. But in the same breath he had told her that the fact of her age and her belonging to an older generation had been occupying his thoughts, though he spoke of it only to dismiss it as artificial and of no consequence. But her instinct contradicted his

brave, reasonable arguments. She was not sure that he quite believed them himself. One's age and generation are not empty conventions which one can deny and discard at will, though one might pretend to for a little while. She knew it because, in Tony's own words, she was so real. And that is why Tony's coldness towards his mother inflicted a vicarious wound and why her feelings were attuned to sympathise, in spite of herself, not with the boy whom she loved but with the woman she did not even know.

CHAPTER TWENTY-FOUR

'I had a letter from Cecilia this morning,' Mr Barlow announced at luncheon, 'she will be arriving the day after tomorrow.' For a moment it felt as if he had spoken to an empty room; his words evoked no immediate response either in speech or looks. Then Tony gave a kind of groan, and Anita quickly tumbled out a few words to the effect that 'that would be very nice' in rather too loud a voice, like air rushing in to fill a void. Again there was silence until Sims who had been standing near the sideboard came forward and relieved it by asking: 'Please, Sir, Alice would like to know which room is to be got ready for Mrs Crawfurd?'

'Which room?' Mr Barlow repeated slowly. He seemed puzzled. 'Ah, of course, Mrs Seiler now has the room my daughter usually occupies. Which room does Alice suggest?'

But Anita interposed quickly. 'Mrs Crawfurd must of course have the room she is used to. I'll move out this afternoon and then Alice and I can get it ready for her.'

'Thank you, my dear,' Mr Barlow said, 'that is very kind of you, very considerate.'

But Tony flared up in protest. 'Oh no, Grandpa, you surely

don't mean Anita – I beg your pardon, Mrs Seiler – to be turned out of her room! It's hers now, has been for months! Ma never has it for more than a few weeks, once a year. It's got all Mrs Seiler's things in it, she lives there. Surely Ma, who's only coming on a visit, can have one of the guest rooms!'

Mr Barlow turned to Tony and looked at him enquiringly till Tony heard his own voice trail away and knew, to his own intense embarrassment, that he was blushing. But he looked his grandfather straight in the face. That room meant so much to him. If you but slipped inside the door, Anita's scent, the exhalation of her person and all her most intimate belongings billowed around you like a cloud of incense – every single object there, large or small, from the big wide bed to the little pink silk cape which hung by the side of the looking-glass and which she wore round her shoulders when she was brushing her hair – everything breathed her presence. That room could not be emptied of her in an afternoon.

'Nonsense, Tony,' Anita said, 'I'll move into a guest room while your mother is here – the blue room is quite ready.'

'But it's the other side of the house,' Tony muttered under his breath.

At last Mr Barlow spoke, slowly and decisively. 'I agree with Tony,' he said. 'It would be very inconvenient for you if you had to move. It was good of you to suggest it, but there is no need for you to be disturbed. I have not been into any of the bedrooms lately, but if you say the blue room is ready and habitable, Cecilia can have that. It will be much simpler. I remember it used to be a very pleasant room, and it has the morning sun. Cecilia will like it.'

It was obvious that the matter was settled and there was to be no further argument. Tony looked at Anita from under his eyelashes. But Anita was not altogether happy about it.

As Mr Barlow had said, the blue room was very pleasant. Like all the bedrooms it was full of chintz and mahogany, but looking out eastwards over the treetops of the rhododendron valley, the blue roses of the curtains and armchairs had not faded in the afternoon sun. It was large and old-fashioned and comfortable, and it had been the easiest room to refurbish. It now looked fresh and clean, and when Anita had put white lace-edged covers on the dressing table and chest of drawers, and had placed a large bowl of scabious and pale yellow coreopsis, interspersed with some spear-shaped, bluish-green foliage, on the table, while Alice did the dusting and inspected the inside of the cupboards and drawers, they agreed that the room looked very pleasant indeed. Nevertheless, Anita was uneasy.

Nichols drove into Waterington to fetch Cecilia in the Bentley and Tony was expected to go with him to meet his mother. But when it was time to start for the station Tony was nowhere to be found. Mr Barlow sent Sims up to his room and Anita went to look and call for him in the garden, but to no avail.

Tony did not reappear until his mother was just getting out of the car, when he explained that he had been at the farm and that his watch had stopped. Cecilia looked up at him and said, 'Why, Tony!' – as if she were surprised to find him here, and Tony bent forward and kissed her on the cheek. Meanwhile Mr Barlow had come out of his study into the hall and Cecilia ran up to him with little tripping steps and embraced him with girlish effusiveness while he patted her gently on the shoulder as if to soothe her.

Tony had remained in the entrance and Anita was at the foot of the stairs. For a moment they all stood there like actors who had forgotten their lines and were waiting desperately for the prompter who wasn't there. Then Anita came forward and Mr Barlow said: 'Cecilia, this is Mrs Seiler.' Cecilia said nothing and Anita felt that any word of welcome on her part would be out of place, so she remained silent. At last Cecilia managed 'How d'ye do.' There was another pause. Mr Barlow, having said his piece, turned to go back to his study, Tony frowned, Anita looked uncomfortable, while Cecilia let both her arms hang limply at her side and looked so forlorn she seemed to be about to cry. Anita was watching her face which, she thought, was so much older than her years warranted: a soft, puffy face which seemed to have no bones in it but which was made of a lot of little silken cushions that had gone crinkly. And now they were crinkling and puckering even more, and her mouth which had no particular shape was trembling. And Anita thought in a flash: 'If only I had moved out of her room. This is much worse than I had feared, this is going to be quite dreadful!'

Then Cecilia said: 'I suppose I had better go up and unpack.' She moved towards the staircase. Tony picked up the suitcases which Nichols had brought into the hall and followed her. Anita escaped into the kitchen to make the tea.

If she felt apprehensive as to what Mrs Crawfurd would say about the change of rooms, she had a surprise in store for her.

Cecilia's expression when she came down to tea had entirely changed. The hurt, forlorn look had gone, her eyes were bright, her cheeks which had seemed so loose were tightened by some muscular effort which was noticeable also in the set of her mouth, her shoulders were thrown back and her movements were brisk. So briskly did she walk up to Anita who was setting out the teacups that Anita instinctively recoiled as if she were going to be attacked. But Cecilia began to thank her and compliment her effusively for the arrangement of her room. Anita made an effort to apologise, but Cecilia would not allow it.

'I'm so *delighted* with the blue room,' she said. 'Of course I was a little *surprised* to find that I was not to have my own – I mean, the one I have always *thought* of as my own – my mother's room, you know – but the blue room is really *very* much nicer. I've never slept there before and I shall *enjoy* it so much. It has the morning sun, as Alice pointed out, and it's such a *pleasure* to have the sun in the morning. And Alice tells me that you have washed *all* the curtains and loose covers yourself! They look so beautifully fresh. And the *flowers*! I've never been able to *arrange* flowers like that, all I do is just put them in water – but you are so *artistic*. Of course the Viennese are famous for being artistic – or is it musical? – but it comes to the same thing, doesn't it? What I mean to say is: it's so *kind* of you to take so much trouble – just for *me*.'

Every time Cecilia emphasised a word she re-tightened her mouth and her shoulders as if determined that neither her voice nor her muscles should be allowed to sag. All through tea she carried on the conversation with the same brittle briskness, answering Mr Barlow's quiet questions about her journey with a spate of detailed information interspersed with little bursts of laughter which she fetched up from her throat like a series of small hiccoughs in a rather alarming manner. They were intended to underline how amused she had been at a number of minute incidents that had occurred – what the porter had said, and how she had thought she had lost her ticket but had found it again in her glove, and how funny the flowerpot hat was that the woman opposite her had been wearing. When speaking of 'home', she would turn to Tony as to the one who would *know* what she was talking about. 'I bought some buns at the little bakery at the corner of Grace Street, you know they bake them themselves and they are always fresh. So much nicer than having lunch on the train. And I had my new thermos with coffee – but of course you *don't* know that though I've had it quite a while. I keep forgetting what a *long* time it is since you were at home.'

* * *

'I'm so thankful your mother took the change of rooms so well,' Anita afterwards said to Tony. 'I was really afraid she was going to be upset, but she was so nice about it.'

'She was upset all right,' Tony answered. 'Alice calmed her down, and then she put on her "brave face" as she always does when something goes wrong.'

'If you thought she would really mind you ought to have let me move as I wanted to,' Anita said reproachfully. 'I still think your mother is being very nice about it – thanking me for the flowers and all that. I do feel so sorry for her, she looks so tired. I want to do all I can to make her comfortable.'

Tony shrugged. 'I know you'll be sweet to her, darling, because that's the way you are. You'd be sweet to anyone who lets you. Poor Ma is not much used to that kind of thing – yes, I'm to blame too, you needn't look at me like that, I know it all right. But you'd better be careful or Ma will be suspicious and think you're buttering her up for some reason or other.'

Anita was almost angry with him. How could he be so cynical! She determined defiantly to be as attentive and considerate to Mrs Crawfurd as she possibly could. In spite of the 'brave face' she was said to have put on afterwards, Anita could not forget her look of helpless despair as she stood in the hall on her arrival and saw no welcoming sign of pleasure on any face. How dreadful to be ageing and unloved, Anita thought, and her heart went out to the poor woman.

It was true that Anita never found it difficult to be warm and friendly to anyone who would let her. As Tony said: that was the way she was. She liked being attentive to others, liked making herself pleasant, and her doing so was nearly always unintentional and as natural and effortless to her as eating and sleeping. The smile of thanks, the genial atmosphere of being liked and loved which she evoked was as needful to her as the air she breathed and the ground she walked on. But to Mrs Crawfurd she *intended* to be nice. That, she thought, would be particularly rewarding – not in the sense that she expected any benefits or favours from her, but simply for the sake of seeing someone so starved of affection respond to a little kindness.

But Anita soon discovered that it was not quite as easy as at first it had looked. Mrs Crawfurd had two faces, or two personalities, and one never quite knew with which of these one was going to be confronted. There was the poor, pitiful woman whom Anita had seen at their very first meeting and who had moved her to sympathy and compassion. She would discover her again from time to time when they were alone together; in the morning, for instance, when Anita brought her her early tea and Cecilia was in bed with her thin, greying hair in a plait and her almost colourless cheek resting on her pillow. Then she would sometimes smile very sweetly and say 'thank you' in a natural way, and Anita would sit down for a few minutes on the edge of the bed and encourage her to have a little friendly chat. Or, again, Cecilia would sometimes be 'off her guard' if she and Anita were alone in the garden, or if she came and sat with her when she was ironing or mending. But then there was Mrs Crawfurd's other face, the one she invariably wore when her father or Tony were present, and very often with Anita as well. Anita recognised it at once, first thing in the morning, when she saw a certain glitter in Cecilia's eyes and heard her voice schooled to recite her 'good morning, thank you, how very kind' with the appropriate emphasis and intonation. Then Anita knew she was being spoken *at* instead of spoken *to* and immediately made for the door.

On the whole, life went on at Milton Place in the same way as it had before Cecilia's coming. She gave no trouble. She was not difficult. She neither interfered nor criticised. She did not assert herself or demand particular attention. It was all the more remarkable, therefore, what a disturbing influence she had on the entire household. She had but to enter a room to set up a current of unease in everyone present. She exuded anxiety like an undefinable but penetrating odour which immediately affected the nerves and senses. She never looked at anyone without giving the impression that she was watching them. She had a way of listening to what was being said, with her head slightly cocked on one side, as if probing for some hidden meaning which she was at pains to detect. A playful little smile was fixed on her lips when she was in company, a smile that seemed to convey: 'I see – I understand' – so that one became self-conscious of one's most natural gestures and one's most innocuous remarks. She had a special 'attitude' towards her father, and a different but also special one towards Tony, and these she maintained conscientiously in all circumstances, undeterred by the exasperation they caused in Mr Barlow and Tony respectively. Towards her father she was all deference and solicitude. She enquired persistently and searchingly about his health. How had he slept? Was the grass not too damp for him to sit out? She was afraid that the pudding they had had for dinner last night had been *very* rich and must have disagreed with him. He was looking rather pale today – the heat, perhaps? She was for ever offering to move his chair to a different position, or placing his lamp at a better angle, or fetching him a cushion, or his stick if they were going out. Mr Barlow, who hated fuss and hated, above all, any discussion of his physical condition, sometimes got so annoyed that he almost shouted at Cecilia to leave him alone, for goodness sake, and not to be a nuisance. Whereupon Cecilia would say, with a little sigh: 'Dear Father – always so unselfish, never considering his own comfort.' And if Anita were present she would smile at her obliquely: 'I suppose Mrs Seiler does all these little things for you so much better than I can!'

But towards Tony she was 'maternal'. When she spoke to him, her actual words were not, of course, baby talk, but the tone in which she said them made them sound as if they were. She always managed to inject a mother's admiration and pride, together with a sort of wistfulness, into whatever she said to him. At lunch it could be: 'I've hardly seen you at all this morning, darling. Have you been *very* hard at work?' Then, turning to Anita: 'He *is* so clever, isn't he? Though, I suppose, I, as his mother, ought not to say so. But I shall never understand how I with my poor silly head [which she would then tap to make it sound hollow] could have such a clever son!'

Or, after dinner: 'Do come for a little stroll with me in the garden, darling. I see so little of you, and soon you'll be going away to be a big rough soldier. I'm always telling myself this is the last of your boyhood.'

And Tony would squirm and shudder as if touched on an over-sensitive nerve and clamp his mouth shut, or mutter something under his breath and, if at all possible, make his escape.

Anita did not wince like Tony, or grow impatient as Mr Barlow did, under Cecilia's mannerisms. For one thing, they were new to her and she was not directly involved. They appeared to her as the mental equivalent of some physical 'tic' – a kind of contortion to which poor Mrs Crawfurd was driven by an inner compulsion which she could not control. There was, Anita felt, real feeling, real love and suffering underneath these tawdry trappings, and Anita genuinely liked her and was deeply sorry for her.

As for Cecilia, it seemed as if she would never be given a chance to meet anyone on their own terms, or to trust, with confidence, her own natural impulses. She, too, liked Anita. She had not expected to like her, but she had expected her to be so very different. All she had heard about her had been told by Emily in her letters; for Mr Barlow, though he had sometimes referred to Anita, had always done so without comment, and Tony had never mentioned her at all. Emily's letters, however, had recently become more and more abusive. Anita had at first been described as interfering and pushing, but she had developed into a 'bare-faced schemer' who was 'digging herself in' at Milton Place and endeavouring by every kind of device to make herself indispensable to their father with a view, undoubtedly, to getting herself remembered in his will. But together they must see to it that this clever little plot came to nothing. Emily already had several ideas how to thwart her, for Mrs Seiler had no work-permit, or even a permit to take up permanent residence in this country, and John would be able to arrange that she shouldn't get one. Also, if Mr Barlow gave up Milton Place, Mrs Seiler's functions as a housekeeper would become superfluous. In any case, so Emily concluded her last letter, written just before she left for Scotland, as Cecilia would be staying in the house for a few weeks, she should keep her eyes and ears open and find out exactly how matters stood between their father and the Austrian woman, and then they would be able to discuss together how best to get rid of her without arousing the old gentleman's displeasure or causing him 'to dig his heels in', as Emily put it.

A pushing, managing, hard-faced woman Mrs Crawfurd had therefore expected to find: someone who bullied her father, for his own good, of course, in the manner of a dictatorial nurse. Instead she found – Anita, and Anita was not only entirely different from the person she had imagined, but not even like anyone she had ever known. Cecilia didn't know what 'attitude' to take towards Anita. She was so surprised by her that she was taken off her guard and found herself actually liking her. And then Anita was treating her to a new experience; she was thoughtful and considerate of her, she noticed what she liked in the way of food and performed little kindnesses for her, 'maided' her as she had never been looked after since her girlhood and, since she had admired the flowers in her room, always arranged fresh ones for her in unusual combinations which gave her pleasure. She was also so easy to talk to and looked really interested and sympathetic when Cecilia poured out to her her endless and pointless accounts about her char, her acquaintances, and her meetings with the Mothers' Union. As Tony had said, his mother was not used to that kind of attention and she could not help finding it very pleasant.

But then she asked herself whether this friendliness of Mrs Seiler's was not all part of her 'plot'. Was she only trying to 'get round' her and enlist her help as an ally – against Emily, she supposed – as she had obviously already got round her father? Emily was probably right – she had always been the clever one – and Cecilia was afraid that she was being taken in. She always mistrusted her own judgment; and then, of course, one never knows where one is with foreigners.

Hence the 'two faces' which Anita encountered in dealing with Mrs Crawfurd, and the tense and disconcerting watchfulness with which she felt herself observed by her, especially when Mr Barlow or Tony were present. Hence the little sly and probing insinuations she would occasionally make, as on the morning when she had come downstairs unusually late and had seen Anita and Mr Barlow come in from the garden together, the old gentleman leaning on Anita's arm.

'Ah,' she said with her most glittering smile, 'enjoying a little privacy at last – with the gooseberry out of the way!' And she produced her series of little barking laughs to show that this was meant to be a joke.

'Gooseberry?' Anita asked, not understanding. And Mr Barlow's face had flushed angrily and he didn't speak to Cecilia for the rest of the day.

But in fact Cecilia did not give very much thought to what her father might or might not intend to do about Mrs Seiler. She had very little thought to spare in that direction. For a different situation was unfolding itself before her eyes and engaging all her attention, causing her unlooked-for perplexity and distress. It concerned Tony, the one and only human being in the world whom she loved – who belonged to her – who was her son. She loved him with all the intensity of her starved and frustrated affections; she loved him with a persistence which no coldness on his part could deflect – she loved him helplessly and almost with despair. Nothing he might do or say, however much it might hurt at the moment, would ever convince her that he did not return her love, because she was his mother and it could not be otherwise. She had not seen very much of him since he had gone to his public school. He spent a great deal of his holidays at Milton Place. She did not blame him for that, it was what she wanted for him: this education and this environment, not the cramped and bitter atmosphere of his father's house. She did not wonder that he was aloof, uncommunicative and stubborn when he was at home; how else could he protect himself against his father's stinging remarks? She wished he might show himself more affectionate with her, but she accepted his coolness as the proper conduct of a boy who considers it 'sloppy' to show his feelings even to his mother. She had never had the opportunity of observing him in anyone's company other than her own; she had not imagined that he might be different with other people from how he was with herself. What she now saw of his behaviour towards Mrs Seiler simply filled her with amazement. And yet there was nothing very extraordinary in it, nothing in any way indiscreet; for Anita had never allowed it to be so from the very beginning of their love. She had always impressed upon Tony that endearments in public were in bad taste and particularly impermissible in their own case. There was nothing of that to offend an observing eye. But for the rest, what to Anita seemed the natural and civilised behaviour of a young man towards any woman in whose company he might find himself, appeared astonishing and disturbing to Mrs Crawfurd's bleak and forbidding standards. Here was a Tony she had never known. He had not changed much towards herself, though he was – yes, definitely, he was – a little softer and more gentle, but she had never seen him smile as he smiled for Mrs Seiler. He was quite transformed: he even looked different – more of a man, and so much more sure of himself. And he had such a way with him – and with her. It was difficult to describe or define it, for it consisted in so many little things, each insignificant in itself, but creating, as they accumulated, a very definite and clear-cut impression.

But what struck her most were the small courtesies and attentions he showed this foreign woman which she would have been so happy to receive from him herself, but which he never seemed to think of where she was concerned. One day he searched all over the house and garden for Mrs Seiler's scissors which she said she had mislaid. Another time, when they had come in from a walk in the rain, he made her sit down in the hall and helped her take off her muddy shoes, then went upstairs to fetch her another pair to put on. Time and again she saw him fetch and carry for Mrs Seiler: her garden chair, or her work-basket, or the vases in which she was arranging the flowers – all this as if it were a pleasure to him, not a boring chore. He did it with smiling good humour, while she, Mrs Seiler, seemed to take it all for granted and to accept it as if it were her due with scarcely a word of thanks or a nod.

Cecilia watched and wondered. Anita saw her hungry look follow her son around whenever he was within her sight, weighing all his movements on some inner balance behind her eyes, registering his every change of expression, every inflection of his voice. She kept her own face bland and taut, almost like a mask, with her studied smile fixed on it a little askew, but her lips sometimes trembled and the corners of her eyes puckered as they had done on the day of her arrival, in spite of herself. How well Anita understood now how irksome all this must be to Tony, but she pitied Mrs Crawfurd at the same time from the bottom of her heart.

One evening they were all sitting out on the terrace after dinner. The day had been very close and now, after the sun had gone down, there was a fragrance in the air and a luminosity in the paling sky that lapped the world in the fulfilment of perfect peace. It was getting dark. No one spoke. Anita lay back in her chair looking across the meadows at the evening star as it brightened into clearness above the fading glow on the horizon. Mr Barlow rose to go indoors. It was getting a little chilly.

'I will stay out a little longer,' Anita said, 'it is so very lovely here tonight. But we will join you very soon.'

'I'll fetch you a wrap,' Tony said out of the shadows. 'I just saw you shiver. You're wearing such a thin dress.'

'Thank you, Tony,' and, as he was going towards the house, she called after him: 'And bring one for your mother, too! I'm sure she wants one.'

Tony went.

Suddenly, out of the depths of peace, in the unsuspected, submerged regions of Mrs Crawfurd's subconscious mind something snapped. She became rigid. Her voice rasped as if forced from her throat under terrible pressure.

'How dare you, Mrs Seiler,' she hissed, 'how dare you tell my son what to do for me! How dare you interfere between us! If I want a coat, I can ask him for it myself without your telling him. But you, you make him dance attendance on you, day in day out, as if he had strings like a puppet, for you to pull – and you show him off to me: see, I can make him do as I tell him, even for you! I don't want a coat! I won't have it even if he brings it, and you can tell him so when he comes back!'

Her last words had come out like a stifled sob. She got up, swaying a little as she got to her feet. Alarmed, Anita jumped up to catch her if she should fall, but Mrs Crawfurd waved her away and walked steadily enough towards the house, leaving Anita dumbfounded, uncomprehending, and not a little shaken.

Tony came out with the coats.

'Where's Ma?' he asked.

'Your mother is very nervous tonight,' Anita answered. 'She has gone indoors. I think I'll go and say good night to your grandfather. It really is chilly, even with a coat.'

CHAPTER TWENTY-FIVE

It was a long time before Anita could go to sleep that night. Cecilia's outburst had shocked and surprised her more profoundly than her conscious mind would admit. It had been so entirely unexpected. Lying in bed, she tried to think about it calmly and reasonably, and as she rehearsed to herself, in slow motion as it were, the incident which in fact had taken barely a minute to happen, the more silly and trivial it looked. What could have induced Mrs Crawfurd to speak to her like that, just because she had asked Tony to fetch her a coat? It was inexplicable; unless of course one took into account that Mrs Crawfurd was, at the best of times, in a state of abnormal nervous tension. Anita recalled how often she had seemed to be on the verge of hysteria, with tears welling up in her eyes and her mouth twitching when she had been speaking of the grievances and frustrations of her daily life – trite, superficial little things which really did not warrant so much emotion. Perhaps she needed to complain so bitterly of trivial things in order to cover up the real, deep-lying causes of her unhappiness. Something of the kind must have been at work in her this evening. The weather had been very oppressive, the air charged with the thunder of a storm that refused to break. Mrs Crawfurd must have been on edge all day and probably waiting, unconsciously, for a pretext to lose her temper. So Anita told herself. It was rather unfair, she thought, that *she* should have been the target for her attack, because she had always been so sympathetic and understanding. And as regards Tony – if Mrs Crawfurd only knew how often she had pleaded with him for more patience with his mother, for more kindness to her, and how she had sometimes even made him angry by taking her part. And Tony really had been more gentle, more considerate of her of late, so Anita thought. Of course she did not want any thanks, but she felt that Mrs Crawfurd had at least no cause to reproach her.

When Anita at last succeeded in settling herself to sleep, she had come to the conclusion that she could feel nothing but pity for Mrs Crawfurd and that she must forgive her. The only thing to do was to ignore the whole affair. Under no circumstances would she speak of it to Tony and she would behave as if it had never happened. By now Mrs Crawfurd must surely be sorry that she had been so offensive, and so she, Anita, would make things easy for her next morning by pretending to have forgotten all about it. She would give her no opportunity to apologise or even to refer to it. So she made some pretext for Alice to take up Mrs Crawfurd's early morning tea, so that she should not have to be alone with her before they met casually in the course of the day. Once they had spoken to each other as usual in the presence of others, no mention of the previous evening need be made by either of them.

And that was how, apparently, it was going to be. For Cecilia came downstairs her usual self, took her place at the breakfast table and answered Anita's 'good morning' brightly, repeating it, perhaps rather too emphatically, two or three times. She made no comment on the change of routine in that Alice had brought her tea instead of Anita. So Anita gave an inward sigh of relief and went about her usual occupations. But as the day wore on and the next one came, and the next, she realised that Cecilia had adopted a new 'attitude', a new technique of behaviour towards her which became more and more disconcerting.

She began following Anita about the house. She went with her from bedroom to linen closet and back, trailed after her downstairs to the scullery and still-room, or out into the garden, insisted on helping her to change the sheets, wash the breakfast things, tidy a cupboard, or pick beans in the kitchen garden. It was useless for Anita to say that she could do all these things more quickly, more easily by herself – that Mrs Crawfurd had far better make the most of her holiday by avoiding household chores. Cecilia answered that she was so impressed by Anita's competence that she must study her methods and learn from her all she could while she had the opportunity, and all the time she kept up a steady flow of talk. Even when there was nothing to occupy her hands, she stood around asking innumerable questions as to why Anita did things this way rather than another, accompanying them with ejaculations of surprise or admiration.

There was now scarcely a moment in Anita's day in which she could simply let herself 'live', for Mrs Crawfurd's ever-recurring query: 'What are you going to do next, Mrs Seiler?' infused even her most spontaneous and unplanned occupations with something purposive and programmatic. It robbed her of the repose and contentment with the passing hour which were such an essential part of her nature, and in which Mr Barlow found his comfort and delight. Now, even when she was sitting with him in the garden, under the eyes of Mrs Crawfurd, there was no peace in her, but she must jump up to attend to something which she said she had forgotten, and Mrs Crawfurd invariably followed her with her insistent: 'Can't I help?'

Until this latest development Anita had not felt the strain that emanated from Cecilia's person in her own nerves. She had observed the effect she had on her father and her son, but she had been, as it were, an onlooker and almost immune from the influence. Her ease and detachment had provided a soothing antidote at moments of intense irritation and had often forestalled an impatient shrug or an exasperated retort. But now that Mrs Crawfurd's attention was unremittingly focused upon herself, she, too, fell a victim to the contagion and it worked in her more virulently than in the others as she had not been partly immunised, as they had, by the habit of years.

Outwardly, things went on as usual. But Anita, made self-conscious by Cecilia's unceasing watchfulness, felt as if her own voice was becoming artificial and her gestures mechanical. She moved in a vacuum, the vital current that had flowed between herself, Mr Barlow and Tony had been cut. She saw them both look at her from time to time with anxious, enquiring looks, while she tried to reassure them with a smile – but it seemed to her as if, in the space which they shared, each one of them was alone, encased in a soundproof, vitreous solitude in which they were visible to each other, but unable to communicate. The air between them carried no messages, words were spoken whose shape was seen forming on lips but whose vibrations died away without reaching receptive ears. So they sat at meals in silence or making only desultory remarks, like strangers met by chance at some railway station or airport and forced to share a table. They seemed to speak only out of politeness, while each one was entirely absorbed in waiting; waiting until this suspension of life should be over and they all could be themselves and on their way again. Only Mrs Crawfurd talked, with a metallic tinkle in her voice, emphasising her pointless points and interrupting herself now and again to invite amusement with her little bursts of laughter which sounded like compressed air being forced out of a pump in a series of jerks.

Neither Mr Barlow nor Tony entirely realised what was happening. Mr Barlow saw that Anita was depressed and on edge, and assumed, quite rightly, that Cecilia was getting on her nerves. Poor Cecilia, he thought, had that unfortunate effect on people, as he knew only too well. He accepted that it would be useless to have any serious conversation with Anita while Cecilia hovered around, but Cecilia's stay would eventually come to an end and Anita would remain. Meanwhile he retired into taciturnity.

But Tony was more acutely distressed. Was his mother intentionally monopolising Anita, or was Anita using his mother as a screen in order to avoid being alone with him? For days he had been trying, unsuccessfully, to speak to her in private, and it was becoming absolutely imperative that he should do so. It would be so easy if only she would allow him to come to her room at night, but she would not give him the usual sign which told him that he would be welcome. Instead, when he looked at her enquiringly, she only shook her head. Why was she keeping him at a distance? What had he done to displease her?

At last he succeeded in waylaying her for a moment alone on the stairs. 'What's the matter, Anita?' he asked hurriedly under his breath. 'You're so worried and jumpy. Is Ma getting you down? I told you she would spoil everything for us, and you wouldn't believe me. But why won't you let me come at night? Have I done anything? I must, I really must speak to you. Let me come tonight – if only to talk. . .'

A door opened and shut. Anita looked quickly over her shoulder. It was Sims coming out of the dining room with a tray of glasses.

'Good Lord, Anita! Whatever is the matter with you? You *are* jumpy – not like yourself at all. Say tonight, Anita!'

But she shook her head. 'No, Tony, not yet. You must wait, darling. I'm not sure yet – wait till I tell you.' And she went quickly up the stairs, as Cecilia came out onto the landing.

Of what was she not sure? Of something she was trying to convince herself could only be her imagination, a delusion of her overwrought nerves. Tired out by the strain of the last few days, she had been going up to her room unwontedly early, although the nights were so close. Leaving the curtains open

for more air – she always drew them across the windows when Tony was with her – she fell asleep quickly, but woke again some time in the small hours as if alerted by an unseen presence. Then she lay awake, listening, yet hardly knowing what it was she was listening for. Sometimes she heard it, or thought she heard it, immediately on awakening; sometimes it was a long time coming, and she had nearly gone to sleep again, now almost sure that she had been a prey to hysteria and deeply ashamed of her own imagination. But then – there they were, these faint sounds in the corridor, this almost imperceptible rustling and breathing outside her door. She felt them rather than heard them. It was so very still in the house at that most death-like, life-drained hour before dawn. In the garden the trees were motionless. There was no moon. Somewhere in the distance an owl hooted. It must be her own heartbeat she was hearing. And yet, in her mind's eye, she saw Mrs Crawfurd come creeping along the passage in her flowered dressing gown and the brown felt slippers she kept under her bed, her hair done up in the little metal curlers she had seen on the dressing table. What a distance she would have to feel her way in the dark, from the blue room where she slept, past Mr Barlow's door, across the landing to the wing where her own and Tony's rooms lay! It was really quite impossible. Then why did she not get up and look, and so dispel, once and for all, this ridiculous, humiliating obsession? But instead she pulled the bedclothes over her ears and hid herself in her pillows. She dared not go and open the door – in case it were true! It would be too unspeakably dreadful.

That night, however, she had been asleep only a very short time when she was wakened by a more definite sound. The door handle was turning. She sat up with a start and switched on her bedside lamp. She saw that it was not yet twelve o'clock. Tony's head appeared in the opening door. He came in and closed it softly behind him.

'Sorry to have startled you,' he whispered, 'but I had to come.'

She did not tell him to go away, but turned out the light and moved over to make room for him.

'Darling,' he said, nestling down beside her, 'I'll be as still as a statue and as quiet as a mouse, if that's the way you want it. But I must talk to you. You've been so strange these last few days, I haven't known what to make of it. What was the matter, Anita?'

'Nothing, really. I was sleeping badly and feeling a bit out of sorts.'

'It didn't mean that you don't love me anymore?'

'Silly!' she said, slipping her arm under his head so that it rested against her shoulder. 'Now what is it you so urgently want to talk about?'

Now that he was close to her, in the dark, and she had not repulsed him as he had been half-afraid she would, he relaxed a little with a sigh of relief. But the words that had been jostling and confusing each other in his mind still refused to sort themselves out.

She waited. It was comforting to have him there – not to be alone any more, worrying about her 'obsessions' – his voice, his touch would restore her balance of mind. 'Well, darling?'

At last he took courage to speak. 'Anita,' he said, in a voice as flat and unemotional as he could make it, 'it has come. My call-up, I mean. I am going away.'

'When?'

'The day after tomorrow. To Exeter. I haven't told Grandpa yet – or Ma. I wanted you to know first.'

'Yes, darling.'

'Of course I've known for a long time that it was coming, and so have you. On the whole it seemed rather a good thing. Things were hanging fire a bit, you know. I wanted to move on. And, then, I felt that wherever I went, there'd always be you – to think about, and because of you I could face whatever happened. But then, when you started not speaking to me – and wouldn't have me near you – and I had to go away and not be sure whether you still cared – oh, Anita! –'

He broke off and she felt his shoulder tremble a little against hers.

'Anita,' he went on, 'even if I have to be away for ages – you will still love me?'

'Of course I will.'

'What I mean to say – you won't fall in love with someone else when I'm not there any more?'

She smiled to herself into the darkness. 'No, darling. I don't fall in love so easily. I'm not made that way.'

'But you fell in love with me?'

'I did.'

'Why?'

'You were somebody rather special.'

'Oh, Anita, really?'

'Really.'

He sighed again, more deeply. These last days he had felt so unsure of himself, so naked to the world, so insignificant and alone. Now self-confidence was returning – more than self-confidence. Life was good. There would be problems and difficulties, no doubt, but he would master them. He was a man whom a woman like Anita could love – not just a silly bit of a girl, but a *real* woman – who knew. . . . Emotion surged up into his throat, welled into his eyes: gratitude, and devotion, but not, to his own surprise, the slightest trace of desire.

Anita knew, by his quivering, that he was crying. And now, she told herself wryly as she cradled him gently like a child, I shall have to comfort him because I am going to lose him, for I know that he will never come back to me. No, she thought as she stroked his hair, she wouldn't even want him back. It was the boy who had enchanted her with his mingled awkwardness and grace, his scowls and his laughter; as a boy she had loved him. The mature man he would soon grow up to be, however fine and attractive, would be a stranger and belong to a different world of commitments and responsibilities which she could not even try to share.

So she mused, until he was quiet again. Then, when his sobs had subsided, she spoke to him softly of his life to come, his plans for the future. He told her he hoped to be sent overseas during his service. More than anything else he wanted to travel and see the world. Later, in Cambridge, he would try for a scholarship that would take him, perhaps, to America. For a long time, in whispers, they spoke of these

things in which, he hardly realised, she would have no part, until, entirely relaxed and happy, he fell asleep.

Then she gently withdrew her arm, for it was beginning to ache. She felt drained of all life and emotion, but quite peaceful. Not a thought of the dreaded rustlings and breathings crossed her mind. She kissed him very softly. 'Goodbye, Tony,' she murmured, and she, too, was lost in sleep.

CHAPTER TWENTY-SIX

When Anita awoke it was broad daylight, past eight o'clock. She had never slept as long as this. Tony was gone, but there was still the slight hollow beside her where he had lain. She felt rested, but as the night's conversation came back to her, she was filled with a romantic sadness which brought poetic images to her mind. We were to each other as the morning and evening star, she mused, and they are both the same, and their name is Venus. The idea pleased her and she dwelt on it dreamily for a little while. Then she sighed and returned to realities. She must hurry up, it was getting late; too late to have a bath now. Alice would be wondering why she did not come down to breakfast – and she remembered the chickens she had promised to fetch from the farm before lunch. Anita sat down at her dressing table to brush her hair.

There was a tap on the door. 'Come in!' Anita called. There was Alice, she thought, coming to see whether there was anything the matter.

But it was not Alice. Cecilia was standing in the doorway. She was fully dressed, her hair put up in its customary net with the elastic edge which made it appear all of a piece, like a wig.

But in spite of this she looked dishevelled, as if she had thrown on her clothes anyhow or had slept in them. Her face, always of a greyish colour, was haggard, her mouth trembled a little and one could see her jaw muscles working as she tried to keep control of it. Anita saw her first in the looking-glass and was shocked by her appearance. She turned round quickly.

'Mrs Crawfurd, what is the matter? Are you ill?' She rose and went towards her.

Cecilia had closed the door and was leaning against it. 'Don't touch me!' Cecilia hissed, 'You – you – Jezebel!'

Anita thought in a flash, 'The poor woman is now quite out of her mind!' 'What is Jezebel?' she asked lamely. Her Catholic upbringing had not made her readily familiar with allusions to the Old Testament.

Mrs Crawfurd did not enlighten her, but Anita soon understood what she had meant. 'I saw my son come out of your room in the early hours of this morning,' she stated, 'in his pyjamas and with bare feet.' It sounded as if this attire, or the lack of it, constituted the greatest enormity.

'Yes,' Anita said, now quite collected as she saw what she would have to deal with, 'yes, I suppose you did. You have been watching to see him for several nights past, haven't you? I really can't understand why.'

'Why? You dare to ask why?' Cecilia almost shrieked, 'You abandoned, immoral creature, you wicked seductress!' She glared at Anita. Her voice shook. But her indignation gave her courage to continue. 'A scarlet woman!' she exclaimed, 'I never thought I should meet one face to face in all my life – and here I find one, in flesh and blood, under my own father's roof! And her victim my own darling boy, my precious innocent child! Oh, the abomination of it!'

She is mad, Anita thought with dismay – she is quite mad! 'Mrs Crawfurd,' she said gently, taking a careful step nearer, 'please calm yourself, please sit down.'

'No!' Cecilia cried, drawing herself up, 'No, I prefer to stand.' She had not exhausted her invectives, and you cannot very well hurl invectives sitting down.

'You plotter,' she went on, 'you disgraceful underhand schemer, with your fair face and your winning ways. Emily warned me against you, but even she did not fathom the depths of your wickedness. She did not see that you were trying to corrupt my boy. Poor lamb, not out of school yet and a prey to your wiles.'

Anita was now beginning to get angry at all this farrago. Cecilia was pitiable and probably more than half-crazy, but such disgusting nonsense was not to be borne. She went up to her, took her firmly by the arm, though Cecilia recoiled, and almost pushed her down into a deep armchair. Then Anita stood over her.

'Now listen, Mrs Crawfurd,' she said, 'all these last days and nights you've been working yourself up into a kind of frenzy about Tony's relationship with me, pursuing me all day to prevent him speaking to me, and spying on me at night to find out whether he came to me. Though why, as his mother, you should be so jealous of his having a lover, I simply can't understand. Don't you realise that though he is young, he is a fully grown man. Innocent child indeed! What you are saying is quite ridiculous. If he is old enough to go into the army, he is old enough to love. Why, you ought to be grateful that I have allowed him to love *me* – that he has had his first experience, not in some back alley, in sordid surroundings, exposed to danger and disillusionment, but with a woman who really cares for him and demands nothing from him in return. If I were his mother, I know I should bless that woman and not revile her. So, for goodness sake, be sensible – and civilised!'

Cecilia covered her face with her hands. Her shoulders heaved. She had been sustained by her anger and had expected Anita to wilt and collapse in the fiery breath of her accusation – to founder in shame. But there she was, standing over her, bold and cool and collected, with not a word of contrition, but telling her to be *grateful* for the seduction of her son, and to be – of all things! – civilised!! What a dreadful word. To be civilised evidently meant to condone immorality. How could she deal with a woman who said things like that? Such a one was quite beyond her experience and understanding. What should she do now? What should she say? 'Oh,' she moaned in despair, 'if only Emily were here! Emily would know how to speak to you. *She* was always the clever one, and she knows the ways of the world. Why did she leave it to me?'

'Leave *what* to you, Mrs Crawfurd? What has all this got to do with Mrs Mannering?'

But Cecilia went on rocking herself and gave no direct answer. 'Oh yes, she warned me about you, Emily did. She saw through you from the first. But even she did not know all the wickedness that is in you. She did not know about Tony. Or she would have told me. She only saw what you were doing to Father. And even that at first I couldn't believe. Because I liked you – I actually liked you! You got round me, too, poor silly me, you're so competent and so clever. How you cosseted and pampered me! Flowers in my room, early tea in the morning – you even pretended to admire my knitting. You very nearly had me under your thumb. If I hadn't found out how you were carrying on with Tony, I should have been as helpless in your hands as poor Father.'

'Mrs Crawfurd!' Anita exclaimed, 'Whatever do you mean?'

'Oh, don't pretend you don't understand, Mrs Seiler,' Cecilia said, drawing herself up and looking at Anita with glazed, unwinking eyes, as if determined now to stare her out of countenance. 'You can't deceive me any more now. You know you've been making up to him for months, petting him and flattering him, making him so infatuated with you, old as he is, till he can think of no one but you. His family doesn't matter to him any more. It's "Anita, my dear" this, and Anita that! No doubt you'll get him to make a nice comfortable settlement for you, if he hasn't already done so. Anybody can see that that's what you're after. You're that kind of woman. Just look at yourself!' she went on, surveying Anita from head to foot, 'Look at yourself, with your hair about your shoulders and nothing on but a wisp of a wrap! I suppose that's how you exercise your charms on an old man for his money, and at the same time on a mere boy to gratify your evil passions.'

Anita was speechless. She drew back from Cecilia's chair, clasping her arms over her breasts as if to shield herself from physical contamination. How utterly loathsome this was! A wave of disgust surged up within her. Feeling her way backwards towards her dressing table, she sank onto her chair and closed her eyes, overcome by nausea. For an instant she had a vision of a distorting mirror being held up to her face in which she saw a nightmare reflection of herself as depicted by Cecilia, in which every fair and familiar feature was twisted and distended to a horrible grimace: covetous eyes, lustful lips, a prying nose. . . 'Oh no!' she murmured, 'Oh no!'

Then she opened her eyes again and saw her attacker slumped in her chair, grey in the face, wrinkled and sagging, looking like nothing so much as a pricked balloon of which there only remains the shrivelled, colourless skin. Cecilia had had her victory, she had seen Anita cowed, but there was no triumph in her and no more venom. For a moment they looked at each other in silence.

Anita was the first to regain a measure of composure. She rose, went to the door and opened it. Cecilia got up as if she had been ordered to do so.

'When my sister comes back. . .' she began, but Anita interrupted her.

'Mrs Crawfurd,' she said quietly, 'you have said enough. Will you please go away now and allow me to get dressed.'

And Cecilia slunk out of the room.

When she had gone, Anita returned to the dressing table and remained seated there, she did not know for how long – it might have been an hour or only a few minutes. Now that she was alone, the full impact of the shock she had received made itself felt and it stunned her. She was, as it were, projected out of time. Not only her mind, but every vital organ and function of her body seemed to have stood still. Then these automatically picked up again, consciousness returned and with it the knowledge that something irrevocable had happened and that everything had changed. Slowly she looked round the room. There was the big carved wardrobe against the wall, the deep armchairs in their flowered chintz covers, behind her the unmade bed. Ten minutes ago they had had the unquestioned permanence and reliability of old friends, now the trust had been broken, there would never be the same confidence between them again.

Deliberately, with precise, self-conscious movements, as if special care were required for each one of them, she began to dress, pondering meanwhile what Cecilia had been saying. She was quite sure that the allegations of mercenary designs on Mr Barlow's fortune had not been Cecilia's idea, but Emily's. Cecilia herself had said so. Coming from Mrs Mannering, the accusation was not less false and offensive, but on the whole not surprising. She must know, of course, that Mr Barlow had been giving her pocket-money – he refused to call it a salary – generously, if not excessively, for she had been buying clothes and even saving a little – for her eventual journey home. But, then, Emily had always disliked her presence at Milton Place, and she would have left long ago if Mr Barlow had not told her very clearly that he did not take Emily's objections seriously and had advised her to do the same. It was the disastrous fusion of Emily's worldly suspicions about money with Cecilia's morbid fantasies which

made it all so particularly revolting. What a horrid brew the two sisters would concoct once they got together, and then they would attempt to serve it up to their father – for his good, as they would assure him. Once more she was overcome by disgust, not for her own sake now, but for his. She was sure he would not believe them, but he would be shocked and upset, there would be a quarrel, and a scandal. No, that must not be allowed to happen. For nothing in the world would she repay all his kindness to her, all the happiness she had enjoyed at Milton Place, by becoming a cause of trouble and discussion between him and his family. More than anything else he wanted, he needed peace – peace of mind and peaceful days, and to ensure that this was not taken from him she must go, go quickly, before the storm broke, before he became involved, on her account, in such ugly scenes as the one she had just had to endure.

By now it was ten o'clock and breakfast would long have been cleared away. She could not have eaten any, had it still been waiting. She went down to the kitchen for a basket in which to carry the chickens she was going to fetch from the farm. She found the kettle boiling and Alice all prepared to make her some fresh tea. She must, Alice said, at least have a cup of tea before she went out. She looked as if she needed it. Was her headache very bad, Alice asked, obviously fishing for information, and when Anita shook her head, 'We're all of us at sixes and sevens today,' she went on, 'it's on account of its being Mr Tony's last day, I suppose. Mrs Crawfurd's upset too. She was not in her room when I went up to her this morning – got up early and went to Mr Tony's room, I expect. Later, when she came downstairs, she was looking all queer-like, and she hardly touched her breakfast.'

Anita drank her tea and said nothing, while Alice pottered around, pretending to be busy. How much had she heard, Anita wondered, what did she know? It would be only natural that she should be on Cecilia's side if she sensed a quarrel, though she had always been very friendly. She was friendly still.

'There's no call, really, for you to go after those chickens,' she said when Anita had thanked her for the tea. 'It's raining hard and Nichols can very well send the boy on a bicycle for them. You don't want to get yourself all wet when you're feeling a bit poorly.'

But Anita said she would be glad of the walk, it would do her head good and she didn't mind the rain. In a mackintosh, with a scarf on her head, she set forth. There was no danger any more of Cecilia enforcing her company on her.

What a relief it was to be out of doors, and alone! The rain fell with a soft, insistent patter on the broad summer leaves of the limes and beeches, collected on them in tiny pools and then splashed down in sudden small cascades. Outside the gates, in the open country, the rain hung like a flimsy veil between the sky and the fields. The wheat and the barley had been harvested. In the distance a wide expanse of some root-crop, potatoes or turnips, clothed a gentle slope of rising land with green. Anita walked along narrow tracks at the edge of fields, skirting hedges, and unlatching and refastening gates as she went. The air smelled very sweet and the rain ran down her face like cool, unwept tears, gentle and pure, without the

302

salt of anguish. By the time she got back to Milton Place with the chickens, she was cleansed.

Luncheon was much easier and more relaxed than one might have supposed. Encountering Cecilia again across the table, Anita realised that the spell of embarrassment and self-consciousness she had cast upon her was now completely exorcised. There was not the slightest emanation coming from her. She might have been a mechanical doll. Anita found herself looking at her unperturbed, with a kind of clinical curiosity. Cecilia avoided her eyes and was silent.

It was Mr Barlow and Tony who talked, chiefly about the different places overseas to which Tony might be sent. Mr Barlow had known them all in his day and described them with many minute details, only to add, ruefully, at the end that they had probably changed out of all recognition since he had been there.

At the end of the meal Anita announced that she was going into Waterington by bus. Tony at once asked to accompany her, but Anita very firmly refused. 'Surely, Tony, on this last afternoon you must stay with your mother,' she said with intentional primness, as if speaking to a child. Tony grinned. And Anita turned to Mrs Crawfurd with a smile and a look that implied: You see, I can still make him do as I tell him.

Before she went out she wrote a short note to her daughter, telling her she was coming home, and in Waterington she went to a travel agent to enquire about boats and trains to the Continent.

CHAPTER TWENTY-SEVEN

Tony left on the following morning and his mother drove with him to the station. Now Anita was alone in the house with Mr Barlow and the moment had come when she must pluck up her courage and tell him that she was going away. It was a sad task she had to perform, because she knew he would be puzzled and distressed at what must seem to him her sudden and unexpected decision to leave him. She felt she had become part of his daily surroundings, of his habit of life, which her going would disrupt and unsettle – and that he hated disruption and change. How she wished she could have stayed with him a little longer, through the winter at least, or perhaps until some other gradual changes occurred which would make the parting seem less abrupt and more in the nature of things than the outcome of a wilful decision. She had to remind herself forcibly what very distressing and sordid scenes were inevitably in store for him if she remained, scenes that would really upset him and strain his relationship with his daughters – or even cloud his kindly feelings for herself –, so that she must at all costs abide by her determination to leave.

She allowed him a little time to recollect himself after saying goodbye to Tony and then, with a heavy heart, she tapped on the study door and went in. He was sitting at his desk in the window, with *The Times* open before him, but he seemed rather to be lost in thought or in dreams than intent on his paper. She went and sat down in the low chair next to his writing table, drawing up her knees and encircling them with her arms as she had done many times before. In this position she could look up into his face which, from this angle, she had always thought particularly beautiful. In the same instant it occurred to her that it would have been better if she had remained standing, for the smile and the look of pleasure he now gave her when he saw her installed so securely at his side, almost shattered her resolution, as did his first words.

'Ah, my dear, how good it is to see you sitting there again at last,' he said. 'How I have longed for this moment! We have had some very trying weeks, you even more than myself, for I have been able to take refuge in here. I know how terribly tiresome poor Cecilia has been for you – and you have been so kind and patient with her – I cannot thank you enough. But she will not be here much longer. She insists that she must wait for Emily's return – says it is her duty to be here when Emily is away, and really, poor soul, I haven't the heart to tell her I don't want her. She's treated too often as being unwanted by that husband of hers – and, unfortunately, by the boy also – without any contribution of that kind from me. And so we have had to bear with her. But it won't be for much longer. Emily returns next week, and then she will be going.'

Anita had intertwined her fingers which were clasping her knees. She tightened her grip till the knuckles showed white and fixed her eyes on them. It was a gesture she resorted to when she was troubled. She did not want to see the smile fade from his face.

'Mr Barlow,' she said, not much above a whisper, 'I have something I must say to you. I, too, will be going away from here.'

He heard her, but he did not answer immediately. This was his moment. He had not foreseen it would be so soon but she was giving him his opportunity, and he must seize it. It must be *now*. For an instant his heart fluttered. Then it settled down to its quiet, determined beat. He felt quite calm. She was afraid he had not heard and was preparing herself to repeat what she had said, when he spoke lightly: 'Are you going to tell me that your visa has once more run out?'

She looked up. His face had not clouded. He was still smiling. Was he going to make it easy, after all?

'Yes,' she said, 'you know how it is. It's been twice renewed already, and the last time I was told that it couldn't be extended again. I've just been looking at it. I'm afraid my time's up at last.'

'And so you think you are going to be turned out? Well, well. I admit I now live rather remote from all the tangles of red tape with which officialdom seeks to complicate our lives, but this is a contingency I had foreseen. I wrote a little while ago to my solicitors about this, telling them I needed a little more time to make arrangements. I have heard from them that the necessary time will be made available.'

She sighed. It *was* going to be difficult, as she had feared it would. Seeing her downcast, he, too, was just a little disappointed. He had hoped for some spontaneous sign of pleasure.

'Do you remember,' he went on, as no such sign was forthcoming, 'do you remember sitting there in that chair, very soon after you had come here, and telling me, as you are telling me now, that you would have to go away? Fortunately, I was able to persuade you then that that was not necessary. I made a suggestion which you generously accepted.'

That almost made her laugh. 'That is putting things upside down, isn't it, Mr Barlow? It was you who were generous. I was so near breaking-point at that time that I had to run upstairs and cry. I don't think I ever told you that – but I shall never cease being grateful. But things are different now. I've been here a long time, and I mustn't expect that you'll keep me here for ever – even if you try to make – other arrangements. That's not the question any more. It's serious now, Mr Barlow.'

She used the word 'serious' in the sense and with the connotations it carries in German, meaning 'real, inescapable'. These overtones were lost on Mr Barlow. But he seized eagerly on the word as on a fitting opening for what he had to say to her.

'It is indeed serious, my dear, very serious, and I want you to give me all your attention. Will you listen to me patiently, please, and not interrupt before I have finished?'

'Of course I will listen to you, Mr Barlow, if you insist. But before you begin, let me beg you, both for your sake and mine, not to say anything at all. Don't let us discuss *any* arrangements. It would be no use. I should still have to go. Don't make me go into reasons and details. Explanations are always tedious and unprofitable, and in the end nothing is changed by them. And you know, once one starts explaining, one is so easily led into saying things one never meant to say and doesn't really mean. Please – let us just take it that this parting is sad for both of us, and leave it at that.'

For a moment she had thought of bringing in her daughter as an excuse – saying she needed her and had written urging her to come back. But nothing could have been further from the truth. Erica, ensconced with her husband in her mother's flat, was going to be dismayed rather than pleased at her return. No, however hard Mr Barlow might press her, she would not put him off with a lie. Besides, those clear blue eyes which were now searching her face would see through it at once, and then she would feel so ashamed.

'Anita, my dear, I don't think it is necessary for you to explain anything,' he now said, very gently. 'I believe I know what is in your mind better, perhaps, or at any rate more clearly than you know yourself. For it is a matter to which I have given much thought. You feel that you cannot remain here indefinitely in the position in which you find yourself. It is not only this wretched visa which stamps it as impermanent and insecure. That is but the outward sign of a situation which you feel to be ambigious and which is therefore distressing to you. You have, perhaps, been trying to suppress this feeling – you may never have put it into words – but I have noticed that you have often been irked by it – and by little things which have reminded you, or caused you to remind yourself, that you are here only on sufferance. Such a situation is contrary to your nature and it is not fitting that you should continue in it. I am not surprised that you feel compelled to put an end to it – and that is why you say you must go away. I understand it very well, there is no need for you to explain yourself any further.'

'Yes,' she said slowly, clutching at this helpful suggestion but rather doubtful whether it would carry her to safety, 'yes, perhaps there is something in what you say, though I did not quite know it. But, please, do not try to get me a permanent permit of employment, please don't do that. It would really make no difference.'

'No, that is not what I mean. Anita,' he said earnestly, leaning a little towards her in order to look more closely into her face, 'Anita, please look at me. I don't think you quite understand in what high esteem – in what tender affection I hold you. If I were a younger man – if I did not fear to sound a little ridiculous at my time of life – I should say – that I love you!'

'Oh!' she answered spontaneously, 'But I love you too, Mr Barlow, I love you with all my heart, and whatever happens, I shall always love you!'

Her impetuous response disconcerted rather than reassured him. It accentuated her youth; it underlined his age. She would not have been so uninhibited, he thought, had he been nearer to her own. But he was determined to persevere.

'I am not asking for love, Anita,' he said, 'I am only asking for forbearance, such as you have already shown me these past months and which I beg you to continue. You do not know, perhaps, how much your being here, at my side, in my house, means to me. What it means to me to see you, and to hear your voice, every day. To know that tomorrow, and the next day, and the next, I shall see you and hear you again. It is a kind of happiness, Anita, an exquisite happiness I have never known at any time of my life which has been a long one. It is a happiness which, though vouchsafed very late, I am still able to enjoy. Do you understand that I would do anything – anything within my power – not to let it escape me?'

His tone was so earnest, almost passionate, that it frightened her. He had always been so calm, so detached. She had never heard him speak like this before.

'If only I *could* stay with you, Mr Barlow,' she murmured, 'if only I could – but it is impossible.'

'Don't say it is impossible, dearest, until you have heard me out. I said I would do anything within my power – though I realise that it is little enough compared with what I am asking of you – but at least your position here would be assured beyond any doubt or question, and you would have some measure of security even after I am gone – if you would consent, Anita, to stay with me – as my wife?'

The silence that fell between them when he had finished speaking was so profound and so protracted that they both found themselves listening to the light wind that was stirring the leaves outside the open window and to the voice of a single bird repeating its call in the dark depths of the great cedar.

At last Mr Barlow stretched out his hand towards her. 'Don't answer at once,' he said softly. 'Perhaps you had better leave me now – and think about it – alone. If I have shocked you – take time – I will wait.'

But Anita slipped down off her chair onto her knees and taking Mr Barlow's thin, translucent hand on which the blue veins made a tracery under the silken skin, she kissed it, no longer restraining her tears. He was very moved, but also much embarrassed.

'Please, Anita, please,' he said, half-rising to help her to her feet. She lifted herself back onto her chair and began searching in both her sleeves for a handkerchief she usually carried there, but could not find it. He drew one out of his breast pocket and offered it to her with a smile. The little paternal gesture helped to ease the tension. She tried to smile through her tears.

'I never knew you cared as much as that,' she said at last when she had blown her nose. 'I am so profoundly touched – and so highly honoured.' And then, as she remembered how Cecilia had accused her only two days ago, the irony of the situation convulsed her. She pressed the handkerchief to her mouth to stifle a hysterical laugh – or sob, she did not know which it was going to be.

He looked at her with some alarm. 'Anita, dearest – what is the matter? Surely you are not laughing at me?'

'No, no, no, not at you,' she gasped. 'I was only thinking what Mrs Mannering would say if she knew you had offered to *marry* me!'

'She will have to know in time.'

Anita gradually regained her self-control. 'I shall now have to tell you something,' she said with some hesitation, 'that I would rather not have spoken about at all. You see, it seems that Mrs Mannering has been very anxious for some time past because she imagines I have been trying to insinuate myself into your good graces in order to persuade you to – to do me a favour – in plain words: to put me into your will. She thinks I am a "legacy-crawler" – as we say. . .'

'Emily said that to you?'

'No, she did not say it to me. She must have told her sister, and Mrs Crawfurd let it slip out – and I could see that she believed it also. I never, never meant to injure your daughters' interests in any way! But what you have just offered me – to be your wife – it would be far worse for them than anything Mrs Mannering has been fearing. She would never believe you had acted of your own free will – but would say I had enticed you and taken advantage of you – by all kinds of wicked devices! Other people would probably say the same.'

Mr Barlow's face had darkened as she spoke. 'Don't say such things to me, Anita,' he said, with anger in his voice. 'Unless you, too, think that I can be driven, or hoodwinked, to doing things against my will. I know Emily thinks I am in my dotage and incapable of managing my own affairs. But you know me better than that. I can assure you that my proposal was not made on the spur of the moment, but after long and careful consideration of everything involved. Of course my daughters will be aggrieved if I re-marry so late in life, and Emily, in particular, will be very angry. Is that going to upset you? Do you care about her opinion more than you care about my happiness? Just now you had the kindness to say that you were – attached to me. Would you refuse to grant me my dearest wish because it would interfere with Emily's expectations? I feel no obligation to sacrifice my remaining years to her greater comfort. Neither she nor Cecilia really care for me and they would bury me tomorrow with nothing more than a few conventional tears. And you do not know everything. Let me tell you that my daughter Emily is planning to turn me out of Milton Place – trying to force me to sell it, because she begrudges me the upkeep of it and of the life I live here. She would have me drag out my days in some poky little flat in the town where she can more easily keep me under her control. And she calls it "looking after me"! But I will not be dictated to – by anyone. As long as I live I intend to be my own master and make my own decisions, and Emily will have to abide by them. If she does not care to come to Milton Place when you are mistress here, I shall be able to bear it – and so, I hope, will you!'

He paused, but still she did not answer him. Her eyes were fixed intently on the carpet under her feet as if she were seeing it for the first time, and for the first time she noticed a slight irregularity in its pattern – a thin red rim that encircled three of its blue convolutions and was missing round the others. She felt a sudden, almost irresistible urge to draw Mr Barlow's attention to this irrelevant detail; a defensive reflex to stem or deflect the swift-running current of passion she had inadvertently released. But her impulse wilted as his power swept over her, bending her to his purpose. At this moment she dared not trifle with him. Thus must he, at the height of his manhood, have bent lesser wills to comply with his designs. She had not suspected this determination behind the gentleness, the tolerance and the detachment she had always known in him.

Almost in tears again, she could only bend her head. In fact, as he looked at her, so visibly drooping under his rebuke, his surge of anger against Emily was already ebbing away. Tenderness and compassion for the woman before him were returning.

'Anita,' he now said in a more gentle voice, more like the one she was accustomed to hear from him, 'I understand your difficulties and your scruples. They are entirely to your honour. But let me reassure you. Neither of my daughters will suffer any hardship on your account, nor will you, I am sorry to say, be rich after my death, for I cannot leave you a large income. But Emily is very well provided for both by her husband and by the money that came to her – and to Cecilia – on their mother's death – and she has no children. She will, of course, have rather less than she expected and that she will resent, but she will not have to deprive herself of anything she has been accustomed to. As for Cecilia, her personal requirements are modest, and she, too, has her mother's inheritance. There is only one person in the world who really matters to Cecilia: Tony. And I shall assure her, quite truthfully, that whatever I do, Tony's future will not be affected in any way. I have long ago established a trust for him, and nothing concerning him shall be changed. His trustees will be able to see him through his university years and any professional training he may choose. The capital of the trust will be at his disposal when he is a little older and has begun to make his way in life – as I had to myself – and the residue of my estate will also ultimately be his. I'm sure you would wish it to be so. If you like you shall see my solicitors and they shall explain it all to you, in figures, independently of myself – if that will set your mind at rest. What I have been telling you may not be clear to you all at once, but give yourself time, dear, to think about it, and you will see that I am right.'

But Anita had hardly been listening to Mr Barlow's financial disquisitions. These money-matters might have been important if they had really been at the root of her difficulties. But to her, struggling desperately with a far deeper, far more personal problem, they hardly seemed to touch its fringe. For she was having to decide, and decide immediately in this very present, agonising moment, what were, in truth, the responsibilities of the heart. She could *not* give herself time to think. To postpone would be to deceive.

'Mr Barlow,' she said slowly, twisting and untwisting her fingers, as she fought with herself for the fateful words, 'you are very kind and generous, but it is not just the money – there are – the persons – I mean, what they would think, and feel, about it.'

'Look,' he said, 'if you are worried about the angry words I said just now about Emily, I am sorry. She does, at times, annoy me almost beyond endurance when she tries to manage *me*, as well as the rest of the world. But I assure you, I have no real animosity against her. I don't find her very lovable, but she has many excellent qualities, and she is not vindictive, even when she is thwarted. She will, in the end, accept what she cannot alter, and she will come, after a while, to forgive both you and me. Cecilia will certainly not quarrel with me. And Tony –'

She interrupted him. 'It's Tony, Mr Barlow – it's because of Tony that I can't accept.'

'But he is quite devoted to you! Surely you do not think that *he* would object!'

Then Anita took a deep breath and looked Mr Barlow straight in the face. 'I am so very, very sorry to disappoint you,' she said, 'I would have stayed with you, indefinitely, if that were possible, without being your wife. But as things have been between Tony and myself, I could never be that. I could never be Tony's – grandmother!'

Her mouth made an involuntary grimace as she forced herself to say the absurd-sounding word, and the blood mounted to her cheeks, suffusing her entirely.

'Anita!' Mr Barlow exclaimed, 'What do you mean? Are you telling me that you and Tony – have been lovers?'

She nodded silently.

Mr Barlow let himself sink back in his chair. 'I see,' he said slowly. 'I see.' And then, after a while, 'Fortunate Tony. I must really be getting very foolish ever to have imagined that I – and blind not to have seen what was happening under my very eyes. But I suppose Cecilia saw?'

'Yes, she saw.'

'She is not a broad-minded woman.'

'Can *you* forgive me, Mr Barlow?'

'My poor child,' he said, 'there is nothing for me to forgive.'

Then Anita rose and, without looking back, went quickly out of the room.

Anita left Milton Place a few days later, on the eve of Mrs Mannering's return from Scotland. She was going to catch the four o'clock boat-train from Victoria, and that meant an early luncheon so that she could get up to London in good time. She and Mr Barlow sat silently throughout the meal, but Cecilia seemed singularly at her ease, saying how much she envied Anita for going abroad – 'only that for you it isn't abroad, of course' – a remark she affected to find very funny and which she accompanied by her very special laugh.

Anita's suitcases were aligned in the hall. They were the same old battered ones she had brought with her, only that they now contained the new clothes she had acquired in the course of her stay. Alice had brought down her coat and gloves.

When they were leaving the dining room, Mr Barlow asked Anita to come into his study. He gave her a ring that had belonged to his mother – a large ruby encircled with pearls in a heavy gold setting. It fitted her finger. He kissed her on the forehead and said he preferred not to come out to see her off.

To Cecilia, she had already said goodbye.

Nichols was to drive her to the station. Sims, Mrs Nichols and Alice were waiting for her in the hall. She shook hands warmly with Sims and Mrs Nichols, and she kissed Alice who was crying profusely. Then she looked once more into her handbag to make sure everything necessary was there. She had a first-class through ticket to Vienna, with a sleeper, on which Mr Barlow had insisted, and the five pounds one was allowed to take out of the country. As she stood on the steps waiting to get into the car, she heard a door open behind her and looked round. It was not the study door, but that of the yellow room. Cecilia was verifying her departure.

Mr Barlow sat in his green leather chair at his writing table and strained his ears to catch the sound of Nichols engaging the gears of the old car, and of the swish of the tyres on the gravel. After that all was still.

It was noon. The sun stood high behind a thin film of cloud, giving a diffuse and muted light. There were scarlet dahlias and purple asters in the flower beds. Their colour, and that of the trees and the lawn, was flat, without highlights or shadows. There was no wind. Just stillness. Mr Barlow sat and listened to it. He heard it seep slowly through the big house, permeating one room after another: the big drawing room, the yellow 'afternoon room', the hall and the well of the staircase. It crept down all the corridors. It seemed to solidify and become almost tangible, an invisible but glutinous substance that filled all space and made it impossible to breathe. Soon it would seep into the study.

Mr Barlow's heart gave a little flutter of fear. That subsided. He leaned forward across the table and drew a sheet of writing-paper from the stand in front of him. For a long time he gazed at the black letterhead embossed on the thick, pal e-grey paper – Milton Place, Sussex. He moved a fingertip gently over the raised surface in a kind of loving caress. Then he took up a pen and wrote:–

'Dear Mr Peacock,

For your information, my solicitors are Messrs Thornton, Thornton and Blake, of 3 A, Clements Inn.'

He paused. Then he dated and signed it.

AFTERWORD

Milton Place was written in the late 1960s but would remain unpublished for more than fifty years. This is the story, a serendipitous one, of how it, and *The Exiles Return*, Persephone Book No. 102, came to be published.

In 2011 my sister, the art critic Marina Vaizey, told me that her friend Edmund de Waal was coming to California on a book tour for *The Hare with Amber Eyes* and I arranged for him to give a talk at Stanford University. I knew the literary executor for Eric Voegelin, Paul Caringella, and he, it turned out, had been a close friend of Elisabeth de Waal, Edmund's grandmother. Born in Germany in 1901, Voegelin was educated in Vienna and had been a professor of politics in the Faculty of Law at the University, becoming a very prominent political philosopher. Although not Jewish, and more a philosopher of the right than of the left, he had written books highly critical of Nazi racial policies. So, after the Anschluss, he came to the United States, where he had a distinguished academic career; his final position was at the Hoover Institution at Stanford University and his papers are in its archives.

Paul told me that there were quite a few letters there from Elisabeth to him. He also told me that he had in his possession, because of his connection with Voegelin, an untitled novel by Elisabeth in English that he thought was very good. He very kindly allowed me to read it and I agreed with him. That novel was *Milton Place* (but at the time it had no title).

After Edmund's talk at Stanford, he, Paul and I walked over to the Hoover where Edmund saw the letters from his grandmother, although he obviously didn't have time to read them. I mentioned to him that I had read his grandmother's novel and that both Paul and I thought it should be published, even though she had been unsuccessful in her attempt to publish it years before; and that Persephone Books in London would be the perfect publisher, particularly as it specialised in fiction by women.

Later on, Edmund wrote and told me that indeed Persephone would be publishing the book and I would be sent a copy. Imagine my astonishment that when I received the novel: it was a totally different one, not *Milton Place* but *The Exiles Return*! Of course this too is a novel supremely worth publishing, as has been demonstrated by its success; and now it is deeply satisfying that this other novel should be available as well.

I believe I understand how this substitution took place. For whatever reason, as far as I know, Elisabeth had not given either novel a title. Edmund and I did not have time to talk about the book I had read, which took place in England, not in Vienna. In *The Hare with Amber Eyes* Edmund mentions that there might be three novels in English and two in German, (although I only know of the two in English and the one in German mentioned by Elisabeth in a letter). In his book Edmund writes quite a bit about the untitled Vienna novel; it was natural that this was the book he thought I meant as it was the one he knew best.

When, some years later, I met Nicola Beauman of Persephone Books I told her the story of the two novels. She was lent a copy of the as yet unnamed *Milton Place* by Elisabeth's son Victor and he agreed that it should be published. And so, not only is *The Exiles Return* in print, we now have the novel that is to be found within the pages of this book too.

Where does this second (but in fact the first) novel fit in Elisabeth's writing career? To a degree that story is to be found in the letters she wrote to Voegelin over the years and also in Edmund's book. As he relates, and as her son Victor de Waal writes in his Preface to this book, she always had strong literary interests and read widely. Her early letters to Voegelin were in German but after November 1939 most were in English, which she knew perfectly from her childhood. (It was quite common among German-speaking refugees, perhaps as a reaction to the countries that had treated them so harshly, to write to one another in English.)

On 1st December 1940 Elisabeth wrote to Voegelin about her writing. She had embarked upon a project of a primer of politics for children, sparked by the questions her sons, then aged 9 and 11, were asking her. 'I have also been doing quite a bit of writing recently, and to my great joy, even poetry has again become accessible. I am sending you three sonnets which are of a group dealing with my spiritual autobiography. My book for youngsters is progressing also. I don't want to submit samples for publication until the bulk of it is finished, and I still have a good way to go.' We do not know if Elisabeth finished the project; but in any case the book was never published.

Later on she worked on her English novel and in late 1967 she sent this to Voegelin for his opinion. In a letter to her on 31st December he tells her how much he likes it.

I have read it in one day, because I could not stop. That is perhaps not the most important point, but certainly not unimportant, because it shows the novel is interesting. Then I was struck by the splendid organization. . . . I admire the careful construction, the introduction of the themes (in the musical sense), their counterpoint and the inevitability of the end. . . . Then I am full of admiration about the degree to which you have lived into the English landscape and town society. The description of the 'grounds', the vocabulary covering plants and gardening, is impressive. . . . And the brief idiomatic characterization of the various types (the old gentleman, the two daughters, the neighbouring lady, etc) is as competent as it is amazing. And finally, the substance. Your sense of presence – the presence that must be gained from a life of planning into the future, that must be captured from activism, before it is too late and there is no presence left. This sense of presence, if I understand you rightly, you find represented in the style of your Mr Barlow – a style that is on the point of being submerged by the new social forces without

direction. In brief, you are in love with England – the England that is dying. In sum, this novel is a fine piece of work.

In reply, on 20th February 1968, she wrote:

You are the *first* and *only* person who has understood what I was really trying to say when I wrote it. There are perhaps a dozen people who have read it; most have found that they "couldn't stop" which is gratifying, because it attests that it isn't dull, but to me the story was only secondary. Some have read it as "light romance" and suggested a woman's magazine, some have said it was "well-written" as to style, and one or two "didn't care for that kind of book". Evidently the three publishers whom I tried were of that opinion, as they sent it back without comment. After that I gave up, as I thought that what I had *really* intended hadn't come through. But if *you* could see it immediately and put it into so many words, as you have done, then it has come through, and that is the most encouraging thing that has happened to me for years! Compared to this, the fact whether at any time any publisher will accept it, is of relatively little importance to me. You have seen the musical construction. (I have wanted to call it 'Trio for Strings' or 'Three-part Setting') and you have felt what you call 'presence', the essence of life embodied in old Mr Barlow, in Anita and even in Tony – and doomed to be engulfed in the "polypragmosyne" [officiousness] of modern society and the welfare-state.

Elisabeth had an abiding admiration for the English and for their conviction and determination during the war that they would eventually triumph, despite appearances to the contrary. *Milton Place* is in many ways a testimony to that indomitable spirit, even though it takes place several years after the war, in about 1950. The two central characters represent all that is best in Elisabeth's world and her most most lyrical writing is about the Milton Place grounds and in particular the flowers that are found there, which mean so much to Mr Barlow and also to his visitor Anita. What also means a lot is the sense of position, responsibility and moral values that are often embodied in an English country estate – if it is well run and the owner has a sense of obligation to others. Mr Barlow is a good man and his house is part of that equation.

We are not told much about the history of Milton Place. It seems to be a classic story in that Mr Barlow's grandfather made enough money in the mid-nineteenth century to become a country gentleman. His grandson was an engineer and had his career in the East, and has retired to the estate. We are not told much about his life, not even his first name. However, we know that several years before the First World War he visited Vienna and fell deeply in love with a Viennese woman but could do nothing as he was engaged already ('it was almost as unthinkable as a divorce') and entered a loveless marriage. His son, who came through the First World War, was killed in one of the military engagements that followed it, and his two daughters, the older an interfering and domineering figure, the other a timid soul, are his only family other than his beloved grandson. The lives of the daughters are observed by Elisabeth with an extraordinary perception of the nuances of English society and its fine and excruciating class distinctions.

The arrival of Anita Seiler from Vienna precipitates the action. Milton Place, although gradually much rejuvenated by her, remains run-down. But it stands for abiding English values, and the central question of the book is whether these values can survive. This has been a constant theme in English fiction, embodied in such houses as Jane Austen's Mansfield Park, E M Forster's Howards End, and Evelyn Waugh's Brideshead and Hetton Abbey.

All these novels turn, to a degree, on the question of who is worthy of the house and what it stands for. In *Mansfield Park* even its squire, Sir Thomas, has defects, and the moral centre of the book turns out to be his poor niece, Fanny. Yet closest in spirit to *Milton Place*, although the house is far more modest, is Forster's *Howards End*. (There is the nice coincidence that Forster when young, although he was an undergraduate at Cambridge much of the time, lived with his mother in Tunbridge Wells, which he disliked intensely, and had gone to school at nearby Tonbridge.) As in *Milton Place*, there is in *Howards End* a mixture of the sensitive and the philistine, those with developed and undeveloped hearts, the Schlegels and the Wilcoxes. Who shall inherit the ancient farmhouse, based on the house where Forster had grown up? The fête in *Milton Place* has certain parallels to the wedding in *Howards End*; the heir in Forster's novel will be Helen Schlegel's illegitimate son, conceived at the time of the wedding, suggesting some hope for the maintenance of the right values in a threatening society.

Then there is Hetton Abbey, Tony Last's nineteenth century Gothic pile in Evelyn Waugh's *A Handful of Dust*. He refuses to sell it to meet the requirements of a divorce settlement and after his presumed death his cousins, his heirs, are determined to preserve the house by running a mink farm. And there is one of the most famous of the country house novels, Waugh's *Brideshead Revisited*, a very grand house based on Castle Howard and Madresfield Court. Like *Milton Place*, these four novels deal with threats to traditional English values, and what is particularly striking is the extent to which Elisabeth de Waal understood these values and made them part of her book. Nor were they necessarily as conservative as they might appear. They were based, it is true, on a hierarchical society, but one in which those who were head of the household knew above all that they had the houses on trust for future generations. The creators of these novels judged harshly those who failed in the duties imposed by being in charge of a country house.

Peter Stansky, Stanford 2018